I'm Your Man

I'm Your Man

F. Sykes

SALTIMBANQUE BOOKS

NEW YORK

Saltimbanque Books, New York
www.saltimbanquebooks.com

ISBN: 978-1-941914-11-3

For AK

Acknowledgments

My thanks to Ron Kolm, Norman Filzman and J. Boyett for their time, support, advice and encouragement.

I'm Your Man

The countries which we long for occupy, at any given moment, a far larger place in our actual life than the country in which we happen to be.
— Marcel Proust, *Swann's Way*

This book is set in Manhattan in the summer of 1994. The atmosphere and architecture of the city, even the smell of the streets on hot July days, are no longer those described here. The world of this novel existed once. It does not now.

I.

WAITING

Times Square early on a summer Sunday is like a sleepy small town in its way; stores that aren't closed are almost deserted, sending music or television noises and the soft, always accented voices of bored clerks out into baking streets and sparse traffic. But this of course is no small town. Those few people who are on the sidewalks by noon are likely to be the addicts desperate enough to come out early to score and dealers small–time enough to take their money. There are the homeless, there are always the homeless. There are the police. There are a few kids from the suburbs who don't know that nothing happens before dark. Any neatly dressed strangers hurrying through at this hour are almost certainly in town for the day from New Jersey or Long Island, heading from the bus or the PATH train to brunch and a matinee.

And Fred is here. About twelve-thirty he leaves his apartment near Ninth Avenue on his usual early Sunday walk. He has money in his pocket and he has his Walkman hooked on his belt, headphones plugged into his ears. He is here but he is not here, the music feeds his head, the music helps keep his feet just off these sidewalks and his mind wherever he wants it to be. The music is the score of a life he lives outside the life he lives; the music helps him be someone, somewhere, else. Inside the music he cannot die. Or fail, for long. He makes his own tapes, cannibalizing with obsessive care favorites he's culled from radio programs likely to play what he wants to hear. He will buy a tape for one song, spend hours half-listening to a background of prerecorded radio junk and chatter, waiting for the one uncollected treasure that makes it worthwhile. The right sound—and he has by now hundreds of hours of right sounds—acts like a drug on his mood, lifting him to just where he want to be, cocooned in the music, just above, just beyond, the world. Today he leaves the apartment with the Stones, "Start Me Up"—"If you start me up I'll never stop…" By the time he reaches Eighth Avenue that's replaced by the Police, "…walk the streets for money, you don't care if it's wrong or right." No order, no sense, only the sound counts, the connection it has to the emotions that keep him just free from reality.

He walks the block, almost empty now, between Forty-third and Forty-second. The peep shows are open, here and on Forty-third; outside one a dirty-looking blond drag queen, eighteen or so—pink Lycra pedal pushers, a man's blue dress shirt tied off above the navel—leans against the wall, the slightly scared look of an addict who doesn't know where her next fix is coming from in her darting, mascaraed eyes. The Koreans whose corner store sells bags, wallets, sunglasses, caps, batteries—cheap goods, always in enough demand—are opening up but in no hurry. The one bar along the block to Forty-second is equally quiet; only drinkers damaged enough to be lost to time and the most self-consciously decadent slummers would be out this early. Fred moves on, past a couple of storefronts selling soda, junk food and drug basics—rolling papers, pipes, cigarette lighters—past the stale grease smell of a fried chicken restaurant, past the subway entrance. He crosses the street to the Port Authority Bus Terminal, where he is most likely to find a trick—that's what he's looking for, a boy, preferably new out here, attractive enough, interesting enough, to let him relax and spend the rest of Sunday doing something other than looking for sex. The Port is also where he's most likely to run into someone he has had and doesn't want again but who will ask for another chance, or at least for money. He dismisses the few early arrivals—no one new, no one interesting, but then no one he has to talk to—and crosses into the newer, uglier of the two buildings that make up the terminal. The effect is of an aging decrepit mall—noisy escalator, cracked yellowing floors, too many empty spaces among too many businesses with too few customers. He takes the escalator up to the second floor and walks down a couple of long hallways to the bowling alley in the older building, its small video game arcade empty at this hour except for the uniformed guard playing something quick, watched by one of the terminal's plainclothes cops. He takes a second escalator down, past the bank of pay phones where half a dozen Mexican youths sometimes hang out, sometimes making themselves available. No one there either.

He goes up another escalator, making his rounds, as two perfect boys just off a bus from somewhere, baseball caps at tough angles, strong tan legs and arms in summer shorts and tank tops, pass him going down the parallel escalator and head for the exit. They are not part of the life he lives. He regrets them and forgets them. They can't be anything to him. Upstairs two men Fred has seen around for years, two of the dozens he walks among and competes with for the same favors from the same boys, slowly trace this route they all take regularly, watchful for any likely newcomers. There are none right now; the only one looking to sell instead of buy is a heavy effeminate young man in a blue warmup suit. He is too old, too gay, too overweight. Fred and the others barely need a glimpse to reject him.

Someone Fred took home once is standing outside the building, leaning back with one foot up on the brick wall behind him, smoking a cigarette. He approaches, embarrassed, ducking his head, not looking Fred in the eye for two seconds at a time, knowing he will be rejected but too needy not to try. Fred must have known his name once but it's lost in a jumble of the half-remembered. Tito? Luis? Something Spanish. Whoever he is he is tall and slender, around twenty, pleasant-looking with long carefully combed curly hair. Fred had been attracted not so much by his nice enough face as by his build, by the long striding walk, purposeful and masculine, the air of confidence. Which turned out to be a lie, so far as this, so far as selling sex was concerned. He was to begin with *too* thin, flabby, poorly muscled, with too much body hair. And then he hardly managed to perform at all, rubbing pre-come from the tip of Fred's dick so hard it hurt, squeezing his nipples painfully, mechanically— doing everything too fast, too hard. Unpleasant sexual details attach more firmly than names.

Now he wants to try again, mumbles a few promises including a hurried, eyes-averted "I do anything with you this time", that is intriguing; but Fred shakes his head, gives his usual "Just walking around right now" line and pulls out two of the singles he keeps in folded pairs in his pocket for just these occasions. The young man slinks back wordlessly to lean against the wall and wait some more.

Fred continues his walk, thrown off his hopeful high by this intrusion, uninspired by Boston, "It's been such a long time"—it has, too, since he's found anyone out here worth the time he puts in. He smiles and goes on. He knows that the music is always effortlessly ironic and tells himself this awareness is one of the things that keeps him from falling beyond hope.

Right now there are no other familiar faces for him to cringe at the sight of, no more "no's" and excuses and evasions and crumpled dollar bills to pass out:

"What's up, Fred?"

"Just walking around right now."

"You be back later? I gotta make, you know, not all that much this time. I wanna get out of here."

"Yeah, well, maybe later."

"What time you be back?"

"I don't know. Maybe I won't. Don't know for sure what I'll do."

"You could buy me a slice? And a soda?"

And so on. Always vain attempts to pin down times and turn brush-offs into promises, always silenced with a couple of dollars. Fred has a problem with simple "no's"; feelings might be hurt, hostility awakened. He can find reasons to feel guilty on his own and he can't deal with hostility.

He starts back up Eighth, ready to go home to rest for another round later—there's always later, always hope all out of proportion to what experience has taught will be there and available. Later there may be someone new. And maybe the someone new will be younger and fresher than the usual pack of used-looking twenty, twenty-five-year-olds. When he comes back in an hour not one person he's seen on this first pass might still be around, although more likely of course most of them will; chances are the men strolling the halls, the effeminate young man waiting upstairs, Fred's former trick, all will be around for large chunks of the day. As Fred will be himself, moving or standing among the shifting population of regulars and one-timers, sellers and buyers, the compulsive and the merely curious, all looking for the one real right thing, waiting out the heat to feed their Times Square daydreams well into the night.

Everything changes when Fred reaches Forty-third street. Sitting on a fire hydrant just west of the avenue, perfect in faded jeans, black T-shirt and a black baseball cap, is a boy Fred has seen before, rarely, for a few seconds at a time—just a tease, a hint of what is possible even on these streets—before he disappeared into whatever world boys like this inhabit. He is not more than fifteen, very slim, curly dark hair in need of trimming, and—at this distance—skin smooth and clear as a child's. Fred has never seen him alone before; the few glimpses he's had have been late at night, this boy a couple-three years too young for the crowd of thuggish adolescents who gather here from early evening on, all noise and pose and wary watchfulness, but he'd seemed to fit right in, this kid, grinning, smoking, bumping shoulders and slapping hands just like all the others. Now he looks too young for that, jiggling a pair of dark glasses between thumb and forefinger, then slipping them on so he can use both hands to light a cigarette with a green Bic. Perfect punk kid.

Fred has no spontaneity, no grace, no natural small talk to fall back on when it's time to make an approach. Thousands of nights, hundreds of boys, but still the presence of someone this instantly, powerfully attractive leaves him awkward, uncertain, tongue-tied, a teenager asking for a first date. The boys he's wanted have always been intimidating; the jocks who'd sneered at him in junior high, the regular guys whose talk of football and girls he couldn't understand, let alone join, the slightly dangerous, swaggeringly attractive high school bad boys whose contempt for him couldn't have been clearer if they'd spat on him. He'd sucked seven or eight hundred dicks without perhaps ever feeling he quite comprehended any of the boys attached. In himself he was still what he had been, the high school nobody, different from those around him in ways that were basic, and never changed. Different from everyone, not just the boys he courted, or tried to court; even among gay men he felt excluded by his preferences, so divergent from theirs. When younger he'd felt these differences as shortcomings, as some lack others might easily detect; there really was something fundamental separating him from all those who fit together so well in groups he could not make himself part of, something that left him feeling in some way less (not just different but *less*) than all those who belonged—which seemed to him to be everyone else. He could still be made to feel less. And the difference here, today, is the most important of all: Middle-aged man from teenaged boy different.

That won't stop him, although now he stands, once again struck dumb at a time when just the right words are called for, on a corner ten feet away from today's promise of happiness. He turns off his Walkman (halfway through the Supremes, "Keep fallin' in and out of love"—more sloppy irony) and looks around. No one else who'd be interested in sight; later there will be dozens of men up and down this block of Eighth and in front of the Port, any of whom would pause as Fred pauses now, excited and uncertain as he is, finding his world suddenly centered on that cap and that cigarette and a pair of clean white Nikes, pigeon-toed now, tapping back and forth among the cracks in the pavement around the hydrant, small jerky movements matched by rhythmic nodding of the head to some music only he hears as he looks up to blow a smoke ring.

Absolute cool. Someone read Fred's fantasies and brought one to life. Suspiciously, dangerously perfect.

Fred's attention is so intense it feels like a physical fact instead of a mental one, so palpable he wonders it isn't enough to turn the boy's head, at least to make him aware as he might be aware of the sun's warmth that someone is there concentrating only on him. But it doesn't rate a glance. The boy stands, cigarette between his lips, long enough to pull up the Levis with a two-handed twist and tug at the waist they don't need, they're fairly snug, not the fashionable baggy style he's probably used to, checks the angle of his cap—perfectly straight, maybe a reaction to all the slants and angles that try too hard—and begins to stroll up Forty-third, elaborately casual. Fred's sure he doesn't know he's being watched; maybe much of his life is a show done to rhythms in his head for an audience only he knows.

Fred tries to decide whether to follow. The boy's walk is smooth and cocky, of course, sway in the shoulders and swing of the long arms absolutely confident, cool as the cigarette, cool as a cap at the perfect no-angle. He goes halfway up the block, past the deli, the gay peep show, the straight peep show, towards the porn shop next to the drag bar in the lobby of the rooms-by-the-hour hotel, discreetly casting sidelong glances into each doorway, barely turning his head and not seeming to care about anything outside himself.

Fred decides. For a show of his own, in case anyone is watching who might think he's after this boy he's after, he looks at his watch as though he's waited long enough for whoever, whatever, and turns and walks casually up the same block. Overtake him. Slow down so they're walking side by side. Connect. The easy part is catching up, but as the boy approaches the hotel a young man Fred has seen before comes out, girl in tow, and greets the boy like a long-lost friend, the usual complicated handshakes, rough macho bump of the shoulders, smiles and words Fred can't quite hear. There is a quick introduction and the boy nods silently, knowingly, at the girl. Fred goes into the deli as if that was his plan all along and buys an overpriced small bottle of orange juice; his throat is suddenly dry. The young man is one of the regulars on these few blocks—early twenties, light-skinned black with short dreadlocks usually as today sprouting from an opening in the red bandana tied around his head. It is early so the hair still stands, tight springs; by late evening it will have lost its body, will be drooping like wilted flowers around his skull. Fred has always found this young man attractive but his mouth tends naturally to an angry line and one night very late he fought with a fat black whore in a doorway up this same block, slapping and cursing her while other regulars egged him on or muttered in embarrassment. That mouth, that fight would be enough to keep Fred away even if this had been someone younger, a boy instead of a youth, and more obviously available.

Fred stands outside the deli and drinks his juice in four swallows, twenty-five cents each. The young man and the girl push past him in a way that's standard for these streets, too close for politeness, forcing Fred, unacknowledged by the slightest glance, to step back to keep from being jostled. He sees now the girl isn't one, but is another of the drag queens whose territory this is too. She's very good, her look almost sweet, almost innocent, and more convincing than most—smooth olive skin, her own hair instead of a wig, no goiter to speak of, a natural girlishness with only the slightest makeup.

The boy meanwhile has followed his friends back Fred's way; looking without pause or expression in the door of the deli and without a glance at Fred he goes back to his hydrant as the other two disappear around the corner. Now, Fred thinks. He saunters back, casually throwing his empty bottle into an orange mesh metal trash container ten feet from the boy's perch—the glassy clonk produces no reaction, no chance to catch his eye that way—and proceeding on to the light pole a yard or so past the hydrant. He dithers some more, conversations spinning whole in his head, before stepping forward to within eighteen inches from the boy's back and saying, "So, what's up?" His usual opening, sparkling as he gets with strange boys—strangers, period—spoken now in a voice that in spite of the juice sounds to his own ears scratchy and barely audible. Nerves. When there is no reaction he adds, "Just hanging out?"

There is no humiliation quite like it, being totally ignored when trying to start a conversation, but he's spoken to the back of this beautiful head, to a black baseball cap, curly brown hair a little too long above a long smooth neck, and not gotten a twitch in return, not even a sense of some stiffening into awareness, an alert refusal to be seen reacting. Fred looks around, no one seems to have noticed, he tries to nonchalant it, look unconcerned, as though his words were someone else's, nothing to do with him. After a few seconds, as the boy lights up a second cigarette, still not looking his way, Fred retreats to the corner, a safe distance, feeling like a fool. Is there still the chance, briefly, briefly, of a delayed reaction, a turning of the head, a smile? Fred can see it, feel it like a memory of sunshine, but of course there is nothing. He lives a few seconds in what could have been—the look, the smile, first words fumbling as his own: The connection, with all that will follow from it, made and understood—but the reality, that slim, black-shirted back he is looking at, is too strong for fantasy and he tries to think instead what he can do next.

As he stands, feeling helpless, a muscular black man of thirty or so, one Fred doesn't remember seeing here before (but he has no reason to pay any attention to thirty-year-olds, so who knows?) turns the corner from Eighth and is greeted by the boy like another old friend. The first words Fred hears from his dream boy are, "Wha's up?"—Fred smiles again, the irony, the endless small ironies. There are more complicated handshakes and swagger as the man claims he's been around the Deuce all night and the boy says, "Oh, yeah, right." Fred takes the opportunity to slip away, still embarrassed by being ignored and feeling his embarrassment, like his desire, so palpable others must be aware of it. He crosses Forty-third and heads up only so far as it takes to be out of sight, then stops and thinks what to do. In that part of his mind where a life more satisfying than this one is possible it's done, the boy has responded to his first clumsy words (they'll laugh about that later), and even now they're talking, joking, on the way to Fred's apartment where they'll find how right they are for each other: The boy who probably needs a father, a teacher, a wise older man who knows life beyond the street (as don't they all, it's the handiest, noblest of the stories Fred tells himself and occasionally almost true), a man who's willing to spend money, of course (there is always the willingness to spend money, that's the source of Fred's appeal to these boys and he never forgets it no matter what he wants to believe) and who really doesn't ask all that much in return. Not much at all.

This is in Fred's mind, somewhere, simmering, as he starts walking again, down the block, right turn, up Forty-fourth, on his way around the block and back to the boy he hopes will be alone again on his hydrant. New lines are rehearsed, and other reactions—some reaction—to the old one. As he passes the hotel he slows and realizes—as his heart sinks and his hopes shift, automatically, to some future meeting, same place, different time, but soon, very soon—that the boy is gone. He walks past the hydrant, around the corner and down the block, then turns and goes back, looking in every doorway, scanning the block ahead and the sidewalk across the street for the look, the walk, that cap just so. Nothing. The man the boy was talking to is gone as well and Fred imagines some date arranged for sex but that doesn't fit the street macho of their meeting. Still— whyever, wherever—they're gone.

Fred won't go home now, not yet, not with this rare beauty maybe on his way back to sit on his hydrant some more and wait for the right words. Fred knows them now, spins them in his head adding just the right response. After all these years he is unsurprised to be a bit relieved by this loss, relieved of the burden of having to charm, having to connect, of being convincing, of saying what he can so much more effectively think and pretend. He can play all the parts in his head with no failure, no rejection, no potential for embarrassment. He's always been able to do that.

He stays close for a while, a few blocks' walk this way or that but always that corner is the center of whatever circle he makes, and every time he approaches hope returns: The boy will be there again, alone again, waiting. Every time the boy isn't. The circles become wider and the hope slimmer and the anticipatory thrill less each time around. After an hour he is almost back to his routine, cruising the streets and the Port as he would on any warm Sunday when the perfect boy had not appeared, had not been approached, had not ignored him and then disappeared. Without giving up hope he consoles himself with the knowledge that there are others. Not perfect, but others.

And there are. One kid of seventeen, eighteen, who's been around the Port off and on for a month or so is there again, loitering near one of the pillars on the Forty-second Street side, a little away from the crowd, but near enough to attract attention. He is very slender and tough-looking, always an attractive combination; there is a hint of contempt in the look he returns to some of those cruising him. Once he'd stood on this block clearly stoned, returning a silly secret smile to everyone, barely able to keep his eyes open. But he is handsome in a cold angry way, freckled the way some Puerto Ricans are, russety brown hair, dressed as usual in a cheap warmup suit that shows off his slim hips and nice small hard ass. He's attracted the attention of one of the other regulars, a man of sixty or so who wears a jet-black toupee and dyes his eyebrows to match; he is said to own one of the new peep shows that have spread down Eighth south of Forty-second in anticipation of the closing of the old established porn shops on the Deuce and the adjacent blocks. The old man stands six feet from the kid he's interested in, tapping a rolled-up magazine against his thigh and looking across the busy street as though he might be thinking about something else. The kid, who has no patience for the customs here, makes the first move, stepping over to ask for a cigarette, and Fred, who had paused at the corner, thinking about an approach of his own, attracted by the slightly dangerous look and the slim hardness, walks on instead, not too disappointed. After the boy he saw earlier this one—anyone else likely to be here and available—would feel like settling, almost like giving up. He doesn't expect much from Times Square anymore—still hopes, but doesn't expect. He's been through a third of a lifetime of this in one place or another; thousands of looks returned, hundreds of advances accepted. And there were many more regrets, innumerable wonderful faces and ripe bodies observed, considered, but not achieved. Perhaps they were impossible because they didn't belong to that kind of boy; or they were lost from indecision or clumsiness or maybe logistics or timing—another interested gentleman standing a little closer, or already in conversation when Fred arrived on the scene. Fred's disappointment was never entirely sexual; something in him believed the possibility that any of these unmet boys—any of those promising backs moving off with someone else, perhaps, any of those untaken opportunities that disappeared while Fred walked around the block, making up his mind—might be *the one*, the boy he would strike that spark with, the spark that would last as it did in his imagination. He knows the truth, knows that the boy he imagines would by definition not be here or in any of the other places boys go to sell themselves. Of course not. But by now he hasn't, if he ever had, the patience, the charm, the ability to flirt and flatter needed to succeed with a boy who is not for sale.

So he walks along the route he's taken all afternoon, returning to that corner more to fuel the stories he's built around it than from any real hope, but at Forty-third he looks down the block and there he is again, his boy, standing—feet firmly apart, cigarette in hand, dark glasses and cool firmly in place—twenty feet from the hydrant Fred might otherwise have approached for weeks with ever-dimming hope and some vestigial twinge of excitement. He's talking to two other young men and as he strolls towards them Fred realizes, with more

14

than a twinge, that he knows one of them. His name is Jeff. He is always available to Fred—or anyone else. He will introduce this boy. Simple as that.

Street etiquette doesn't allow a trick to approach a boy with his friends on the street; Fred would never overstep that boundary. He passes the small group—the third is a bearded biker type, blond, tattooed, twenty-five, of no interest—without taking his eyes off Jeff. Jeff's gaze slides to him briefly, sufficiently; any eye contact is enough. Fred walks twenty feet further up the block, crosses over, and strolls back down to wait at the corner, across Forty-third from the first sighting. In perfect confidence.

The idea—to Fred a fact, accomplished as soon as he's thought of it—of having Jeff make the introduction—not pimping, exactly, only helping—makes him giddy with relief. All the strain he'd feel is gone—having to say hello to a stranger on his own is a strain, the approach, introducing himself, making small talk; he can't just wave money at them, though that would be simpler, maybe more honest. This is a gift. He looks at his boy again where he still stands with the others, his back to Fred. It's difficult to tell what he might look like under that black T-shirt worn loose over the pale blue Levis. Fred has memories of others of course to provide clues. But the whole point is this is someone new, something different—a quality of skin all his own, shoulders, nipples, navel, toes, pubic hair, underarm smell of sweat or deodorant, dick circumcised or not, balls small or large, ass flat or rounded—everything new, and what Fred does see is fresh and sexy as it could only be with someone this young, just ripening. Fred will need as much freshness of mind to make the stories, Fred's stories, work, become fact. That's where the troubles always come. At the least all his memories will be improved upon, given new bits and pieces to conjure with. He concentrates on the clothes, since that is what is he has now. The jeans are not the usual too-new stiff denim but worn to a boy-baby blue; Fred can almost feel their softness as he begins to fit this boy into the stories he has ready for every boy he longs to meet.

After a moment Jeff detaches himself from the other two and strolls down the block and across to where Fred stands. Fred's boy and the biker drift over to talk to a slim, feral black hustler, always around, in a dirty white T-shirt and tight blue nylon shorts. Jeff is an olive-skinned Puerto Rican with very curly black hair that always seems to need cutting. He has on a cheap-looking shiny green polyester warmup suit (the previous summer he had said to Fred, "Green's my color for the season"; apparently the season isn't over) that probably passes some street fashion test. Jeff is soft-spoken and with Fred never pushy or demanding but he's on the street now and shows it; maybe for the benefit of anyone else who might be watching he comes towards Fred with a rolling, limping gait so exaggerated he might have one wooden leg. He is chewing on a toothpick and smiles sideways, looking at the pavement, as he follows Fred down the block and around the corner onto Eighth where his friends are less likely to see them shaking hands.

"S'up?" Jeff's speech has a clogged, phlegmy quality, always congested.

"Where you been, Jeffrey? It's been a while." Fred knows where he's been.

"Jail. Two months on Rikers." He might be embarrassed or he might be bragging. "The juvie part, right?" He snorts and coughs once, an eternal habit.

"For?"

Jeff shrugs as though it's obvious. "Drugs, what else?" He looks at Fred and smiles his shy sideways smile again. "Fuckin' DT, looked *my* age, all strung out and shit. Fuckin'...." He shakes his head ruefully, still smiling; those here for whom arrest is certain now and then are usually able to find humor in the inevitable.

Fred won't pass up an opportunity to sound knowing. "Only way they can get along. Don't make you believe them, they're back in uniform. Just got out?"

"First of the week. First time I been here for the longest." He gets to the point. They have only one subject. "So? Wha's up?"

16

Fred shrugs, suddenly shy about asking, not wanting to embarrass Jeff or hurt his feelings. That lasts only a second. "So who's your friend over there? Kid with the shades?"

Jeff looks briefly confused, then shrugs and says, "Oh, him? Nah, nah. I don't think he'd be interested." He looks up at Fred curiously, head again tilted towards the sidewalk.

"Won't hurt to ask."

"Uh-hnn. Him and me, we had some trouble with a trick. He didn't like it."

"What kind of trouble?"

Jeff shrugs, not looking Fred in the eye as he goes on. "Guy took us all the way the fuck up in the Bronx, wouldn't let us get our money unless Shorty there fucked him. Wound up we stood all night, wouldn't even give us extra for carfare."

Fred's fantasies had had the boy inexperienced, but fantasy isn't illusion and he sheds this one with a pang but no pause, as he has so many before. "So? The guy got what he wanted?"

Again the slanted curious look and shrug. "Kid didn't like it, though. And like it's my fault, I knew the guy and shit."

"You know me better, right? Tell him I'm okay. You can come along if he's worried."

Jeff shakes his head stubbornly. "I know he's not gonna be interested, is all."

"How you know if you don't at least ask him? Maybe money's the only reason he's out today. Wants to get out quick as he can." Jeff shakes his head some more but he's giving in. "You can come along, okay? Just bring it up to him, see what he says."

Jeff grumbles a little more and finally says he'll try, but when they get back to the corner the boy is gone, again. The biker is sitting on the hydrant now, drinking beer from a brown paper bag and flirting with a dyed blonde drag queen in shorts and a sequined halter top, poorly shaved goiter bobbing above a red ribbon necklace. Fred can still see the boy—his boy— in that spot where he seems to belong. He had convinced himself—this *will* happen, they *will* be introduced, they *will* be together, and he has made himself believe they will turn

17

into something, the two of them, so the simple unfairness of his not being there, the impossibility of it, as if they'd come to the corner and found the kid floating away, ten feet above the pavement and rising faster and faster into the blue city sky, is a shock, a tear in the reality Fred has woven out of the desire born an hour before with the first sighting and has built into something almost solid since seeing Jeff and his chance. Jeff doesn't notice his distress—he wouldn't, Fred is very good at seeming blank—and after a quick look around says, "Come back in a few. I'll see where he went."

So this time Fred walks around the block the other way, south, then east, then north, then back down to where the sightings have been today. Before the end of the first block he hits play on the Walkman and comes up with the Supremes again, smooth emotions, hope over experience, just right for anticipation of a meeting that will be more than another trick, desired too much not to disappoint. When he returns to the corner Jeff is talking to a street pimp, very slick in a sleazy way, copper complexion, Mephistophelian goatee, long oily hair, actually wearing a purple hat and matching suit, pants held up by paisley suspenders but with a sleeveless white undershirt and sneakers spoiling the uniform. Jeff manages an inconspicuous shrug as Fred passes. No luck.

So Fred starts again the boring familiar round of places he knows too well, places whose interest is only in the changing faces and possibilities for an encounter, a little contact, some brief satisfaction, enough to free his mind for a while. For now the hydrant is the center of all. Jeff is there and then he is gone too. Fred goes home to use the toilet and then stands at the table, attempting to read the Sunday paper, but what if he misses it, this boy's reappearance? What if Jeff greets him next with a helpless shrug and a "Where were you? He was here but he wouldn't wait, left with this other dude." The thought is enough; smiling ruefully at the imagined disaster—it would be just like him, just his luck, he wishes he had someone to share the joke with—Fred closes the paper and goes down to the street.

The thing to keep in mind is the difference between fantasy and illusion, between the fiction that is longed for, lovingly rehearsed, and the fiction that is believed.

Fred is already tired, he sees the whole day slipping away in another futile search, another missed opportunity, but he goes out anyway, back to the block which once again he approaches with hope in the form of visions of how it will be. It isn't. Neither Jeff nor Fred's boy is in sight. "You're just a memory," Mick Jagger sings in his ear, maybe with a mocking smile. It is late enough now—mid-afternoon—to be crowded; a dozen men, regulars, are scattered along the curb, singly or in small chatty groups, alert, watchful, taking in anyone new and likely with a practiced, covetous gaze that does not become intrusive enough to bring retaliatory insults from the more aggressively macho boys on the block, or those who want to seem that way. Strung between the doors of the Eighth Avenue peep shows and porn shops are a few clearly available youths, too familiar by now for the watching men to even notice. They pose, shirts open or too tight, hands suggestively near crotches, pretense gone, without much pride about it anymore, about the fact that they're for sale to any man who approaches and makes a reasonable offer. Any offer.

Fred wonders if his boy has returned and been snatched up already; he would seem like a shocking, perfect gift to these jaded chickenhawks, as he does to Fred. Fresh meat thrown into a den of lions expecting rancid fat and gristle. He shakes off the thought, replacing it again with the way it will be, the approach, the small talk, the offer, the shy acceptance…. He goes no further now, the fantasy only begins, over and over. At the corner of Forty-second he stops to look across the street to see if Jeff is in front of the Port but he isn't. Fred turns and starts back down the block, falling in behind two regulars he's always been too nervous to approach; attractive, twentyish, present usually for glimpses, with no need to linger, they would likely dismiss his fumbling approaches. Both are now shirtless, showing off the hard sculpted bodies that Fred assumes could only come from hard work but that for some people seem to be natural. One is tall with reddish gold curly hair and café-au-lait skin, the other a short Hispanic with a large gap between his two front teeth. Once either might have been Fred's boy on the hydrant. Now they are the arrogant elite here, fully aware of their own appeal, free for now, for a few months or years more, to say no in confidence other offers will come. They swagger along, the center of attention, greeting friends with loud surprise and solid handshakes, acknowledging old tricks with barest nods. Fred walks behind them, admiring the shifting muscles in shoulders and backs tapering to hard well-shaped butts under the thin summer jeans, and thinking his boy, not dragging years of these streets behind him, will be that much better. He's thought about these two before but he dismisses them now. Too old. Used. Second-rate to begin with or they wouldn't still be around at their age. When they turn into the pizza and gyro place halfway down the block he passes without a sideways glance.

Fred walks through the Port again (nothing new, no one interesting), back past the hydrant (nothing) down the block going the other way, west, on Forty-third, by a small playground and basketball court where frequently neighborhood boys—strictly off-limits but he can look, dream—can be seen sweating in tight shorts, a pleasant enough cheap thrill. Today there is only one black kid shooting baskets, handsome enough, but chunky, with a block for an upper body and a big bubble butt, not Fred's type at all.

He goes to Forty-second heading back towards Eighth and as he passes the post office here comes Jeff, hesitant, stopping, pretending to tie a shoe as Fred approaches.

"Wha's up?" Jeff asks, pretty much of the shoe.

"Any luck?"

"He's around, just not, you know." He stands and taps the foot a couple of times before looking Fred in the eye.

Fred doesn't know. "Did you try? Did you ask him?"

Jeff looks at him as though just now realizing something. "Damn. You really want this nigger, don't you?"

Fred nods and says with implied quotation marks he's not sure Jeff will hear, "Yes. I really want this nigger."

Jeff does understand—a lot of people are smarter than Fred thinks they are—smiles, looks away, shrugs, and says, "Pass by over there in twenty minutes or so."

"He's around?"

"He's around. Okay?"

"Twenty minutes. That corner of Forty-third." He doesn't want any mistakes.

Jeff nods and saunters off. Now that it seems again like this might happen, Fred imagines reasons it won't—somehow Jeff won't produce the kid; Fred can hold that fact over Jeff's head, until some future day when he will feel obligated to come through. Even then this boy will be in his future. Maybe today. He enters the bus terminal through a side door and goes up the escalator next to the airport bus office. On the second floor, only looking, on his way to someone better than anyone he's ever seen available here, he runs into James, who's always been around, had been a trick of Fred's ten, twelve years before, when the scene was still two video arcades on Broadway, Playland and Fascination, that were a meat market for men like to Fred to shop in. That had ended; the arcades had closed, the buildings they were in been torn down and replaced by flashy towers, and the next wave of boys—there had been so many once—found other things to do, scared off by AIDS, Fred supposes, by the police. It is not his imagination that there were more of them then or that it was new younger boys—fourteen, fifteen—who had stopped coming around, while too many others had aged without going further than the next cruising spot. He remembers with the sort of nostalgia others have for senior proms and drive-in movie dates the nights he walked into Fascination at midnight-one AM, passed through the numbing, rhythmless din of pinball machines and Pac Man, the flashing lights making weird pastel shadows on the dingy walls and worn dirty linoleum, the crowds divided between the serious game players and players of other kinds—hustlers, drug dealers, boys looking for money and men looking for boys. Seeing a new boy, circling him, watching over his shoulder as he pounded the buttons and made the screen dance, hoping he'd sense a presence and turn and their eye contact would last that fraction of a second too long to mean nothing. Score.

James has AIDS now. He is thin and looks unhealthy but he was always thin and never seemed to take care of himself. There had always been something unkempt about him— clothes slightly wrinkled, fingernails untrimmed, hair wild; he was young enough once that it didn't seem like more than a phase. He is very dark—though lately he's had a waxy pallor that doesn't go away—and claims to be mostly American Indian although his features don't say so, but then he's someone who lies, for money and respect and sympathy and often for no apparent reason at all. He has a purplish burn-like scar he claims is from surgery to have a cyst removed from his throat; it shines slightly, still a raw sore down one side of his neck, jaw to collarbone, and he makes no effort to cover it. He greets Fred like a best friend but everyone gets that treatment; James has always been everyone's best friend. They shake hands and James, with considerable pride, holds up a white plastic bag.

"Wanna see my new movie?"

"Another one?"James has been in two others Fred knows of, cheap, sloppily-made gay porn. The one Fred has seen consists of several unrelated sequences; James—in the credits under his street name, Duke—has a solo turn. Dressed in a leather vest, a large expensive-looking hat and nothing else, he masturbates expressionlessly, standing in front of a wall as blank as he is, looking over the camera at nothing. Fred did not find watching this an erotic experience; the too-thin body—narrow shoulders, undeveloped chest and legs—was overwhelmed by the big dick he manipulated with one hand, all the flesh slightly gray in the poor quality film. Not attractive, all in all. "I don't know how soon I could watch it."

"No?" James feigns disappointment. "'Cause I need it to show around. I'm gonna make a lot of money from this one. They promised me a cut."

"In writing?"

"I can trust these guys. Here, look." He takes the boxed video from the plastic and shows Fred the back cover. "See? Me and Manuel."

Fred doesn't recognize Manuel, a lightly bearded Puerto Rican—no whites or blacks need apply for this particular series of videos—standing shirtless next to a fully clothed James in the garish color on the video box. "Got a co-star this time?"

James smiles. "Customers like the couples better. And now it's all, you know, safe sex, right?"

"I hope so."

Returning the video to the bag James asks the inevitable. "You got a couple dollars? This place is dead. I'm gonna get me a slice and go on home."

Fred pulls out two singles and gets a quick hug and pat on the back in return. "You better start collecting on that percentage," he says with an edge of real irritation. James waves him off with an inappropriate laugh and goes on his confident way.

As Fred turns back to the escalator he sees one of the regular uniformed Port Authority cops has been leaning against a pillar watching them. James waves to him as he passes and gets a nod in return; Fred avoids his eyes, feeling the chill of embarrassment at being known for what he is by someone who disapproves. It is an embarrassment he hates and fears. And endures, another part of his life.

Back on the street Fred approaches the sacred corner once again, but this time with more hope than expectation. But he rehearses finding Jeff and the boy together, another meeting, more small talk, ideally ending with Jeff begging off because of a previous appointment or something. Fred doesn't much like being with two: He only really cares about his own pleasure and having to pay attention to anyone else is a distraction from that; he worries about how he looks to the one watching him with the other; he worries about not seeming to show favoritism. Of course it's his money, after all; why should he have to bother, or care? That's one thing about boys, Fred thinks. Female prostitutes—and even the young men who've been around here forever and pretty much lost hope—just want the money and don't need shows of consideration and fairness; they've learned to expect nothing. The boys Fred likes still have their pride, though, require attention and respect and will likely be hurt if they don't get it. Maybe angry. Maybe dangerous. So he has to try at least.

He is of course as he approaches the corner ready for disappointment, for neither to be there, for Jeff to have failed, even for the agonizing thrill of seeing his boy's back as he walks off with some other man, one of the regulars Fred prefers not to think of as his rivals. So it is a breath-shortening pleasure to turn the corner and see the two of them right there, standing next to the hydrant, Jeff in his green warmup, the boy in his boyish jeans, T-shirt and cap, sunglasses hanging from his belt, smoking again. They are waiting. For him. Jeff catches his eye and Fred nods and continues across Forty-third and around the corner onto Eighth, slowing, trying to seem cool in spite of his hard-beating heart as he nears the middle of the block and waits for them to catch up. The boys are cool by nature, without thought or effort, sauntering along in no hurry at all. Much too cool to hurry. As they meet Jeff mutters an introduction and Fred only half hears the name he's given. He shakes his hand and the boy—Alex? Alan?—favors him with a "Wha's up?", a smile—very white teeth, a crooked gap on top, sexily crooked, one upper tooth misaligned with the others enough to be noticed—and a conventional handshake, nothing fancy, not the streetwise three-part kind Fred doesn't feel he can get right anyway. He doesn't know the formula for the street version, fingers there first, thumbs there next. He needs practice he will never get.

"What's up?" Fred replies, ever the wit.

"We could get a drink?" Jeff asks, leading the way.

"Sure," Fred says, and then to the boy as they follow, "Was that Alex? or Alan?"

"Adam. A-D-A-M." His voice is slightly husky, soft, with a little catch to it, the way a boy's voice can be before settling into a man's. He looks Fred directly in the eye, his own dark brown beneath long lashes and thin, almost straight, eyebrows. He has a humorous curve at the corners of his mouth, the kind that seems always about to become a grin. Fred can only smile back, excited, almost giddy, he can't believe his luck, but of course he doesn't know what to say, if this frank boyish witty look is expectant it will be disappointed. Fred thinks sooner or later any boy will be disappointed in him and will disappoint him in return. This has come to seem like no more than realism, although the moment itself is always a blow.

In the deli on the corner of Forty-fourth Jeff and Adam argue over which is healthier, flavored milk or Nutriment. Jeff gets chocolate milk, Adam a container of strawberry-flavored Nutriment. "You could buy me a pack of cigarettes?" Adam asks.

"Sure."

"Newports." Of course. Everyone out here smokes Newports.

Fred pays. They go out and across Eighth towards his apartment, the boys drinking from their cartons with no straws. Jeff comes near enough to quietly say, "I told him thirty apiece. That okay?" Fred barely thinks how much more this is than he'd usually spend on one. He nods and Jeff moves on ahead a few steps.

"I saw you out there earlier," Fred says to Adam, who makes a face as he sips his drink. "You didn't notice me."

He doesn't seem to notice now, closing the flap and holding the container away from his body to shake it up before drinking some more. "This tastes sour." He offers it to Fred to sniff. It smells artificial, as close to strawberries as its milky pink is a to a strawberry's color. "You don't want it?" Fred asks. "Nah." Fred takes the full carton and tosses it into a wire trash barrel near the curb. It lands with a thunk and he's grateful it hit its mark without spilling; no small embarrassments here, no regrets for an impulse turned klutzy. "Thanks," Adam says, and Fred makes this word into something: A well-brought-up boy, a habit of manners, very clean in his black Colorado Rockies T-shirt and matching cap, the immaculate faded jeans, the shining white Nikes. Adam gives a tug to the pants as he had earlier, a quick two-handed motion practiced on much looser garments than these Levis; he has a Guess watch on his slender wrist and a fancy belt with the Guess logo trailing along its length.

They cross the street, pass doorways and basement stairs where crack smokers can be seen some nights in the shadows, quickly illuminated by the flame of a lighter held to a glass stem, then shadows again themselves. It is now a still clear summer afternoon; the air seems bleached. Jeff has started talking to Adam about some rap group Fred has never heard of, although he always tries to seem knowing about street slang and hip hop, to be able to drop a name or even a snatch of lyric in such a way as to seem right up on the interests of the boys out here. To himself he always sounds phony, even snide, he can hear himself stumble, reddens with the effort of pretending, he knows how little he knows, how much he wants simply to impress with a few facts and none of the effort of real knowledge. But often it seems to work, at least a bit, to twist the view some boys have of him, bring looks of surprised curiosity, if not of admiration, to separate him from all the other men hanging around, competing for the same favors from the same boys. In this conversation, however, he hasn't a clue—something about some rapper leaving one group for another—and waits for an opening. Fred had thought from his look that Adam was Puerto Rican, Hispanic, but his speech has a streety black lilt in the way certain sounds are emphasized, particularly at the ends of sentences; as they enter Fred's building he says, "This is a nice building," hitting "build" with an extra stress and smiling at Fred.

"They keep it up pretty well." He unlocks the inner door and automatically looks towards the super's apartment at the end of the hall next to the elevator to see if the door is open or even if any light shows from under it indicating someone might be home. Fred has had enough boys here, has had enough little troubles with them, to want to avoid being seen with even a prize like this one. Not that everyone would consider Adam a prize.

Fred's apartment is something he usually apologizes for although none of his tricks ever complain. It is a long narrow studio, bathroom to the left of the door, two closets and what passes for a kitchen—a small counter with a sink, ancient waist-high refrigerator, pitted and worn gas stove—along the hallway to the single room for living, fifteen by ten feet or so crammed with everything that won't fit in the small closets. Jeff has been here before, of course, and leads the way to the blue and violet futon bed against one wall. He sits and almost immediately begins to unlace his shoes. Fred turns on the fan in preference to the noisy air conditioner, hoping it's enough for the warm but today not stifling room, and automatically picks up the remote control and turns on the television, tuned to the Weather Channel; he winces—dull white guy TV—and tries Showtime. Kid's movie with a dog and cat talking in cute British accents. He goes to most boys' favorite on Manhattan Cable, at least when it's too early for the sex channels—The Box, music videos by request, almost all rap. It's the right choice. "All right, Gravediggaz," Adam says. Fred hasn't heard of them but glances at the screen, knowing that later on he would not be able to pick out what he sees and hears from dozens of others.

Adam sits next to Jeff and begins to unlace his shoes as well. Fred stands over them, unable to think of anything much to say—the usual small talk flits through his mind, filler—but unwilling to let this be just a sexual encounter, no other connection made.

"I could use the phone?" Adam asks suddenly.

"Sure."

The phone is on top of the dresser next to the futon. Adam goes through his jeans pockets and comes up with a rolling paper, a number scrawled on it in pale pencil. He holds this in one hand and the receiver in the other as he pushes the buttons, then listens. "What's your number here?" Fred tells him and Adam listens briefly, then punches in more numbers and hangs up. "Called his beeper," he says to Fred. *Beep*-er. And then to Jeff, "I can ask him to meet us at six, pay us what he owes." He sits back down next to Jeff and begins to take his shoes off in earnest. One of Jeff's is already off, tossed under a chair. His socks are dirty; there is the faint odor of feet in the room. "We can be done by five or so, right?" Adam asks Fred.

Fred looks at his watch. "It's only just four. Sure." And because he still can't think of anything else to say he begins to unlace his own shoes. Adam is entranced by a new video, a light-skinned black woman singing a love song, and doesn't seem to miss the conversation.

When Jeff stands to take off his pants Fred motions for Adam to get up while he maneuvers the futon from the couch to the bed position and throws a sheet over it. He is used to Jeff, who although he is young enough and handsome enough is too familiar and not in any way more attractive or satisfying than a half-dozen others Fred knows just as well. He has in fact a persistent hygiene problem—he never seems quite clean, there is always the slightest odor, never rank, but noticeable, the smell perhaps of someone who showered yesterday but not yet today, not quite recently enough. He is one of those Fred settles for when nothing better has appeared, remembering him younger, not so hairy, the small dick something that still might grow.

Undressing for sex with someone new is one of the few reliable thrills—stomach-tightening, mouth-drying, breath-shortening—that Fred knows. He begins, silent, fingers working quickly on shoelaces, buttons, zipper, belt, without ever quite taking his eyes off Adam, who works at the same things with oblivious care, checking his sneakers for scuffs, folding his T-shirt, shaking out the jeans and putting them over a chair, revealing as he does a body that is all long lines, waiting to fill in. Though he isn't, Adam seems taller than Jeff because of his slender build. The long arms and legs seem unfinished, waiting for the rest of him to catch up. He wears boxer shorts with a design of random red and white triangles—boys from the Deuce usually wear boxers—and sits on the futon, now a bed, in those and clean white socks, which he pulls up as far as they'll go.

28

In addition to the sheet Fred has taken the necessities—a towel and a jar of lubricant—from the drawer in the old dresser, setting them on the floor within reach. Jeff has lain on one side of the bed. Fred lies in the middle and Adam, lifting his hips enough to remove his shorts, on the other side. As he stretches out Fred puts a hand on the boy's side and trails his fingers down until it rests on his thigh. Jeff has begun to masturbate in a halfhearted way, stroking his small dark dick with one hand while the other, balled into a fist, supports his head so he can see the television. "You want to watch music or porn?" Fred asks Adam.

Jeff stops what he's doing. "Music or what?"

Adam props himself up on one elbow and talks over Fred. "Porn," he says. "Porn."

Fred thinks this is his answer to his own question rather than Jeff's and says, "Porn? Okay."

"No, no," Adam says quickly. "I was talking to him. I wanna listen to music. I don't like porn."

"Yeah, the music," Jeff says, returning to his dick and the video.

"It's a good porn movie. Some other time." Fred doesn't argue; the tiny misunderstanding will not be forgotten by him even if the others have forgotten it already. He slips off his own plain white jockey shorts and trying to be fair reaches out one hand to each of the boys. Jeff moves his jackoff hand so both are under his head. There is a faint tang of sweat from his armpits that is exciting, a whiff of boyishness as Fred thinks of it, and Fred's fingers comb through a slightly moist tangle of pubic hair to find the half-erect penis which he squeezes lightly and strokes with the tight up-and-down motion he prefers for himself. There is little response; Fred can see Jeff continuing to watch the thumping unintelligible jumble of cocky black men and jiggly lighter-skinned black women flickering by on television.

Adam's skin is smooth and dry, almost cool. The thatch of soft pubic hair reaches no more than a couple of inches towards his navel. His cock rests dark and ready against one thigh, and hardens a bit when Fred begins to stroke it. Fred looks at Adam's

29

face and finds him looking back, humor lively in his eyes, which quickly turn back to the TV screen. His thick very curly dark hair grows relatively low on his forehead. His skin is indeed still a child's, smooth and delicate.

Fred takes his hand off Jeff, leans over and kisses Adam on the shoulder and is rewarded when he looks up with a grimace, an amused wrinkle of the boy's slightly broad nose. He moves his hand to Adam's balls, seeming large in their loose sack, and then runs his middle finger along the short strip of skin leading to his butt. Adam resists this slightly, with a rejecting shift of his hips, so Fred slips his hand out and back onto the thigh. Hoping but not really caring that Jeff is amusing himself, he moves his head down, trailing his nose and lips along Adam's smooth hairless chest (tiny dark nipples centered in dime-size pinkish brown) circling his tongue around the inverse nipple of the navel and passing the soft hair with its quick whiff of soap and—what?—powder? Adam's dick rests half-hard on his thigh, paler than expected it turns out, seeming larger perhaps than it is because the boy himself is so slender, his body so young. The effect of the few hairs sprouting around the smooth balls is perfect to Fred.

Fred kisses each thigh and takes the dick in his mouth, trying to find a comfortable position between the two boys on the narrow bed. There is little response to his sucking, a slight stiffening, but he glances up to see Adam intent on a new video that has started, louder and more violent than the last. Boyz II Men don't play on this station, nothing even that atmospheric. Fred decides that whether he cares or not fair is fair and moves from one to the other; he briefly sucks on Jeff's now flaccid dick, a tan shoot in a tangled black thicket, noting again the faint sour smell that permeates much of the sex he has, the smell of almost clean young male.

Looking up, Fred realizes that Jeff is asleep, or pretends to be. Adam notices him noticing and playfully, grinning, reaches over Fred to jab Jeff in the ribs, making him jump and grunt, "Yo, yo, man. Chill." Adam does it again. "Chill, man." Jeff doesn't

30

open his eyes and that's good enough for Fred. Jeff's sleeping—maybe real, probably faked—has been a feature of their last few tricks and Fred has taken it as permission, the sort of license he cannot resist; he has twice halfheartedly tried to fuck the apparently sleeping Jeff, rolling him onto his stomach, slipping grease inside him, mounting him, only to be rejected, bucked off almost, with the same sleepy remark: "You're too heavy."

Now he has a license for something else, to ignore Jeff altogether and concentrate on Adam. Tactful Jeff. Considerate Jeff. Fred turns the other way and sucks Adam's dick again, then moves back up to embrace him, but as he does the phone rings and Adam without hesitation jumps to answer it.

This is the moment, perhaps, when everything changes, when fact so merges with fantasy the two become confused, entangled, inseparable, when this trick stops being only that—one more among the hundreds, to be filed as a memory that will deteriorate, blur, become a barely differentiated part of a larger memory that involves innumerable images, hundreds of snippets of boy that flash through his mind, detached from the human beings they had been part of. (Some, a few—as likely despised as loved—he has remembered as individuals, though no longer quite complete, pictures faded and indistinct with time.) Anyway, Fred will claim as much later, will even tell the story (and he hasn't ever told these stories, except in his mind, that's how amazing he finds the moment); it is a vision he will return to again and again, himself on his side of the bed, watching Adam standing an arm's length away, slim and nude, his three-quarter erection bobbing a little as he makes points on the phone with smiling animation in his crackling soft voice. Fred could reach out the two, two and a half feet to touch him; he could take the dick in his hand, could stroke the boy's side or thigh or ass, could even lean forward enough to suck on Adam some more; he briefly imagines the grin of surprise on Adam's face. But he waits. The surprise could as easily be that of someone intruded upon; this vision of Fred's could be an assault to Adam. So Fred resists his temptation; he has learned from too many small embarrassments spread over too many years what fragile unpredictable things a boy's ego, a boy's pride, a boy's affections, can be. He could tell stories for hours. He doesn't.

So he only looks, and sees, and that is his moment, imprinted for good as what it is—that vision of perfection he's carried around for years, here at last though even now just out of reach—and what it might be. He will remember that he might have made that move, could have bridged the gap to touch, kiss, suck all he wanted. *His choice* was all that came between himself and perfection. Maybe.

The call lasts a few seconds, arrangements are made, and Jeff wakes long enough to hear the results: The two of them will meet someone at Rockefeller Center at five-thirty to collect some money they're owed, the balance on some deal or other—Fred assumes for drugs. He wants to tell them to be careful who they deal with, to always sell COD, not to trust anyone. He wants to say the things that will make Adam think he's streetwise and knowledgeable, can be trusted and respected. He quickly rehearses a little speech but Adam looks around for a clock, fixes on the time on the VCR and hops back into bed saying, "You can hurry a little so we won't be late?" The moment has passed, fortunately; later Fred will feel prickly embarrassment recalling he'd thought of setting himself to advise these boys on the tactics of street life. Thinking he knows the world he trolls for sex has always been his most dangerous pretension.

Jeff stays awake now but is taking care of himself, one arm over his eyes, showing no sense of urgency, no apparent awareness anyone else is around as the other hand deals with his erection as though it were a chore. Fred returns his attention to Adam's body, kissing his way back down to the soft hair around his penis, then sucking a little more before asking, "How do you want to come?"

Adam shakes his head. "I can only come when I fuck," he says, the hard word sounding even harsher in his percussive speech.

Jeff turns long enough to look at him. "No. Really?"

"I always been like that. Only when I fuck. I never jack off or anything."

"I never heard of that before," Fred says, disbelievingly—he knows this is a lie, can only be a lie, but not why or what it means. He's excited by the new thought that this boy with his pubic hair and a dick already bigger than his own might never have come at all and uses this as an excuse not to show he can't. Why else make this story up? It's too much to be possible, if not to hope for: Sexually experienced but still somehow a virgin. It does let Fred off the hook of having to give good head, more trouble than he's usually willing, able, to go to, and with some relief he moves around so he is parallel with the boys and begins on himself. He reaches down again briefly to stroke Jeff, but no more than enough to be polite, and then he turns all his attention to Adam, and to himself. It is immediately awkward; he uses his left hand but Adam is on his left, and so in this position he can masturbate or he can fondle Adam but not both. He tries reaching over with his right hand but can touch no more than the boy's arm and chest. He jettisons the last pretense of fairness and asks Adam to move, which he does, making a show of climbing over to Fred's right, Fred moving to the side of the bed as the two boys poke and shove each other playfully until they're settled.

Now Fred can begin. The boys are whispering and he says, "I can't concentrate if you're talking," says it with a smile to Adam, a smile that says (he hopes) "I'm not like this, not pushy and fussy, just hurrying so you can get out in time"—a lot for a smile to convey. Adam smiles back, avoiding eye contact now, closing his lips over the upper teeth; he is really sensitive about that crooked tooth, which exaggerates his sexy—to Fred— overbite and sensuous upper lip. Fred adjusts himself, Adam on his side facing him, Fred's right arm under him, around far enough he can stroke Adam's slim firm ass. Now is when he regrets Jeff. If it were the two of them he could ask Adam for all sorts of things he would never do with another boy in the room but might—who knows? worth a try—on his own.

As it is, Fred won't even risk embarrassing him by slipping a finger into his ass or asking him to suck his nipples. He looks at Adam, is disconcerted to find him looking back now, pushes his head down so it rests next to Fred's shoulder, and continues. On the other edge of the bed, Jeff finishes with a few sighing gasps; Fred raises his head enough to see him sitting up halfway, reaching for a Kleenex to wipe up the small spill of white foam that has dribbled into his pubic hair. Jeff holds himself, wilted and dripping, in one hand and delicately cleans up with a few squeezes to bring out the last of the come. Adam looks over his shoulder and laughs a little, childishly, at the sight, then turns back to Fred and watches his working hand. Fred stops and picks up the jar of lubricant—recommended as the best for this in some book he'd thumbed through once—from the floor and takes out just enough. He begins in earnest, feeling the smooth skin of Adam's butt under his fingers, wanting more, wondering how much he might ask without asking too much.

"Put in it on my leg," he says softly after a moment to Adam, who understands and reaches down to move his half-limp but still impressive dick onto Fred's thigh where it rests like a flower offering on an altar. Fred pulls the boy closer, wanting as much of this skin as possible, wanting to smell Adam, to taste him, to see and feel the slightest movements of his body as he shifts and breathes. He wants to concentrate to the exclusion of all else on this boy, for his senses to perceive nothing that is not somehow Adam. He has always wanted this; with boys less purely beautiful he can never even hope it's enough, his fantasies taking over where their appeal ends, he must fill in what they lack and do all the work of turning the inadequacies in his arms into what he needs. He doesn't come because of them, he comes because of what they should be. Nothing else is possible anymore; even meeting someone for the first time, flattering him, looking for the right boy in him, the boy he wants, he knows it's one more fantasy.

But sometimes he doesn't know. Now he doesn't know. This boy is too good not to be perfect. Adam has the look and the smell, the sound and the smile, the grace and the charm that promise everything. As others had, too, but promises don't all come true.

So Fred works on himself. Adams's head is on the sheet next to him, held away from his shoulder, it would be perfect on his shoulder but he twice tries to shift the boy's position and both times Adam moves slightly and refuses to touch his head to Fred's body. Beyond Adam Jeff again seems asleep, maybe is asleep. Fred will try to forget he's there. He spreads his legs, relaxes, feels the skin Adam offers him, right leg slightly bent at the knee over his own right leg; dick palpable on his upper thigh, inches from Fred's own; from pelvis to shoulder they are one, sweat from the boy's hairless tawny skin mixing with Fred's, tiny squishing at the slightest move. Fred goes on. The hand on Adam's ass drifts to the narrow opening and probes a half inch in, met by another clench and a shift of the hips. He opens his eyes to see Adam give a half humorous shake of his head so he strokes the solid skin around the opening, reaches far enough down to stroke that tiny strip of moist flesh from asshole to balls. It is hairless, too. A boy.

Fred looks at Adam again, his eyes closed now so he can be watched without embarrassment but Fred doesn't, the angle is too sharp for comfort, so as though he were with someone of no interest he closes his eyes feeling all he can feel as his hand works, first fast, then slow, full strokes followed by massaging just the head, a pause or two to empty himself of everything else—the too-loud TV, the fact of Jeff, Adam's stiff reluctance. These shouldn't register—it should be all Adam, Adam, Adam—but the reality isn't working. Not quite, even with the boyish scent of strawberry drink on his breath and the smooth promise of his ass. With each pause Fred looks at him who does not look back.

So when he finds it it is like most of his others, except the boy he holds is closer to the center, so close to his own center of desire, his own fantasy. It's like this the first time with someone sometimes but by now usually he has realized he is with the wrong person, the boy who looked so promising is not *the* boy, only another pretender; at the instant he comes, before the first little explosion has even landed on his stomach, his mind has already detached from the desire, the act, and sees the boy he has used for the inadequate thing he is. Adam is not inadequate. Jesus! He should be enough, more, but now by himself is not enough. Fred wonders if Adam has come at all yet, this "can't come except when I fuck" line sounds like a macho kind of excuse for something not quite so macho, but still the thought excites him. He looks down at the boy's sleeping dick, the small puff of dark hair around it, and pulls the body encircled by his right arm a little tighter. And there it is. He closes his eyes and it is the next time and they are alone. Adam has never come but now he can, now he can at last, he pumps and strains in Fred's mouth, just the barest sharp smell now of him, of sweat and energy, a boy playing ball maybe, and he loves it, Adam does, loves the slow rising, the accumulation before the explosion. Now Fred looks at him quickly again, bringing it closer, himself closer, he pulls his boy tight to him and continues, eyes closed again, tastes and hears and feels Adam's coming, his first spurts in Fred's mouth and has it happen again and again, each time bringing himself closer until he hears himself sigh and stretches out one leg and lifts his head off the sheet, gathers it all in, groaning as he comes six, eight inches up his stomach, sighing, fondling Adam's ass as he finishes.

He stops after the usual eighteen, nineteen twitches of pleasure, away from what brought him there even as his hand coaxes the last juiceless sensations. He breathes deep, sighs again and looks at Adam, who looks into his eyes with a smile, perhaps half-scornful, perhaps looking for agreement on how funny this whole sex thing really is.

Jeff and Adam are in a hurry to get to their appointment and Fred is afraid he will be forgotten, a blip on this boy's radar that will disappear as soon as they're apart. He walks them to the elevator and back down to the street, a bit disappointed this time to be offered the standard handshake; he hasn't impressed Adam as someone whose cool knowledge of such things as three-part handshakes can be assumed. He holds Adam's hand longer and more firmly than needed so he can say, "You be around later in the week?"

Adam's mind, already elsewhere by the time he'd tucked two folded bills, a twenty and a ten, into his sock before they left the apartment, refocuses as he looks Fred in the eye, then away, and shrugs. "Sure, okay. Wednesday's all right?"

"Wednesday's fine."

"Over there around seven, okay?" He jerks his head in the general direction of the street where they met. "Where you were today."

Fred agrees and they shake hands again. Then he waves to Jeff a few feet along his way, getting in return a quick odd look and a two-finger wave good-bye before the two follow their long shadows down the afternoon street.

Done. Done, with the promise of a future.

Afterwards Fred imagines a first meeting on his own, with a slightly different Adam:

Fred: You come here often?

Adam: (Shrugs) Just, you know, sometimes on weekends, see what's up.

F: You do a lot of this? Make money out here?

A: Nah, nah. That one time with Jeff is all.

(The best Fred can hope for. Jeff is no longer with them, has had a better offer or something. Airbrushed out.)

F: You've got to be careful.

A: Yeah, that's why I don't like to. I need the money, you know. (Rubs thumb against the second and third fingers of his left hand. Quick eyes-averted smile.) Gots to have money, but.... (Gots? Fred can't remember just how black Adam talks, doesn't know whether he'd say gots for got. There were some be's in there, though. "We be...." "I don't be....")

F: I've seen you around a few times, late.

A: Hanging out. Just chillin' is all.

F: You can always come over and chill out with me.

A: (A look. Quizzical, ready to be amused or flattered,

broken off when it meets Fred's own serious ready look.) I don't be too good at keeping appointments sometimes. (The p's in appointments struck like a gong no doubt by some memory of appointments missed.)

F: Worth a try.

The wait begins. It is constructed from conversations he might have someday with someone, maybe even Adam, Fred going again and again to where he wants to be; the same questions, requests, confessions, confidences run again and again through his head like prayers. Things he would do anyway, selecting fruit or cleaning the bathroom or walking to work, become elements of the story (it is all the one story. Fred and Adam are together, the bond between them a weld, and everyone knows and is startled and admiring), a story of ways of being close to this boy, of impressing him with kindnesses, generosity, knowledge, with savvy and experience of every useful, every admirable, kind. These fantasies form a parallel life—from the morning alarm all the way through the day's work to reading a few pages before bed to reassure himself there is more to his first, his real life than the boys he might find on a few Manhattan blocks—everything he does alone involves two people, an alternate Fred with an imagined Adam next to him, both being watched, maneuvered, supplied with words and things to do, kept handy at all times to give Fred the life he would right now like to live. And Fred has waited already, might say he's pretty much waited his whole life for this chance, to have this boy to wait for. Not that this life of waiting hasn't been rewarded other times; he has found before what he'd thought he was waiting for, and has lived through and gone beyond the reality of finding, eagerly embracing, what he'd wished for, only to find that although it looked right, felt right at the moment, it wasn't, not really. Maybe this time is different. He has to think so. Until now each hope he's rushed to has left him where he started, still waiting. Or maybe waiting again, although in retrospect it seems like one long stretch, an unbroken life of longing. Not in the passive sense, Fred does not sit alone in a darkened room, expecting his future to seek him out. His waiting is restless, searching. Even sitting alone in a darkened room, in his mind at least he is always on the prowl.

It has been two lives as long as he remembers. The wait. The conviction there is out there someone worth waiting for willing to be—well, loved, Fred guesses is the word. He would have to show some affection in return of course, this boy, when finally found. That would be the minimum. And while waiting Fred rehearses, cannot keep himself from practicing how it will be.

And then there is the life he actually lives while the wait goes on. This is where the hundreds of unsuitable boys come in—wrong the way Jeff, say, is wrong; that is, almost *right*, right at first glance—perhaps no longer in the mid-teens (the perfect age) but young enough, good-looking enough, boyishly built, not threatening or contemptuous or dirty (Jeff with his definite odors pushes the limits, clean-and-dirtywise) or too hairy— almost right. It rarely takes even fifteen-twenty minutes in bed for the truth to become clear; usually the look and the sound are subtly wrong from the moment he comes close enough for conversation. It's rarely the physical flaws that spoil a boy for him, although there are hardly any Adams available anymore; Fred's problem is finding a person he wants to be close to. He doesn't need innocence exactly—a good thing he doesn't, on the streets of New York—but he wants a boy who lives *his* real life a certain distance from the street, from all that sex and show, and who can turn his mind to Fred, though not (let's be sensible) to Fred alone. There've been few who've come back for him and not only for the money, and so he hopes for the temporary best from each encounter—a good time, no problems, someone who at least won't become a nuisance, one of those hazy memories of disappointment materializing on familiar street corners day after week after month, asking for one more time, for a couple dollars. If he can't have the boy he wants—(Boy is too much to hope for most days. Young men, more often; Fred makes careful distinctions: Adam is a boy, Jeff a young man)—if he can't have the boy he wants, a young man who'll give him a no-regrets good time and then disappear will do. If love is not to be had, pleasure should be possible, losing himself, forgetting the wait for the time it takes to enjoy the sight and smell, the feel and taste of someone new.

But now, three days' wait, for the promise of a specific boy to be in a specific place at a specific time, is like a gift. There is no need to find a face to fit the story. He has the face. He has the boy and at least once more the chance for one reality to live in, the second life converging with the first.

Everything feels different with a real boy to wait for. They are together when Fred wakes up, there is sleepy soapy business in the shower, Adam drowsy but hard leaning against the tiles, Fred making him come—his first time?—the idea recurs in little electric thrills—while Fred in himself absorbs the sensations his other self comes by so easily; Adam is willing to do things for Fred he would never consider for someone else. There are no disappointments yet, so much that might actually happen.

Much of the pleasure, the satisfaction, in the second life comes from the reactions of others, Fred's triumph reflected through those who—let's face it—never thought that much of him before. Let's face it. He is impressive only within himself, little Walter-Mittyman that he is, with these secrets he can only imagine others knowing, actually believes might impress rather than repulse. Now he takes Adam through the day with him, every person met meeting two, every real act parallel with and inferior to that act with Adam, and inferior to the best of all: that act with Adam and witnesses. So there is a kind of third life here, in addition to the everyday and the everyday with Adam—the everyday with Adam and others watching: The looks, the whispers and shaking heads. They're together? That kid is gorgeous. And so sweet and affectionate. Hard to believe, isn't it? Even laughter would seem like recognition, if Fred could convince himself it wasn't deserved.

He bounces to work Monday morning happily not quite alone, with a secret he can't tell but can show in glimpses and carry around in a story, the same old story, turning the day-to-dayness into another life as he always does, treating reality like water he must push through, changing its shape as he passes and not turning to see it is the same still all around him. There is no one he works with—he's been here for years, known these people for years, likes some, doesn't care about the rest—no one here who *knows*, he thinks, really knows. Although sometimes he wonders. Sometimes when a boy has been in and Fred has noticed, has looked, has maybe moved from where he was for a better view, enough to get an idea of what he might be under the shirt, under the jeans, an idea made again of choice memories of some of those hundreds he has known—sometimes he thinks he's been too obvious and expects to see the knowing smile, the embarrassed eyes sliding away from his own. Knowing. The thing is of course he would not want to be known, exactly, not just like that, not exposed, only longs to tease the edges of the awareness other people have of him, what he is, what he might be.

The assumption is he's just another queer. That's all right, in New York it is, can pass without comment, if not without notice, like being lame or Jewish. Fred has had a stiff rapport with others of whom the same assumption was made, as though they might accept him and he them, men with something in common. But he knows better, feels his difference from them, too, at every moment. In fact there is no one with whom his nervous, uneasy awareness of difference does not intrude; there never has been that he remembers and by now the awareness is so deep there never will be.

The closest he has come to the truth has been with certain women he has known, almost sympathetic enough, he has thought, for confessions, but still he has never done more than circle around the truth, the dangerous truth. He has never had a simple moment of complete honesty with another adult. Partly it's that he is not sure they will see his passions as something worth considering, they might not like him enough even to try, he is unwilling to risk that they might understand and turn

41

away. And the lifelong habit of secrecy is too strong to break. And there is a mystery, glamour, almost, in having a secret. Having this secret.

Fred works in a middle-size bookstore in such a busy location it doesn't have to be very good, although he has pretensions he can project onto his job, such as that he is an important employee in a real literary establishment. He is big-fish-in-a-small-pond important; he's gotten that way by working harder than other people, most of whom are just there for the money, and by knowing more about books than those around him, most of whom don't know much about books at all. He feeds his ego by having enough obscure Gide and Horatio Alger, small-press histories of the French Revolution and the American labor movement, to impress some people. Even himself, when he doesn't look too closely.

So this is his life at work: He is usually happy to be left alone, and he is. He sometimes seeks out conversations with others (they don't often with him), or he joins conversations in progress that might not have started if he'd been present. He thinks obsessively about how others react—might react, have reacted—to words and actions of his, but he rarely thinks in wider terms, thinks himself into someone else's general view of him. If he did his exclusion from the run-on conversations among people he knows, works with, has known, in some cases, for years, might loom embarrassingly in his thoughts. There is nothing in him that responds for long to the flow of real talk, he loses interest, never has enough interest in anyone else to listen for long; he waits for his chance to make jokes, points, an impression; always in the flash of time between thought and speech he seems to have the perfect words and sometimes he's rewarded with smiles, nods, a change in the general tone. At least as often he completes his own thought, adds to some part of the ongoing conversation with himself others can't be expected to understand when he brings them into it. Real talk is rarely what he has imagined, he is never thought as funny or as clever as he expects to be. Afterwards, when his attempts have been met with blank incomprehension, as they too often are, he wonders sometimes what he could have been thinking. He knows that other people—reality—are only a distraction for him; they take him away from where he wants to be, in that parallel life where he's so much more comfortable than he is in life as it's actually lived; in his second life, for one thing, he is a social success. He may not know that usually his discomfort shows, he is not quite present to others, he slips away to where he wants to be and they are left talking to an odd emptiness. He tries to respond in a regular human way but his words— which flow so well in his mind when he controls both voices— seem false, even to himself, when part of actual conversation with another person. Perhaps he doesn't fool anyone, he doesn't really know; sooner or later maybe it becomes obvious that it is not him speaking but someone he isn't but wants to be seen as. Something anyway sooner or later turns almost everyone aside, if not completely away from him—the falseness, or the wariness he's developed from fear that the falseness is noticed, or the way that without all he keeps to himself his part of conversations becomes inappropriate. Something. The fact is he doesn't care much or for long at a time. This life isn't life.

So he is solitary even with these people he knows and sees daily, moves through a routine so regular as to be almost military, built from the bits and pieces of work he has claimed for his own over the years here, as he has taken over jobs small and large, gradually making himself indispensable. On Mondays, say, like today, he will go through the first half of the alphabet in the bookstore's Mystery section and through all of Poetry and Plays, straightening, stocking and making up orders all at the same time. He has no computers, no lists of standard stock, only what he knows and remembers; he knows and remembers quite a lot. He is happy to let everyone else think he knows enough, is good enough, to make this store something special. He knows better. But he is more than willing to hear the odd, barely deserved compliments. "It's so good to find a bookstore where they've actually heard of Djuna Barnes." He smiles, nods, shrugs modestly; he has heard of her, though he's never read her. "This is our computer right here," is how he, with some regularity, is introduced. He lies when he doesn't know something, claims false but plausible reasons for being out of this or not carrying that, lies quite a lot, in fact, and well. It rarely hurts him any. At worst, another lie can always cover the first.

Life at work in other words gives excuses for another kind of second life, another near accomplishment. He is good enough to be thought really good. It is still a second life because he knows he is in fact only just good enough, only good enough compared with what others here can do. Most of the time, when no glaring gap has appeared in his stock, no shortcoming been uncovered, he can live this version of a parallel life: Not just good enough, but good.

He has the luxury of this freedom and prestige, of being a big fish, because the couple who run this particular small pond are happy to see him as what he claims to be. He is an ornament, smart enough to be convincing, and there is some pleasure for them in being old-fashioned bookstore owners with an old-fashioned bookish trivia fountain for a clerk. And Fred wonders sometimes how much he is an excuse—"Why spend all that money, we've got Fred"—for them to avoid investing in computers and inventory software, the expensive necessities of any modern bookstore.

He knows it's just as well for him they don't. Computers would level the field. He could no longer interrupt other people's conversations with corrections and answers if the answers were a few keystrokes away for anyone. If he could be checked on that easily he could no longer be quite as confidently, carelessly wrong as he sometimes feels free to be. He shakes his head along with his co-workers when they ridicule the owners' refusal to invest in a computer. But he knows his own interests.

At work today Fred is a man with a secret. He smiles, he whistles and sings to himself—he'd had a Beach Boys tape on the Walkman on the way over, a choice, their bouncy threads of love and disappointment too thin to hold real pain—whistles and sings (to himself), "Let's get together and do it again" and hopes everyone notices, imagines everyone noticing.

And some people do. But from shyness or fear, all that accumulated habit, he can't make the most of it. He is coy and smug instead. "Well, you're in a good mood today. Have a good weekend?" is one of the first things said to him, even said with a bit of a leer, what he wanted to hear and how he wanted to hear it, but Fred just grins and shrugs and says, "Very good. Quiet." As though he'd been to a movie he'd liked. He doesn't leer, he isn't the leering type, but he can't even work up a good hint he isn't afraid will be followed up by questions that will spoil his secret with embarrassment. So the reality is just, "Very good. Quiet." Again, still, it's his second life he'll look to for pleasure.

The first two people he sees at work are the two he's known longest; he thinks of them as friends, as much as he thinks of anyone as his friend. Frank, the one who mentions Fred's mood, is the lone black employee, and has thrived here, thrived among whites in general (he prefers the company of whites) by being a sort of anti-stereotype, someone for whom the whole racial thing is a bit of a joke, a joke he is in on and most blacks, most whites, are not. "I know them better than you do," he might be saying, sly, a spy in the other camp, "and all your suspicions are true. Except about me." His discussions of race are likely to end with his dismissal of the complaints of "foolish Negroes." He wears military caps and jackets, tries to harden his round teddy bear face with massive sunglasses, owns a motorcycle—an American one, he's quick to say, a Harley—and guns he insists on his right to. His image seems to require a string of flashy white girlfriends courted behind the back of his flashy white fiancee. And all of that's softened, made almost attractive, because Frank sees himself: He's in on the joke he might, with a little less self-awareness, become—an unpleasant bumptious bigot. He is truly genial, lightly self-mocking. And the edges, the edge of anger, edges of money worry and worry about women, Fred suspects even worry about being seen by the superficial as what he most despises, as "another foolish Negro", stay almost hidden under the face he wants to be known by.

Greg is something different altogether, he is what those who don't know better think Fred to be, a gay man standing near the door of the closet, unwilling to call attention to himself but not hiding, either. Fred envies Greg his unglamorous secrets—the boyfriends (always referred to only as "friends" or, in the case of one who died after they lived together for years, his "roommate"— never lover, never anything implying more, however evident the more might seem). Fred envies Greg something else as well, something substantial Fred uses to round out his second life but which he knows he lacks in the first one: An ability to be there for others, in health and sickness, grief and pain. It is Greg, not Fred, who has nursed dying men and gone on to take care of all that comes after, Greg who has come back to rebuild his life, Greg who lives what Fred only daydreams—a life with others. Greg is Fred's age, slight and graying with a quick rabbitty smile and a tendency to be annoyingly, single-mindedly thorough. Greg is a living reproach.

Aside from working in the same place, Frank and Greg have little in common except that Fred doesn't want to be thought of badly by either one. So it's, "Very good. Quiet," with Frank. And Greg is preoccupied with his work, puts on his little half-glasses to study an order form, not noticing Fred's mood—or at least not mentioning it; if there is anyone Fred suspects may be aware of him, his tastes and glamorous secrets, and disapprove, it is Greg. Even if not Fred will call no more attention to himself in this. Not in real life.

Today, another day, glides by, greased lightly by the unshared knowledge of Wednesday, renewed constantly because Adam can be brought through the door at any second in front of anyone, everyone, can be made to say and do whatever Fred wants, the effect always perfect. All these years, decades, polishing what works and what doesn't, what feels good, feels right, have left those few always reliable stories—all the same story or two, really—and they hurry the day by, cushion the fact he is alone and has no idea if Adam will keep his appointment, obscure facts so well they may never intrude at all. He will have three good days.

And nights. Without the "yes", without some promise, however shaky, of meeting Adam again, Fred knows he would have haunted the streets Monday and Tuesday nights, made a fetish of that corner where he'd seen his boy first, that block where he'd been glimpsed the few odd nights Fred had seen him before. The story Fred lives now, Adam out there in a certain place at a certain time not far off, soothes two ways, giving him a life to live that makes the life he lives smooth and full, and giving him a hope that makes any effort unnecessary; if he can believe, even only just, that they will meet, he doesn't need to walk the streets, looking and hoping. He has what he hoped for.

By Wednesday afternoon it's grown thin, the promised life. As the day goes on Fred begins to prepare himself for disappointment, which becomes the first act in other stories, happy endings delayed by circumstance. The meeting he has planned and rehearsed is there still, ready when he needs it, but now the time has come to prepare for the possibility he will stand on that corner, walk that block—and the next one and the one across the street—for hours. He is ready for this, too, ready for Adam, the Adam who is with him always but not tonight, who tonight will be late, will not come, will need to have his absence covered in order to make Fred's disappointment only a pinprick. These stories have all been used before; now they include Adam. There is the simple late and sorry story. There are the unable to come story and the injured, arrested, somehow helpless story, Fred finding out, showing up to rescue him from threats and disasters. There is the arriving late in trouble story; Adam chased, maybe, threatened, in danger anyway, and there's Fred, loving and unafraid defending him in words, even fighting, risking danger himself, walking off with his love in spite of the gun at his back. There is even the spite story, Fred rejecting the penitent boy who shows up too late for excuses, or on a different night altogether, Fred barely consenting to notice the genuine remorse, the genuine pain, the genuine desire they should be together. That one is for much later on an empty night. After hope. There is even rattling around the attic of Fred's mind a story of another man, Adam somehow in thrall to someone he of course much prefers Fred to but can't quite get away from; Fred becomes Adam's refuge, his secret lover. That story has all the glamour he could want, and secrets to keep, and the lush pain of a boy his own but still shared. That one is for later still and passes quickly, observed but not considered. Actually thinking about any of them would be too embarrassing even to Fred, would make even him smile at his own distance from reality, from any sort of sense.

Fred doesn't want to appear as eager as he is, of course, he must seem cool, so he makes himself wait, eats a light early small dinner—God forbid the middle-aged man's after-meal bloat when he is alone with Adam for the first time—and reads the paper with bare attention. He washes himself in the important places and changes into a black T-shirt and slacks that don't make him look stumpy and fat. He hopes he'll remember to be less stoop-shouldered than usual, looks critically at himself in the mirror to find nothing has improved, the slight roll of fat shows above his belt, the overall effect is not he knows attractive. He smiles at his reflection and gives himself the usual out: He's the one spending the money, that's as much attraction as he needs. There are moments like this when he sees perfectly clear the self who has nothing that might keep a boy except cash and whose tastes assure he may never be happy or even safe with these boys he chases—moments when he knows the truth, smiles back at it, at the homely chunky unimpressive self in the mirror. Smiles. And then turns way and puts his stories back on, his parallel life, the way he'd replace skin-tight Lycra with something that allowed for secrets and doubt, something roomier, more flattering, than the truth.

He is early, so he hovers nearby, across the street and down the block, eyes trained on the magic corner, waiting for the time to come, stories of things going right jostled by the ones he's rehearsed just in case. Seven comes and goes and the first doubts become solid, begin to take on the deflated shape of disappointment. The stories bounce through his head as he stands and walks in the pre-theater crowd, and somewhere in the part of his mind that remains in reality, keeps him functioning day to day, is the knowledge that he had seen Adam before, he will see him again, some night, on these blocks, a surprise to both of them (Fred's been through all this before—Adam had made his promise unthinkingly, forgotten it before it was even out), Adam reminded by the sight of Fred that there is money to be made. And then it begins again. He shakes his head, remembering how he hates it, the time it takes, the nights of lost sleep, of walking and waiting when there is so much else he might be doing.

This night, unlike the Sunday before, is real New York summer, hot and sticky, the air visible in the middle distance, blurring the world a dirty gray. Greasy stains on the sidewalks in front of the fast food joints flavor the air and half-closed garbage bags waiting for the next day's pickup add their spoiled stink. Fred feels damp, his shirt sticking to his back, sweat trickling down from his armpits, assaulted on every block by human smells, rotting food smells, the lingering pockets of exhaust from trucks that drove by minutes before. He squints, contact lenses feeling dry, and looks for his boy.

For the first half hour, Fred, tensely hoping, walks only as far as that corner is visible, as far as Adam could be recognized through the heavy air. But Adam isn't there to be recognized. Fred moves halfway up Forty-third and back to Eighth, down Eighth to Forty-second and back to Forty-third. He crosses to the other side of Eighth and stands near the subway entrance, slightly back from the corner but able to scan the entire block, alert for the walk, the attitude, the cap set perfectly straight. There is no shortage of any of these, but not together. Not Adam.

Heat and the streets go together, heat and restlessness, heat and sex, and the block Fred watches is busy tonight, a mingling slowly changing crowd barely rippled by passers-by going up to the theater or down to the Port Authority. This is part of the whole scene Fred is so familiar with; unsupervised peep show booths showing three minutes or so of porn for a quarter are popular spots for the twenty-dollar blow jobs the more desperate hustlers specialize in, and some of the men and youths who earlier in the afternoon might have been in front of the bus terminal have moved up here. At least one young man lounges in front of each of the block's three porn shops, ready to accept almost any cash offer to duck into a booth inside. They are regarded without much interest by the older men who've already had them. Some of these might be less particular later on, but it's early, there may be other possibilities. From his vantage point across the street Fred can pick out a dozen faces he recognizes from his hundreds of days and nights walking the short stretches of sidewalk that matter in his own hunt. They are where he would expect them to be, doing what he would expect them to do. The sellers strut and pose and strive for eye contact. The buyers watch and wait, forming little groups here and there, chatting with their favorites, talking and laughing for a few minutes before moving off again alone. Fred's eyes shift from man to man, group to group, anxiously registering every face, head, back, walk, as a negative: Not Adam.

As the evening passes and expectations die he moves a little further from the corner, but not too far, walking and watching, hoping no one bothers him. He begins without music, keeping the Walkman headphones on his ears as an excuse to ignore approaches. At first his eagerness had been so strong, the stories he had so loud the music would only have been a distraction. As hope fades the music comes back and provides its usual background to less possible, less urgent daydreams. He was uncertain enough bring the quiet stuff, he has James Taylor and Patsy Cline, voices that break in the right places, balancing yearning, happiness, regret. They can help Fred find balance, too, find the story that keeps some hope but allows for the throat-tightening satisfactions of watching his own sadness.

The stories are spun—the late story, the too-late story— until it gets late enough Fred is stuck with the wrong-night story and the forgot-altogether story. He realizes how much of his disappointment comes from the knowledge that he will be sliding back into that old life of his; Friday nights, Saturday and Sunday afternoons, are one thing, but it's years now since he's felt so out of his own control that he's unable to keep away from these streets at all hours. In that unlamented past he'd been kept out by the knowledge that, after all, what he wants he's found here before, or close enough for hoping, and maybe will again; any time of the day or night could be the one. Now it's knowing Adam has been here before. So. Any time of the day or night.

Tonight will be a late night, the first of as many as it takes to find Adam or give up on his being found except by chance. Fred walks, stands, walks, stands, doesn't take care the way he usually would to make his path a wide circle so as not to be noticed enough to be approached by the bold and the shameless, with their lies about good times. He walks up and down the busy side of the street avoiding eyes and faces he knows, not seeing Adam, until the crowd thins down to the most desperate of the almost young and the most hopeful and reluctant, maybe loneliest, of the older men. A dozen times he sees himself turning that corner and finding his boy back on that hydrant. He listens to what he wants to hear. "Why can't I forget you and find somebody new, instead of dreaming sweet dreams about you?"

Adam has been here before. And could be again. At any time of the day or night.

Fred sometimes wonders why he's always able to sleep, no matter how miserable he tells himself he is. That isn't the way it's supposed to be, broken hearts and sleepless nights are cause and effect in every sad song he knows. "You'll walk the floor the way I do…." "Four in the morning, crapped out, longing…." Walking after midnight because you can't sleep, not because you're still out looking for sex. But sleep he can, and does, as always, lulling himself with what might yet happen. There's tomorrow night, the night after that, the night after that. He wonders at himself, but he knows; it's the stories that keep his heart whole, the parallel life that lifts the full darkness of his own midnights. Tonight he sleeps like a well-fed child.

And then he does what he's always done, what he can't not do. He walks through the next day even less present than usual, somewhere else almost every moment, blocks and a life away, the work he does flowing from some part of his mind that operates on its own. Another man might wonder if his lack of interest in those around him is so evident it's like a sneer, part of the reason all his connections with others seem to short out sooner or later, to wither instead of develop. If they begin at all. Fred doesn't wonder. A song he's carried with him down the years has been slipping through his mind lately, as it does from time to time when, he guesses, he's thinking about some new boy who reminds him of the one he'd first connected it with, and the day after Adam doesn't show up he finds he's singing it to himself, not all of it, he doesn't remember more than a phrase or two and that not for sure, but there it is: "In a white room with black curtains near the station." While thinking of Adam he remembers a boy whose name he's forgotten if he ever knew it, an untouchable boy in the neighborhood where he grew up, a boy who mowed the lawn a few doors down, shirtless in cutoff jeans, dark skin growing darker in the sun, black hair sweatstuck to his forehead. Fred never even said hello, he doesn't think, tongue-tied always by desire, by other people, making excuses to walk back and forth on the block where this wonder strained and sweated, unaware. In Fred's mind—there only—they came together, in a dingy hotel room with little more than the bed they shared the few times they could meet. "Yellow tigers dance down moonbeams in your dark eyes," he sings in his mind, the other line he thinks he remembers. There is something satisfying there, thwarted lovers struggling to be together, the boy of course wanting to be with him, and it feels just as right brought forward these what, thirty years? to become him and Adam forced—why? whyever—to share brief tender moments somewhere they can hide. It isn't even a story, more a feeling, hope, a movie matinee glimpse of implausible passionate possibility.

Fred's next evening waiting for Adam is just what he was afraid it would be. He passes the corner, their corner, early, on the way home from work, circles, passes again, waits, reluctant to go home (any second of the day or night), while telling himself, I've never seen him this early except Sunday, telling himself to pass by occasionally, not to linger. It's always hard to talk himself into being reasonable when he can only think of the one thing. When he does go home it's to eat quickly and wash, and then he's back. Part of the streets.

It's a long evening. Standing, walking, standing some more, walking some more. The block, that corner, are never out of his sight for more than a moment. Fred has his music and a version of Adam that has settled into place, a new face he's fit into the world carved out for all those boys before. He lives his second life here again, listening to love songs ("Like a snowball rollin' down the side of a snow-covered hill....") and loss songs (Even, "I've seen the needle and the damage done" can fit into a briefly satisfying story of his boy caught half against his will in some drug den, needing rescue) and avoiding eye contact with hustlers and dealers and men who share his taste. Again there is the tired helpless feeling as the evening disappears—and one quick moment of joy: A familiar boyish build and walk, a familiar head of dark curly hair, this time a striped shirt worn loose over dark jeans. Not familiar enough it turns out; this boy, this young man, is, seen from the front, older, darker, less: Not Adam. Fred feels pointless embarrassment yet again.

The real Adam doesn't show early or late or in between, probably, although Fred is nagged by the thought of himself at one end of the block as Adam passes by the other and disappears, or standing idly across the street looking right as Adam strolls up from the left to be instantly approached and made an offer that whisks him away before Fred ever thinks to glance that way. He is haunted by possibilities, they keep him there from early till late: Maybe Adam had both the night and the time of their meeting wrong, maybe he comes most nights, late, maybe he'll just happen to pass by. Only he doesn't this night. Or if he does he comes unseen.

Fred's day Friday is the same only less. The urgency is calmed; Adam, gone, may just become another story, although somewhere in Fred is a certain unaccustomed confidence: He's incorporated into all the stories the knowledge that he's seen Adam on that block before, not knowing him, having no connection, and so he will certainly see him again—won't he?—the connection made, all that first meeting stuff over, will only need to catch his eye before any of those others who will be trying, with the extra reward of taking this prize from those jealous old queens, a possibility that makes a story all its own—he sees their jaws dropping in the stunned realization they've had something rare snatched from right in front of them. They'll have to settle for one of those stale regulars, regretting Adam all the while. This shift of his thinking, or daydreaming, has taken him from necessity (he has to see Adam the second he comes around, not risk missing him) to the comfort of inevitability (Adam will be back when Fred is here. Sometime.) So he can begin to relax, in his fashion, in the cocoon of what should, might, will be. Waiting. He can do that.

So by Friday evening it's already routine, this new extension to Fred's life of waiting. The humid heat has settled in on the streets, Fred's midtown streets, hot enough for long enough by now that the smell of summer—greasy smoke and overripe fruit, auto exhaust and day-old restaurant scraps—can be assumed, inescapable as the hot still air itself. Its presence is one of those clichés—like dirty streets and crowded subways and the danger of crime—New Yorkers boast/complain about with pride; what they're willing to put up with to live here proves they're worthy of the city and its secrets, even if they can't agree on what those secrets are. Fred does it; this sharing of extremes is one of his standard lines of conversation, one of his few means of human connection: Too hot or too cold, rain or snow, anything outsiders might find intolerable, mentioned with an understood wink, a proud smile of city solidarity.

It's hot for walking back and forth when he arrives, before sunset, and he's tired to begin with, so he claims a spot half in shadow by the bank across the street from Adam's corner. Usually he is either on these streets in the hunt or he isn't on these streets at all, but tonight he's purely, literally waiting, and waiting—once initial hopeful daydreams have faded—gives him more of a chance than usual to catch some of the street life that otherwise would barely register as his mind raced forward, intent on a boy glimpsed in the distance, or on dinner or on a world he'd made with a memory and a possibility and the effect of … Rod Stewart, for instance. ("When the rains came I thought you'd leave/'cause I knew how much you loved the sun." Real romance.)

Fred knows all he wants to about the middle-aged and elderly men who cruise the streets as he does; most seem happy socializing even if they rarely get lucky, this might be a card game or bingo, the recreation as important as winning, although of course they still want to win. Those who have been coming around for years may have quit expecting big winnings; they will stand and talk to other older men, to the almost young men who wait outside the porn shops, young men they know and are no longer interested in, all the while eyeing every newcomer with brief hope—not of much, perhaps, but then they won't be much disappointed. Most of those newcomers, most of those out to sell and not to buy, learn quickly to be respectful of the order of things here: Stake out a position, wait for that first eye contact and for some acknowledgment (a smile, a nod), inviting an approach, then small talk leading to this or that or maybe nothing at all. There are constant shifts, comings, goings, one by one or two by two. Always, around and among these are the hustlers too desperate to take the time to observe the rituals; the addicts with no idea they leave the impression of being barely under control, ready to burst into violence or maybe tears; the self-absorbed beauties who know noise and motion mean attention and think too much of themselves to wait as if they were ordinary.

With time to kill Fred can look beyond this circle of men, old and young, whose routines he knows, and see the rest of the human traffic around Times Square—discounting theater-goers and commuting office workers and all those others just passing through (this is Manhattan) who might take any street or avenue on their way somewhere else. He watches those who pause or hang around or leave and return, those who want or expect something from these blocks. There are some different faces tonight, but it doesn't matter, those lingering here now fill the sidewalks for the same reasons they've been filled the nights and weeks, months and years, before, most of them most of all to be near the illicit and illegal, sex and drugs, crime and criminals, where so much is possible, where lives must be more thrilling than the lives they live.

Fred is one of them, or at least this place is part of the life he lives. Tonight as on nights before he will attract his share of attention—especially standing near his corner, watching; as a moving target he'd be harder to approach, could slide away, but since he doesn't move everyone knows he's waiting for something, they are suspicious or else they want to have what he's waiting for, to sell him—to be—what he's looking to buy. He shakes his head when approached, says no as firmly as he can without arousing anger. "Yo, wha's up? Wha's up? Watchu lookin' for?" "Nice young girls?" "Sellin' nickels." "Yo, pops, lookin' to hang out?" Shake his head, look the other way, turn the Walkman up so he can pretend he doesn't hear. Listen to "I got a peaceful easy feeling," listen to "If I fell in love with you, would you promise to be true?" Pretend it drowns out the sound of the streets. Doesn't even say, "Don't call me 'Pops'."

As he stands and waits and watches Fred notices again what he has noticed before, how few of those who linger, of those who reappear, alert for whatever brought them here and brings them back, are sure enough of themselves to face these streets without a face prepared for the faces they'll meet. The men seeking boys as Fred does have their masks, stretching truth in their own ways; theirs often center around their hair—dyed, combed over, added to, covered—hair trying to be young enough to match the youths they're after. It's the others Fred wonders at. Some sort of play-acting is natural for the young, like adolescents everywhere wearing selves borrowed from TV and movies, rap videos and street corner thugs cool enough to emulate. The adults though—the time so many of them spend in front of mirrors perfecting the look they want the world to know them by shows how much they care; it's an effort, this arrogance, this swagger. "You talkin' to me?" every one of them has sometime said to a mirror, maybe without a touch of irony, maybe believing that was the way men met other men. Maybe they're right. Few are immune to the need for an image that will keep them afloat out here, some vision of accomplishment or potential—mastermind, kingpin, player, mover, shaker; tough guy, intimidator, gangster, seducer, stud. Winner, in short. Something worth being.

From a distance the adults are almost indistinguishable from the adolescents. Jeans and T-shirts, sneakers and caps. All play by the same rules—street rules, which are prison rules, junior high hallway rules, playground rules: The biggest boast, the hardest push, the loudest threat, the nastiest sneer wins. Tattoos and muscles count. Ex-cons who can't adapt to the straight life can feel right at home with other men whose lives grind against the law. Their women (and most men here would think of a girlfriend, a wife, as "my woman") are like best suits of clothes, maybe brought around to show off but not for everyday; they can only complicate a man's life on the street. Most women regulars are addicts or whores; the occasional streetwise entrepreneur tough enough to hold her own among men is rare. Men who can't thrive elsewhere, or won't try to, have lives out here, careers as thieves or as small-time players or pimps, selling drugs or sex; their working tones are usually a little lower key than they'd use among themselves, whispering "Smoke?" or "Got coke" or "Nice young girls here" to the likely buyers who don't look like narcs (Fred hears a lot from them), their working manner still and watchful, though even the stealthiest, the stillest, can usually be spotted by the quickness always in their eyes.

These professionals compete with those few from Brooklyn or the Bronx who, coming to the city to sell their girlfriends or sisters, can be seen coaxing and arguing the girls into an arrangement. It's the money that counts, everyone agrees on that. There are even a few of the classic purple suit and feather hat pimps, almost distinguished in this company—their professional need to impress women as well as men has smoothed them out over the years, and they are older now, not necessarily here to work, more likely to stand around with their peers, burnishing the glow of claimed accomplishment, than to add to the general feel of violence just suppressed, crime just waiting to happen. They seem to think their look and the lives they've lived have earned them their share of the streets' chief honor, respect. Most of the youths here haven't gotten past the violence yet, the glamour of the criminal life, maybe want no more than to be around to see the explosion that always seems imminent, are hooked on the idea of it, the thrill the very thought shoots through them, their testosterone fantasies.

And there is violence, but not much of the tabloid guns-and-knives variety. Not enough to wait around for. Mostly it's the small, nasty explosions of anger over territory, even if it's a square foot of pavement that belongs to no one for more than a few seconds at a time. Belligerent standing and bellicose walking can make a stroll down the avenue an adventure. Be always alert for someone's sudden shift from walking to standing still in your path, forcing a detour or a confrontation—a sidewalk charging foul. Watch for the angry young men—one or two a night, always—walking with intent, aiming for shoulder bumps and brushes, excuses for the thrill (that word again) of exploding anger—self-righteous "What you looking at?" "Watch where you're walkin'!" anger. They stare down any approach or as they come close maybe look contemptuously away and pretend not to see, even the small victory of forcing someone to move aside an almost druggy delight. Watch closely: See the lead shoulder square and lower a bit for the blow? The arm stop swinging just before the hit? Fred sometimes manages to avoid these without seeming to, shifting his path slightly far enough ahead of them it might be a coincidence. When actually bumped he moves on and shows no sign he cares, or even notices, withholding that satisfaction is his own little victory. Who knows if he fools anyone—not himself, his fantasies of angry words (his own devastating, searing) provide him with an adrenaline rush just like theirs. Still, he can be surprised by someone older, almost always black, anger undiminished by time and experience, throwing himself around like a kid.

There are others. There are the few military men, in reality or in their own "You talkin' to me?" dreams, white men no longer young, in brush cuts and Fu Manchu moustaches, pieces of army fatigues, wire-rimmed sunglasses, looking like B-movie extras, usually hoping for someone to listen to their stories, true or otherwise. And there are the buyers to make it worthwhile for all those sellers, men looking for whores and drugs and stolen goods, cheap. Everyone thinks of the score, claims to think only of the score.

As Fred looks around this night he realizes how seldom he registers the men (they're almost all men) who are here every day at least from dawn to sunset working in stores and at food and newspaper stands. From where he waits he sees the two dark small Hispanics (the job description for fruit stand and pizzeria work) keeping an eye on outdoor displays for the market on the corner where he stands; the vigilant Orientals preparing to close the bags-and-sundries store opposite in the next block; the crazed-looking bearded man, always smoking and mumbling to himself as he tends the salt-and-garlic-smelling meat at his corner stand, its smoke giving this block an odor unmistakably its own.

Late at night (and Fred is still here late this night, to his own annoyance) all these are joined by the drag queens and their hangers-on—wannabes without the nerve yet for heels and wigs on the street—and their suitors, those who admire and yearn for the fictions they represent, or perhaps (the younger) just not ready to handle the real thing, feeling safer with someone they can treat like a woman without the risks they'd run talking to an actual girl; here at the slightest threat of rejection or embarrassment they can retreat behind contempt, yelling, "fag," ridiculing an Adam's apple or touch of five o'clock shadow—whatever it takes to protect their unformed manhood.

And the drag queens love a little drama, even that kind, some crave it even more than the toughest of the kicks-hungry boys do, the slightest touch leaves them screeching for their wounded dignity. Most, though, want most of all to be taken for what they try to be, for one night at a time: Another corner girl looking for some fun.

After Fred has been standing watching for a few minutes there's a commotion across the way; one person walking down the sidewalk can be enough for a commotion and this one moves through the crowd oblivious as a dog. He's young, thin and black (Fred's seen him on the streets before); hair dyed yellow teased into strings like Michael Jackson's, teeth capped in gold, he moves like someone late for his own coronation, grinning, bouncing to whatever music is in his head and never needing to speak or look anyone in the eye, his world is so complete. Others might be caught up in their own music, but not so much the world has gone away. He moves on, not slowing or seeming to notice anything outside himself, certainly not that he's one of the few sights out here that leave some amazement behind.

Even as he'd worked on it Fred had known his ability to convince himself of Adam's inevitability wouldn't keep him from staying late again. As someone who took no pleasure in school Fred developed early on great faith in the promise Fridays held of freedom from all the school-day be-there-and-do-that under the eyes of teachers who didn't like him, freedom to follow his fantasies, freedom to fill his time with a more satisfying life than the one he lived every day. What began as a child's living for two weekly days of release has been inflated and glamorized over a lifetime; his adult Fridays have a special tingle of possibilities: Fridays out here might mean— more than once have meant—boys whose own itch for Friday excitement would allow Fred to obliterate a dull empty week with the thrill of the hunt, even the thrill of success. Fridays in his mind have opened out in all directions.

This Friday he becomes bored waiting, watching, and with a mid-evening return of energy expands his range for a time from the one block to loose wide circles, the hydrant still their center, altogether about the same as the area of his usual weekend prowling, hunting walks. Some of the young men have noticed him around enough the last couple of nights they decide it's worth trying to catch his eye as he passes; the snake-thin black youth he'd seen Adam speak with on Sunday falls in step beside him with a half-whispered, "Yo, pops, wha's up?" Fred looks at him sideways—shirtless in tight blue nylon shorts and dirty white sneakers, chocolate pudding skin, satisfied stoned grin, no shame—and shakes his head and keeps walking. Maybe another night although the blatant approach, the all but naked body offered without the usual dance of eye contact and hesitation, makes him nervous. This kid might do anything. And Fred really doesn't like being called "pops".

And there are more of the ones he knows; he has allowed himself to forget his usual stock of singles for getting rid of them and they're not used to his saying no without some little bribe to make rejection palatable. First Tony, once very attractive Tony, whose life from seventeen to twenty-two has been a hard steady slide: A pretty enough boy—curly dark hair, freckled, slimly ordinary—nervously, rather sweetly, willing to be coaxed into using his mouth, he's now another fixture on the street—sallow, teeth rotting pursed cracked pleading lips. Willing to do anything, yet again. Saying no to him means guilt; he looks stricken, wags his head from side to side and makes whispered ultimate offers. Fred shrugs and says maybe next time, that old lie, and moves on. Someone else, whose name he can't quite remember, if he ever knew it—tall, twentyish, black, all confidence and no skill, even once was a mistake—at least has the pride to hear a no and walk away.

Fred moves among them, the new and the old, the cool and the anxious. He is alone every second, and every second he and

61

the person he wants to be with are together where he wants them to be. Not here. He stays through the slow shift from the early evening crowd larded with the curious and casual to the late-night collection of rejects and denizens. As usual all but the most extreme are strained out by the later hours, by ten-thirty, eleven, a few hardened or desperate hustlers are left, the drag queens and their courts, pimps and scaggy hookers, dealers and thugs and the few for whom the sleazy glamour of the street is never exhausted. Again Adam never shows. Again, maybe.

Saturday he is ready for a marathon, out, around, home, then out again, planning to schedule himself so he can do something else—clean house, read, something—but he knows he will be out, period. Adam has by now begun to fade into the picture, the general line of Fred's story has opened enough to take him in and fit his name, what is remembered (already Fred is forgetting) of his face and body, his voice and manner, into what is always there. Fred even looks with some interest at a new young man near the Port, dark, twentyish, a dusting of moustache and beard, smoking, carefully paying no attention to the early few who circle him, dance closer and closer, intent. Nice, but not nice enough, and Fred walks away, back to his corner and up the block, around onto Broadway past the last of those arcades that used to hold nightly promise of willing boys; for years now the arcades have ceased to be welcoming, even possible: He wonders again where they've gone, those (mostly) straight kids intrigued by money and new thrills and the very idea of sex (sex is sex to some boys, coming is coming), encouraged by others who'd done enough hustling to assure them it was easy money. So many boys then but now there are only a few, special treats, not a regular thing, for Fred and the others who hunt alongside him. Being there then, knowing at least once a week there would be someone new and young, desirable and available, was reward in itself, this block brings it back, how anyone might have been there for him, his offer of a quarter for the next video game understood to mean a little walk after and "hanging out," the universal code for something else.

It happened often enough to make night after night of nothing worthwhile. Times Square didn't welcome boys looking for fun and trouble the way it once had. Adam would have been lost in a crowd once. Well, no. In a crowd, but not lost. Not this boy.

And he isn't now. As Fred walks back to the corner he sees the familiar stance and back (unmistakable this time, he's instantly certain) as Adam stands talking with two young men Fred maybe has seen before or maybe hasn't—it doesn't matter, he's not interested in them—both black, one too heavy, the other homely, both too old. The only idea he's had all week is here, that's what matters. Suddenly Fred's as light and alive as if not a minute had been missed, the sight of Adam has erased all that doubt and waiting, hurt and disappointment. And in a way of course they've never been apart.

All he needs is to be noticed. Fred slows as he reaches them, on the right block but up a bit from the holy corner, Adam's back to his approach. Nothing will do but standing where he'll be seen; no greeting, no signal the others might detect, is possible. That code of the streets Fred prides himself on knowing. So he goes around them and into the little storefront where he'd bought the overpriced orange juice the weekend before. Seeing Adam he really is thirsty, throat dry with excitement, and he buys another orange juice and steps outside to pause in Adam's view to drink it. There it is, an adequate instant's eye contact, and Fred crosses the street to lean, perfectly confident, one leg up, against the wall of the old hotel opposite to sip the orange juice and wait. As he looks back he sees Adam look his way and give him a sign, right hand out at waist level moved up and down a couple-three times: Wait. He can do that. The best moment in his week of waiting.

Minutes pass, Fred pretending no interest in the little group across the way. He can catch few words but knows the gist, street talk, girls and drugs, sneakers and basketball, cops and scores. The three don't know each other except on street terms; the talk is loud and the gestures big, everyone anxious to impress. Adam is the youngest by maybe three years but the least loud and the most watchful. He isn't uncomfortable, though, he holds his own, Fred thinks, seeing himself someday welcome to stand nearby, silent, a question Adam doesn't mind having asked. For now he listens to the explosions of laughter, the loudest lies from across the street.

Adam pulls back, there's a backslap-hug and three-part handshake for each of the others as he moves off, knowing where Fred is, crossing the street down the block from Eighth and heading for the corner without looking back. Smiling at the cool of it, Fred follows at his own pace, fast enough to catch up at first but slowing deliberately, wanting to savor this, all the daydream seconds coming true, and to watch the walk, learn it so from a block away he'll know when Adam is around. It's a bit much right now, the walk—an extra rolling of the shoulders and hips is the conversation he's just had carried into movement, another way of talking loud, filling space with himself, as much the street as the boy.

Adam stops in front of the store near the corner and flashes his crooked-toothed smile at Fred, then averts it, his self-consciousness taking over again, and offers his hand in a conventional single handshake, again both a disappointment and a relief. "I'm out of cigarettes," he says. Not one of the lines Fred had rehearsed for, but no surprise.

"Newports. Right? That all you need?"

"Box." The accent makes the word harsh. "I'm okay otherwise." They go together into the little corner store and Adam hangs back a bit as Fred stands in line behind an elderly French couple, gaunt and precise in matching blue nylon warmup suits, buying yogurt and coffee. Adam looks out the door and Fred looks at him, his jeans today stiffer, a darker blue, this time baggy in the hip hop fashion, a tangled Warner Brothers cartoon fight on his black T-shirt, worn loose over the pants, same baseball cap as last time.

Adam takes the cigarettes, tossing the matches into a trash basket and slipping the pack into his front jeans pocket instead of opening it. "You missed our appointment the other night," Fred says.

Adam looks at him blankly, but recovers. "Oh, yeah, I was … I had to go see my father and shit." The lie is thin, something to finish the subject, Adam forgets it as soon as it's out. From him there will be no apologies. "So, um…." He looks at Fred from under the bill of his cap. "You paid both of us thirty last time, right?" Adam has one subject with Fred, so far.

"Thirty apiece," Fred answers, correcting him without seeming to, not saying the double payment was a premium for the introduction, for a chance at this moment, the two of them.

"So that's sixty, right?" Adam's smile is bright, crooked tooth forgotten in his eagerness.

Fred looks at him, surprised, half expecting the smile to turn to a laugh, but it stays, bright and—no other word—greedy. "I don't think that's the way it works," he says reasonably, hoping his doubt will make a difference.

"I'm not worth it?" Adam's smile shifts a little around the eyes, still certain, but trying harder. Fred has an answer ready for this question, one of those he's rehearsed for years, but the answer is, "People who think they're worth that much never are," one of his stock of waiting-for-a-chance putdowns. He doesn't use it now.

"Well, you know," he says. "We'll see." That seems good enough for Adam, who takes the cigarettes from his pocket and taps the pack four times quickly on the back of his hand before peeling open the cellophane and opening the foil. He has gum in his mouth, a small pink lump he pushes into one cheek with his tongue as he uses a clear blue Bic to light up with the single-handed flourish Fred had first noticed on the corner the previous Sunday. The money bounces around in Fred's head—he never has enough, even when he seems to have plenty, not tossing it out the way he does in small bills and big wads. Even while thinking this, he settles on another story, one that has also gone by before, even been proposed, never worked. A quantity discount—he might even call it that, this boy's got a sense of humor, maybe not about money, but still. "See me," Fred will say—how often? "Twice a week.

Forty dollars per. It adds up, right? You'll make more that way than sixty once a week." He has this conversation where he has most conversations and sees his offer accepted before he and Adam have crossed the street.

Fred's usual lack of small talk again leads to the weather ("At least it's not so sticky today") and school (Adam hedges, changes the subject, generally sounding like someone who should be in school but isn't—perfect for the fatherly lectures and displays of irresistibly practical advice Fred would like to be able to carry off. He doesn't try these now, of course, lets the subject drop as Adam wants it to, because Adam wants it to, fully aware this is real life, what works so well in his parallel life would be interference to Adam, making Fred rigid, uncool, adult, to be dismissed, even—God forbid—avoided).

Before the elevator has gotten to the right floor Adam has made it known he has to be somewhere—not right away (maybe he's calculated how much of his time is worth sixty dollars)—but soon enough. And this is a relief to Fred; he finds the gap between the conversations he has in his smooth second life and conversations in reality too great to bridge. Almost all the time, talking with almost anyone he feels the distance between himself, flesh, and the other person, flesh—gestures, smiles and frowns, nuance and inflection, all the signs and clues of the everyday, are a language he speaks a bit uncertainly and doesn't quite comprehend, like a second tongue imperfectly learned; he is never quite sure if he is understood as he intends, if the words he hears mean just what he thinks they do or refer to something else he has missed. Small embarrassing misunderstandings come often enough he is always wary, tries to measure his words, think, for God's sake, before he speaks, but things happen, the tone goes wrong, questions are asked and his answers skewed somehow, he tries to be witty and ends up being flip, he freezes because he doesn't want to seem flip but doesn't know what else to be—he can't quite be himself, that's safely—isn't it?—buried. Or later, only too late, he realizes that wasn't what the question meant at all, or what he said not what he meant at all, or was what he meant but not what he should have said. Too late.

He doesn't intend for that to happen now. Saying little, sticking to the obvious, is a way to avoid it—unfortunately also a way to seem dull, to be dull, and to seem to have nothing to say. Fred has much to say, but nerves and uncertainty keep it in that other life of his, the second world that accompanies him always, next to him not only in his straight, respectable everyday routine, but even now, when the lives exist in the identical time and place and with the companion he has longed for. But he cannot bring them together. So it goes, so it goes, precisely where he has wished himself and still he has to try to be something, someone, else, if only slightly other than he is. He might be in an office with strangers, not his apartment with a boy he wants to love.

Adam knows why they're here and sits down, businesslike, to unlace his sneakers. Fred hovers for a moment, not wanting to be noticed hovering, savoring Adam's presence: Details, details—thin quick fingers picking at the knots in his laces, tongue flicking past that crooked tooth to moisten the upper lip. Fred hadn't noticed how full Adam's lips are, had been too intoxicated to take in the first time all he now wants to soak up and memorize—those lips, the nose—nicely shaped, a bit broad—the eyebrows, as remembered, oddly thin and straight. Adam checks his new white high-top Nikes for marks, stopping what he's saying—something about going to a birthday party in the Bronx—to brush at invisible scuffs with the heel of one hand, intent for the moment on only that. He looks up and smiles, lips closed over the offending tooth—it isn't that bad, it's a charming flaw, a little crooked, a little gap, just enough to emphasize his slight overbite, and Fred finds an overbite adds perceptibly to attractiveness, making the so-so appealing and the appealing irresistible. Still, Adam doesn't like it, the gap, the crooked tooth, Fred seizes on that and it becomes a story, a Fred-and-Adam story, the first (as he thinks) that is only them, not just Adam fitted into the same old stories. Fred will pay for the dental work, he will be the one to rescue his boy from his discomfort—Fred has no money, he doesn't know a dentist for more than checkups. But for the instant, another instant that will be repeated, he can make the offer, see the gratitude, be the man who changed Adam's life, and all casually, like so many other just-right things he would do. Adam will be publicly grateful. Fred will talk to people about it. He will say to the dentist (who would know, at least suspect Fred's interest in Adam), "Close the gap but don't touch that overbite."

This develops in the dream time where Fred lives, glides through his mind like background music while he carries on the conversation, adds a layer of pleasant possibility to the reality of being in the room with Adam, who has stood and pulled his T-shirt over his head, and is as perfect as Fred remembers. Above his boxers, blue-and-red-checked this time, pulled an inch or so above the top of his pants, he is smooth, still; a growth of soft hair is noticeable on the arms and in the armpits Fred has a quick glimpse of as Adam lifts and folds the shirt before setting it on the dresser. Fred notices again that Adam is slim, all slimness, torso descending from boyish wide shoulders down a wedge of back. The elastic band on the boxers stops just below the tight knot of his navel; the too-loose (fashionable) jeans— Levis again—are held up, just, by the wide black belt he'd worn Sunday, with the Guess logo repeated in white letters; without it they would slide on their own down Adam's slender ass. As it is he removes them, careful again, standing in socks and the boxers to fold his Levis over a chair, safe from wrinkles. He sits on the futon and pulls up his clean white socks as Fred turns on the television, this time instantly switching to the Box, again the right thing to do: Adam's attention snaps to the screen as he hears the beat. He even stops chewing gum for a moment, the pinkish lump visibly held by his tongue against his front teeth as he's engrossed for the seconds it takes to identify the scene, the group, the song. Some hip hop something; Fred would have to concentrate more than he could ever be bothered to understand half the words, but he's heard of the group and can name one of their other songs and that should be enough to leave just a hint he knows some of this stuff.

But Adam is ready. As soon as he places the video he loses interest and turns his attention and a "So wha's up?" to Fred, who can only lamely answer with a shrug and a "What's up?" of his own—he can't quite do it, can't quite break his conversation down to grunts the way anyone Adam's age does automatically. Adam takes charge, standing and surveying the futon, trying to remember how it opens into a bed. Fred moves behind him, taking the opportunity to touch him, placing both hands at the top of his boxers for seconds, seconds only, hands half on the puckered elastic, half on smooth cool flesh, shifting him aside with a quick nudge, feeling a stirring in himself he has not felt until now. Until now the excitement has been something else, it has been the hunter's thrill, anticipated victory, as though he'd been kept from Adam by forces he'd had to overcome through cunning and determination. He did what he had to do, fought through the jungle. Now sex is the thing.

Fred pulls the futon out flat and throws the sheet he keeps just for sex over it. Adam climbs on to smooth the sheet so it covers the corners, reaches from side to side, on his knees, thin cotton stretched tight over his butt. Fred looks with longing but does not do what he most wants, doesn't even dare touch, let alone slide a finger under the cloth, squeeze the muscles, feel the softness—moist—the freckling of soft hair, just beginning. That would be still somehow not part of the arrangement, a liberty, so he looks and imagines the touch, pulling down the shorts, Adam cooperating, not moving, perhaps looking back at him with a grin of complicity as Fred strips off the boxers leaving Adam only in the white socks—dark slim boy wearing nothing but white socks is one of Fred's dreams—for Fred to touch, to push down flat on the bed, to open, hands pushing legs apart and tongue up and in (Adam will be clean, clean is one necessity, the sad reality of humans, all unhygienic, is one reason fantasies are a necessity), before turning him over.

As Fred imagines this all in an instant, beginning to undress himself, Adam finishes with the sheet and flops down on it, leaning back on his elbows to watch the TV. Fred moves aside, out of the way; he doesn't like being seen naked anyway and Adam isn't even slightly interested. When Fred is in only his white briefs he joins Adam on the bed, stretching out full length beside the boy, who looks for another moment at the dancing on the TV screen, uncertain now, not willing to begin, that's Fred's job. With a playful look Adam stretches and almost snuggles into the mattress before looking at Fred. "Wha's up?" he asks again. Then, never far from the thought, "So, sixty's okay, right?"

Of course it isn't. But Fred smiles back. "What do you think? Are you worth sixty?"

Adam grins and rolls over onto his stomach, buries his face, rubbing it in the sheet and stretching like a cat, back arched, before relaxing. Then, amazingly, he twists around to pull the boxers down and off and says, kicking them away, "You could give me a massage?"

This is so unexpected Fred hardly knows what to say. "Um, sure," is what he manages, rolling onto his knees to hover over Adam, who—he's done this before—moves both hands down by his thighs, waiting. Fred has no clue. He tries to think what he's seen on TV, anywhere, and begins where the shoulders meet below the neck, pushing his thumbs carefully into the dry firm flesh that gives a little here and moving out to the shoulders and the soft relaxed upper arms, drawing his fingers through the warmth of the armpits.

"Harder," Adam says. "In the middle more."

Fred had thought he was pushing hard but he tries again, going over the same small area with more force, not wanting to hurt but suddenly not sure he can do it right, maybe Adam is used to this kind of pampering, always gets massages from his men and will find this one inadequate. Fred should have some sort of massage oil handy—next time he'll be ready, quickly sees himself ready, the warm oil making Adam's skin glow slick under his hands, his boy's body lost in pleasure as Fred kneads his back, butt, thighs, then turns him over to find he is ready, too. Well.

70

Of course this is this time. Adam wiggles back and forth directing Fred's hands to the exact spots he wants massaged, never sounding quite satisfied as they work down his back, Fred straddling the slender naked body he barely has the chance to admire, he's so convinced he's failing. He's trying thumbs and fingers and the whole hand, inward, out, around. He's rubbing as hard as he can.

"Massage my butt." Adam's exact words. Fred moves down to rest astride his thighs and begins. It seems almost plump, Adam's ass, with him on his stomach. He begins, digging his thumbs deep into the rubber-firm flesh, the pressure of each push opening the cleft slightly; the opening is round and seems deep—it doesn't open enough to be fully spread. Fred, suddenly only interested in pleasing Adam as Adam expects to be pleased, does not at first even try to make this his sex instead of Adam's massage. "Harder," Adam says again. Fred works harder, fingers inches away from Adam's dick, thumbs an inch from his asshole. His erection begins to return and he pauses, quickly, almost furtively, almost as though it won't be noticed, to shed his thin white briefs, pulling them down his thighs and calves, leaning first one way, then the other, until they are off and dropped to the floor. Then he resumes his position, straddling Adam's thighs, half-hard dick hovering over his ass, both hands holding the boy's hips as his now-tired thumbs move rhythmically up and down.

"Now massage my calves," Adam says.

There is the sweet smell of the strawberry gum Adam chews. There is the sound of the Muzaky music on the porn video Fred puts on when Adam is annoyingly distracted by some new rap something, and the whir and rattle of the air-conditioning that sends a thin ribbon of cool air to cut the heat of the dim room—amber light through the closed blinds, the flicker of the television. There is the distance in this intimacy: Fred and Adam lay together on this sheet Fred keeps only for sex and Adam says yes or no. Mostly yes; Fred knows enough not to ask the definite "no" questions. Yet.

71

But they start with a no to a question Fred hasn't thought to ask. As they lay together after the massage ordeal—parallel on the bed, face-to-face, Adam, on his right side, arms folded across his chest (and what signal could be more obvious?), Fred on his left side with one hand on Adam's left shoulder, the other just under him, in the hollow above his right hip—Fred begins with a quick kiss on Adam's full closed mouth, as natural he thinks as smiling. Adam pulls back. "I don't kiss on the lips," he says. Not angry, firm, explaining, waiting for what's next.

What's next is disappointingly what it would be, with the extra twist that Fred doesn't want anything with Adam to be usual. He had wished it too much more. The old stories haven't had this life in years, the hopes haven't been so high. And Adam naked is everything he should be. But he's just another boy looking for money and maybe a good time and not thinking he has to do more than undress to earn it.

"You got condoms, right?" Adam asks, insisting on one before he'll let Fred put his mouth on him. When Fred comes up for air, mouth dry, saying, "I hate the taste of latex," he gets a grin. "You don't suck or anything?" Fred asks wistfully.

"I don't do any of that shit. I'm always just there for my tricks is all," Adam says, as though it's all he needs to say, as though he's said it before, has had to say it before. Says it and smiles.

Fred goes on. Adam seems indifferent to attempts to excite him, looking down at Fred with interest but no sign his hard-on is more than an adolescent reflex, no indication anything Fred could do would turn his natural excitement into the little frenzy that would make him come.

So Fred gives up momentarily and begins on himself, moving up to lie next to Adam and stroking the boy's stomach and legs. Freed of Fred's attention, Adam finds what he needs in the porn video on the VCR, as a stupid-looking young man walks around a room fucking four girls—spread, waiting—in succession, his face as blank as if he were sorting mail. Adam rolls over onto his stomach and begins to move, bouncing his hips up and down as he rubs his dick against the sheet. This is what's going on, Fred thinks, this is why Adam claims he can't come, he's embarrassed to have his friends see he still beats off like this, instead of with his hands. Fred had done it this way himself, always face-down on the bed, did it for years, maybe, when he was thirteen, fourteen—almost Adam's age. Now he raises up on one elbow, one hand still stroking himself, and watches: Adam, arms at his sides, eyes closed, upper body still as his hips bounce up and down in quick bursts, interrupted by glances past Fred at the apathetic fucking on the screen. Movements slow to a rhythmic grinding and then quicken again, shaking the light futon. Both hands remain open, palms up, by his thighs. Fred watches the long legs and the bobbing slightly raised clenching and unclenching ass, touching them tentatively after a moment, then more boldly when he finds his hand doesn't break the boy's rhythm—feels the working of Adam's tight muscles, telling himself it might not be only his hand there, works on himself with the dark opening he has hovered over and the legs he has held between his knees, the slightly sweat-slick skin he could lean over and lick but doesn't need to. He comes quickly and seconds later turns his head to see Adam—eyes still shut, head lifted from the sheet, mouth slightly open, upper overbite catching lower lip in a soft smiling sigh—do the same.

Later Fred will find the condom Adam has used to make himself come quicker, then rolled off his dick and dropped in the trash, and hide it away, limp, squashed and ugly as it is. He doesn't think why exactly. Souvenir. Trophy. Something to help him other days, when Adam's not around, just because of where it's been.

Afterwards Adam sits on the toilet, bathroom door open, Fred able to look in from down the hall and see knees and toes, a hand with paper folded over it, the profile of a dark face with curly hair, as his boy leans forward to talk about the last thing Fred wants to hear, how much more money he can make tonight. "I can make, like, maybe two hundred in a night, right? I go out right now and meet someone else, then one more after that." Fred is able to blot out the words, or what they mean, and the fact Adam lied to him about having to be somewhere, lied to hurry him along. He turns away as Adam wipes himself, listens to the sounds of rushing water, then the squeak and splash of the shower. Now is the moment, now more than ever, more than on the street or even in bed, when he is alone with Adam most as he wants to be. Adam is in there—the water level is raised and lowered, Adam's voice takes on a harsh edge as he chants loud unintelligible words in a rap rhythm, sounding like those people on the street singing along with their Walkmans with no clue how unmusical it sounds. Adam is somehow both elsewhere (in the shower alone where Fred doesn't have to chat or charm or impress) and here (in Fred's apartment where no one else is or knows where he is or can touch or talk to him). Fred can make him, can make *them*, himself and Adam, anything, because they are together though just enough apart that Adam, real boy, can't interfere with Fred's Adam. Who certainly isn't going out looking for any more tricks tonight.

Go out Adam does. To something. With fifty dollars in his pocket. (Fred has gotten away with pleading partial poverty, doesn't think the time is right for any long-term arrangement, doesn't want to scare Adam away by being too eager.) Again they have made an appointment. Fred, deciding a weeknight is too easy to find excuses for, makes it for the next day, impressing two o'clock Sunday on Adam as firmly as he can without seeming to care too much. He's let himself be seen to care before, with others. It's been a mistake.

And he doesn't follow his boy, doesn't slip out behind him and tag along to see if he does go back to the Times Square streets to look for someone else or if he just goes on home. Fred has before, with others, lingered out of sight nearby and gritted his teeth, hoping other men would pass on by the boy, whichever boy it was then, as though his own presence, unseen in some shadow, would be like a spell that would keep what was his, his. Now, though, he is satisfied, it was just enough, just good enough, he doesn't need the reassurance of knowing for sure. Adam out of the shower, nude and dripping, drying his face and hair oblivious to Fred's greedy eyes taking in the rest of him, is another vision he can live on. He tells himself the fifty is enough for Adam's night. He tells himself Adam really does have some party in the Bronx to go on to.

All toes are ugly. Adam's are a bit on the long side, thin, the skin like almost all his skin a dusky off-white. The smallest toes on each of Fred's feet are curved from fifty years or so of shoes, the tips of both big toes have reddish caps from ingrown toenails; otherwise his toes are clam white or pinkish, blushing from under their tiny tufts of hair.

Adam's feet, which Fred has also massaged ("That tickles. It's not hard enough if it tickles.") seem long although somewhere in their conversation it turns out they both have the same shoe size. They seem long because they are slender. ("You're going to be huge," Fred has said too enthusiastically in the quick forgettable during-sex conversation, misled by this slender illusion.) Fred's feet seem lumpier, with bluish veins and almost horny patches on the soles, the sides of the heels.

Adam's calves, so slim when he stands, seem bigger, loaf-like, but stiff with muscle under Fred's fingers when he lies on his stomach having them massaged. There is no hair on the delicate pale bridge of skin behind the knees, and little down the back of each calf, down the thin rope of tendon leading to the foot. In front of the calf there is the hard ridge of bone (to be massaged away from) with a couple of fetching small straight white scars Adam doesn't remember the origin of, and more soft hair, still not much, a dusting. Fred's calves are thick from walking, solid if any of him is solid, blue-veined white under reddish hair.

A knee is a knee. Thin, fat. Dark, light. Knees.

Adam's thighs. They seem long but substantial—everything is more substantial intimately, from inches away—dense, sensitive when kneaded between Fred's hands.

He can find muscles like buried rope with his clumsy fingers. Near the tops of course, outside, front and rear, is the smooth flow of flesh to the curve of the hip, but inside, inside, the most delicate smooth pale baby's skin. And between, from balls to asshole, the fine untouched connection feeling to Fred's exploring finger powder-dry, flawless. When Fred sits his thighs look like furry turkey carcasses, ready to be singed clean and cooked. Fred could take Adam's dick, soft, and his balls in the circle of his middle finger and thumb, like a napkin ring, and hold them captive, soft and flopping, bird-warm in his hand. But of course when Adam is hard it isn't possible and when they finish Adam is anxious only to leave so afterplay, aftertalk, is not possible. (Not that Fred expects more, he's used to this, too, as he's used to all the talk about other things; these boys after all don't want to think of themselves as part of this, talk about what they're doing makes them think about what they're doing, and why, and most of their lives—maybe Adam's too, Fred can't quite really tell yet—can't bear much thinking about, it's bad enough to live never mind thinking about it.) They want to do this and get the money and get out. So Fred looks and touches only what he can during those minutes he has before and during, to learn this boy. The balls, the soft loose sack holding them, delicate ovals swinging in a little more room than they need, more baby-smooth skin. Adam's dick is large—Fred thinks how big it might become, another fantasy in itself—circumcised, with the aureole-dark circle of skin a quarter of the way down from the tip a familiar mystery. Fred has managed, almost surreptitiously, to lick, almost a fetish, his favorite places—where firm becomes loose as dick meets balls, the joining of the inner thighs.

On the right side of Fred's abdomen, just above his crotch, barely discernible under hair, is the thin brownish scar, three inches or so, of a hernia operation. Maybe from the hernia, maybe not, one of his balls is swollen slightly larger than the other; both are tight within their usually shriveled sack. One, the left, tends to slip up when has a hard-on to rest uncomfortably on the pubic bone next to his dick. That dick is small, smaller than his pinky finger when flaccid, although adequate when erect. He has sometimes wondered if it's too small, but since it doesn't need to attract or excite or satisfy anyone, how could it be? He never really worries about it. As far as that goes it is, as the song says, money that will make the monkey dance. Of that he has enough. Some anyway.

Fred has always had a weight problem, nothing serious, but as he's gotten older the heaviness has settled above his waist; now a roll of fat, there's no other term for it, makes his shoulder-to-waist silhouette pear-like and hides his navel under a tight-lipped smile of flesh. And he almost has tits, soft tissue that ripples when flicked, and hair again, even on his back, which like the center of his chest has a few pale dimples to commemorate his decades of acne. Adam has no marks from navel to neck that Fred can see; he is almost too slim, but the definition is there, the thin hard fifteen-year-old chest and seamless stomach. His nipples are pinkish bronze, not sensitive, barely if at all swelling during sex.

After his shower Adam stands in front of the full-length mirror, smoothing, adjusting, coming at himself from all angles till he's satisfied, a last look and nod, with the impression he'll make. Fred goes down to the lobby with him, out of the building. On the sidewalk he holds their good-bye handshake a fraction and more past its natural rhythm (three-part handshake, Fred can do this, actually, he only a little awkwardly follows Adam's lead, thrilled at this sign of—what? Acceptance? Or is Adam's smile satiric at the corners of his mouth?), turning it into a promise from Adam they will meet—no excuses this time, no forgetting—Sunday ("That's tomorrow, right?" "Yup. Tomorrow."). Then he watches as Adam walks away—another two-handed tug pulling up the jeans and much less show than earlier, when he left his friends, a quick straight-ahead walk that will not step aside or stop short of its goal. Whatever that is. Fred sees how the clothes hide what he for the moment has almost memorized, show the shoulders but hide the shape of the back, barely allow suggestions of the hips, leave legs to the imagination altogether. Fred no longer has to imagine. For the moment he remembers.

However close to the earth he remains, Fred believes in the existence of other possibilities, feathered ones that might carry him off at any time to some lighter, airier, better place. Adam comes with feathers for him (well, so to speak), and Fred floats on his possibilities for the twenty or so hours until he again will stand on a street corner hoping for this new reality to continue and grow. For now it is Saturday night, summer in the city, and he goes out to fly while he can.

He is not alone, of course; he takes himself and his double, and the boy his double has captured, down to the busiest New York night streets, where so much that is not for him might be. He floats obliviously through the dull midtown streets, then moves through Greenwich Village, headphones in place and music loud and right enough to provide even more lift than Adam's promise has already given him—Springsteens's "Promised Land" and Dylan's "Mr. Tambourine Man" and the way Van Morrison builds from tentative pleasure to strangled joy ("Spread your wings") in "Ballerina."

Village restaurants, bars, clubs, stores are open and crowded in the late evening hours when he arrives, having walked those dozens of dark, empty, unwelcoming midtown blocks to where the welcome is constant. Fred doesn't accept the general invitation—doesn't feel welcome (but why should here be an exception?). With Adam he would; for the moment he sees the two of them in this restaurant, that fashionable klieg light of a store, part of something together. Alone he barely pauses to look in doors and windows at people living lives together. Glamour to others is the life of the rich and privileged. Glamour to Fred is the life of anyone who can be comfortable in a crowd. It's that foreign to him; he's the cartoon character who says everyone feels out of place somewhere and when asked where he feels out of place himself answers, "Earth." For now walking by here is enough, on his own Fred doesn't feel a need, even a desire, to stop, linger, join in at a bar or his own table in one of the restaurants. Knowing all this is here, that life goes on, boisterous and constant, is enough. He feeds his parallel life, reassuring himself that all this is ready if the life he lives next to the life he lives becomes real and he can join a world, this world, just like a normal person.

He walks himself exhausted and on his way home of course passes by the Port and the block he has haunted waiting for Adam. He is anxious at first, slows and looks for that familiar cap and walk, but Adam isn't around and Fred can tell himself their afternoon and the promise of tomorrow has been enough. He walks back and forth a few times anyway, a habit, as though his feet would take him back here even if he didn't think about it. But he does think about it. Has he met the perfect boy? Well. Adam is experienced, perfect would be willing and interested but inexperienced. There was that forgotten appointment, there's the solid eager greed.

And of course even perfect would never mean the only possibility. Fred, who usually plays the Walk/Don't Walk signs like an expert, catching light changes and missing traffic by half seconds, lingers at an intersection he could easily have crossed, watching a young man—almost a boy, seventeen, maybe, eighteen—ambiguously near the Port, on the other side of Forty-second. He might be waiting for someone to approach him, maybe not even knowing what sort of offer he might hear. But he has a full backpack, maybe he's just off a bus, waiting for his ride. (He has a full backpack, maybe he's just off a bus and knows no one here, has nowhere to go.) Fred hangs back through another cycle of the light and watches, wondering. Young enough, slender (slim and slender are good, thin and slight seem weak, insubstantial) and blond, his crew cut too long, almost shaggy. His pale cheeks show a few reddish eruptions and a nick where a rash hand on the razor tried a little too hard to even off the sideburn over one of the slightly hollow cheeks. His brown eyes stare ahead, empty, and the thin red lips with their peeved teenage pout are parted slightly. Fred moves closer, unnoticed. It's a sign of something that this kid is not looking at the sidewalk crowd but at the street, and sure enough the light changes only once before a gray van driven by a girl too much like him to be anything but his sister pulls up and he comes to life with a light relieved curse before opening the door and slinging his pack into the back and himself into the passenger seat. Fred watches them pull away and continues his walking tour more relieved than not. Another challenge he doesn't need to try to meet. One more look around and he goes home, for once both alone and (for him) complete.

The next morning he is as anxious as a virgin bride. The first meeting must have been a trick like any other to Adam (Fred is able much as hates it to be honest about his boy's experience and motives, before pushing them aside as he does most malleable inconvenient reality), and the second, luck, easy money. He mustn't know how hard Fred wished and nudged either encounter into being, Fred knows enough not to let on to that, though the problem always has been not what he knows he should do but what he's able to avoid doing.

Fred is ready and out in plenty of time, time to stop at the cash machine for a refill, enough for the day. (He has to bring up this quantity discount thing; even though he sticks the receipt in his pocket without looking he knows the balance is alarmingly low to someone who always likes a nice cash cushion.) And he goes to meet Adam.

Who is, wonder of wonders, right there, right on time, waiting, Fred knows with a tingle of pleasure, just for him. Fred has slowed rounding the corner onto Forty-third, not expecting this, thinking even if he remembers Adam will have to be cool, show who's in charge, keep Fred waiting just long enough perhaps to be put in his place. But here he is, in a white T-shirt this time, very clean, with a horseshoe-shaped logo Fred doesn't recognize and new sneakers, dazzling white in the afternoon sun. The jeans might be the same—dark and stiff and loose—as the previous day's, but probably aren't; Adam seems like the fresh clothes daily type, to himself that's part of who he is.

The block is as deserted as the week before except for another young man Fred has seen around either very early or very late, looking for someone who might follow him into the peep show next to the hotel. His eyes meet Fred's briefly but Fred's slide off and go to Adam, leaning against the hotel wall, one foot up, just as Fred had stood waiting for him to finish talking the previous day. Adam catches his eye and with a follow-me jerk of the head begins to walk, but not across the street and back towards Fred's apartment. Instead he goes up Forty-third to Seventh, Times Square, and turns north, moving quickly enough Fred can't quite catch up, even speak to him without shouting, which of course is out of the question here. So Fred follows. After a block, maybe far enough Adam thinks no one he knows might see them (someone seeing them—even the twenty-dollar hustler back there on Forty-third—is one of Fred's fondest wishes, to be seen and known with Adam), he slows so Fred can catch up and turns as they come together to offer a smile and a quick handshake and the usual "Wha's up?"

"We going somewhere?"

"I need to ask a favor, okay?" The smile again, gap and all.

"What kind of favor?" He knows, instantly he knows.

"I gotta have some new sneakers for my sister's birthday party. It's tonight. I can't—"

"What kind of sneakers does your sister wear?" Fred asks, deliberately misunderstanding, hoping Adam has the humor to see the little joke. He doesn't.

"Not…. They're for me. To wear." Adam shows a flash of irritation at Fred's thickness.

"Those look new." Fred looks down at the unscuffed Nikes with the faint gold swoosh but Adam shakes his head with a little dismissive twist of the mouth.

"Not these. I mean, new, yeah, but I got a red shirt for tonight, maroon more, they got to have some color like that in them." They haven't stopped walking and Adam inclines his head indicating an Athlete's Foot store a little further up Broadway. "They should have them here." He takes a couple more steps before remembering he hasn't had an answer yet. "I'll make it up, okay? We can take it out of next time's." He smiles again with a sidelong glance that takes in, Fred supposes, both his doubts and his reluctance to say no. *Next time's?* "I need the cash today, too, though, for her present."

Fred shrugs helplessly; "no" seems somehow impossible right now. If Adam needs these for tonight then either Fred buys them or Adam will rush him through their time and go out to find someone else so he'll have the money by the end of the afternoon, and Fred can't force him to that, can't let him down now—later they can talk money, make that part of things regular so it won't get out of hand, but rejection now of this first favor, when they barely know each other, they're just starting out, would take some months to get over—might even mean they wouldn't have the months, Adam would pass him by for someone who'd be willing to spend the money, to trust him. And "no" would make Fred a different person than he's been in all those stories, all that parallel life, the one where he and Adam both have "next times" to make everything clear.

Fred doesn't quite say yes but Adam knows he's won and leads the way into the store, immediately becoming absorbed in the men's sneaker display along one wall. Fred doesn't see anything in red and says so, but Adam just grunts and moves off, picking up a black Reebok held to its display by a stiff cord. "When did this come out?" he asks of the yawning young black clerk, who takes it from him and looks at the tag.

"Last week, I think. Couple weeks." Adam replaces the shoe and picks up another, white with blue and maybe a hint of red near the heel. "That's new, just yesterday," the clerk says.

"Whose is it?" Fred sees the swoosh and almost says "Nike," but fortunately is saved that embarrassment when the young man answers with a name Fred recognizes, just, as belonging to a basketball player. Fred retires a few feet away, his mouth risklessly shut, as Adam asks for these in his size, which, Fred is amused to find himself pleased to hear, is the same as his own. Any connection is something. Does he see a quick glimpse of a life of Adam's flashy barely worn hand-me-down sneakers regularly showing up on his own feet? Yes.

Adam drifts near enough to Fred to give him another quick smile. "Not much red in those," Fred says.

"Just got to be, you know. Enough. That shit is ugly," he says, changing the subject, pointing to a boxy pair of Asics before sitting down to wait. His back is to the shelf along the wall and Fred quickly lifts the Nike he has chosen to check the price—$79.95. Not a fortune by fancy sneaker standards, but twice what Fred would spend on himself—Modell's has tables of sale shoes for thirty, forty dollars. Not sneakers out this week, though, not with the right ball players' names on them. Fred might have guessed that Adam and out-this-week went together.

Adam is very serious here, trying on the shoe when it's brought to him with careful bouncing up and down and—mostly—study from all angles in the shoe-level mirrors before nodding his approval and putting them back in the box. Then between the bench and the counter, he picks up a package of white tube socks, cheap enough, asking for them with barely raised eyebrows and getting them with a shrug from Fred. Then at the counter, "Oh, shit, I need a cap. That'd be perfect." *Perfect.* A baseball cap, black and, Fred must admit, the shade of the small spots of red on the sneakers he's about to pay for.

"You really need a new cap?" The one Adam has on today is red, too, though a much brighter red than the one on the wall behind the register. In response Adam asks the female clerk taking the security tag from the sneakers for his size. Fred's never owned a fitted cap, but then he isn't much for caps.

Adam carries a little over a hundred dollars' worth of stuff in an Athlete's Foot bag out of the store and leads Fred towards home. Leads is the word; Fred prides himself on walking quickly but he can just keep up with Adam's young legs as he weaves through the crowds on Broadway and cuts the light as close as Fred would have on his own. He doesn't let himself be caught until they're on Fred's street when he lets up a bit and Fred pulls abreast.

"Thanks." Adam makes the word harsh. "I needed these."

Fred almost says, "Don't expect this very often," but even that seems too … adult; he's never wanted to be someone who pulls aggrieved faces, someone who's tight with a dollar, like a parent. "You want to look good for your sister's birthday party" is what he says, and is rewarded with another of Adam's smiles, cut off with the lips closing over it and a flick of the tongue moistening the upper lip.

There are differences from the day before. Again Fred rubs a hand on the boy's slightly sweat-slick butt as Adam comes and this time takes the opportunity of rolling the condom off Adam's dick himself, oddly thrilling, somehow an honor, unveiling him still half hard, a shade darker than the used Latex, although later Adam flushes the squished rubber when he goes to the toilet, spoiling any chance for some sort of collection. Probably just as well.

For himself Fred is prepared to be content again with small pleasures and waits his turn. Adam is about where he'd been that first time, next to Fred, face-to-face and body to body. He still holds his head away a bit on the pillow next to Fred's and won't touch any of the places Fred would like to be touched. And when Fred, desperate for something, for contact, just contact, touch me instead of me doing all the work, asks Adam to play with, pinch, his nipples, Adam does—nipping Fred's right nipple painfully between the untrimmed nails of his thumb and forefinger and reacting to Fred's yelp of pain with a small hard smile and shrugged, eyes-averted, "I thought that's what you wanted."

"Not so it hurts." Fred rubs the sore nipple, no longer erect as the sting subsides, looking fragile enough to have been severed with a bit more force. There seems a message here. In the momentary pause to recover before he begins on himself again he asks, "So what do you think of all this you do with men?"

Adam's brown eyes catch Fred's blue ones, inches away, but quickly slide off. "I think it's nasty." Husky voice, disdainful wrinkle of his broad nose. "*Nasty.*"

For now all that they are, all there is to Fred and Adam is a bit of sex and, apparently, Fred's right to buy the occasional clothes. In Fred's second life they simply continue from there, himself and Adam, as though there were more. But Adam, as soon as they're through, says he needs to go. Fred this time is a bit disappointed; things aren't developing, just continuing, and getting more expensive. They haven't even mentioned money this time and Fred's sure Adam is assuming the amount will be the same. Plus sneakers and a cap. Next time? Next time's wouldn't nearly cover it. Now it feels too late to cut the money, eliminate it, he can hear Adam's "Why didn't you say so? I was counting on that." Fred's mistake, Fred's fault, and how can he argue?

So Adam takes another quick shower, and comes out—another of those images that will stay—naked but for Fred's big yellow towel, now wrapped around his still uncut hair like some African headdress. He has found a can of talcum Fred keeps in the medicine cabinet and seems happy to have it. Climbing onto the futon, he sprinkles powder carelessly on his big flopping dick (the excess spilling down on the bed as Fred cringes at the thought of cleaning it up), and then rubs it in, leaving his dark flesh smeared with white and his dark curly pubic hair dusted with powder. He seems oblivious to what he's doing, talking all along about the party—somehow a different one than the birthday party he started out discussing.

On the way down Fred—handing over fifty dollars—makes a weak joke about being paid back for the shoes ("Guess I'll have to take it out of your wages." Jesus, what is he thinking sometimes?) that Adam blows off with a knowing ghost of a smile and not a word. Wednesday, again. They'll meet at seven on Wednesday.

Fred moves light-years ahead of any reality he might legitimately claim. He has a relationship now—doesn't he? That's the word, he guesses, hating its Oprah/Chopra women's advice column tone. A relationship. Some sort of sex three times and a pair of sneakers. He hasn't even asked Adam's last name, in the street world a real confidence, and Adam hasn't asked Fred's phone number, which would not mean a commitment, something less than that, more along the lines of a steady trick, but Fred refuses to think of himself and Adam that way. He would think of it as a step. When it happened he would. His second, parallel life is still full, though feeling no closer to the actual than it did; unlike parallel lines these lives should tend to converge. There has been no connection made with Adam deeper than quick sex and money, where Fred starts out and usually finishes with the boys, the youths, he becomes involved with. He has to provide the rest, and he can, he does, he always has, he's gotten good at it. Knowing what he wants, he can satisfy his real audience, himself, as long as the raw materials, so to speak, are there—the boy he wants near enough and possible enough to be made into a story. But the story can't much outlive its own plausibility. Fred is already worried, Adam hasn't moved closer to him these few chances they've had—closer to Fred's money doesn't count.

At work Fred with a relationship is still Fred. Same small signs something's changed, same unwillingness to go an inch further. He parades his relationship the same way he'd paraded his first infatuation, by being unaccountably, silently pleased with himself, hoping everyone will notice and think it must be love, hoping no one will ask embarrassing questions he couldn't actually answer. Knowing in fact no one will be interested enough to spend much time piercing his coy armor.

He bounces around smiling at nothing and singing under his breath—standards keep running through his head today, Cole Porter and Irving Berlin, good for something that's only begun—"I've Got You Under My Skin"—or even for an exquisite, bittersweet finish—"What'll I do if you don't love me too?" Adam would never know these songs. More to teach him, if he'll listen.

Frank notices what Fred has put out to be noticed. "A roller-coaster ride, isn't it?" he asks with a grin. It takes Fred a moment to understand this means he'd been less cool than he'd thought the previous week when Adam had failed to show up and he'd put himself through all the stories he needed to get back to his usual state of hopeful self-delusion, living out the remotest happy possibility.

Fred is too surprised by Frank's insight, by his own transparency, not to reply in kind. "The best of times, the worst of times," he says; a grin of his own, a shrug, and they're linked in the brotherhood of exasperated—but ultimately successful—lovers. The kind of bond that's supposed to be common but that Fred never feels, or not for long. The conversation ends there, complete.

Greg seems to notice nothing. There is something about him, his calm self-sufficiency, the apparent ease of his satisfactions, that makes Fred want to go further with him, to shock it a bit, that smooth ordered resilient life. They have never scratched the surface, the two of them, not even on the few dull dinner-and-a-movie evenings they've had. They've talked movies, books, other people at work, politics, retirement plans—all the things strangers on a train might, never approaching the membrane that separates the friendly from the truly personal.

Greg comes in on Fred singing, "I Concentrate on You" as he fails to concentrate on an order form at the small desk in the basement office they both use. Fred has stretched the second life to include someone else, an observer who doesn't just suspect but knows, who might be—impressed? No. Who might be agreeably scandalized by the plain truth. He's begun to think, rehearse, how to say it: In the form of a request for advice, Greg would always dispense advice, he'd feel it a duty and duty defines him. "I know this sounds ridiculous," Fred would say. "But I've sort of fallen in love with this fifteen-year-old male prostitute. I don't know what to do." That's too bald, of course. It shocks but misses all the romance. And since he hasn't managed to refine it into something he could actually say out loud he takes another tack.

"You always seem to be—um, well—involved with somebody," he says, genuinely fumbling his way around Greg's tendency to use words like "friend" and "roommate" in a way that implies more. "Or am I reading too much into these friendships of yours?"

For the years they've know each other and the warmth and intimacy Greg has clearly shown some old acquaintances of both sexes who've dropped by the store, Greg is always wary of opening up to Fred. It is Fred thinks his own old problem—his lack of authentic interest in others, his failures to hide his own transparent self-absorption behind the smiling mask he tries to maintain—that dooms him to a permanent isolation. Greg now is clearly taken aback. He smiles an embarrassed version of his nice rabbitty smile and says, improbably, "I like to wrap myself in an air of mystery."

Fred is impressed, it's the sort of thing he'd like to say himself, has said in various smug ways when it's seemed appropriate. Greg isn't smug, he's smooth and careful and throws Fred off. "Well, I feel a little mysterious myself," Fred says. "I might, well, be getting into a problem I could use your advice on, is all. Not right now but…"

Feeling duty call, someone who might be in need of help, Greg turns instantly serious. "Something wrong, or…?"

"Well, not yet, you might say. I'm in a situation where things might go wrong." He lets that hang there and makes a few vague observations about how difficult things can be between people of different backgrounds, ages, so forth—chickening out—and then Greg is paged to take a phone call. Fred decides this has been a successful conversation, establishing his own mystery, a touch of danger, putting the glamour of his second life into the story of his first. A step towards combining the two.

Adam shows up on Wednesday, late, unapologetic, leading the way again but needing this time only cigarettes and to be gone quickly. Fred has rehearsed the reasonable request, that at least part of the sneaker money be repaid, spread out over their next few meetings, but Adam will have none of it. "You don't understand, I got to have this cash today. I can't be—it's like I'm wasting my time here, I don't leave with enough to go right home." He can't go much further without risking Adam's not coming back, so Fred tries to shrug it off with a bit of humor ("Can I at least have them when you're through? We're the same size.") that Adam doesn't even smile at, it would have been a nice touch, a tiny natural bond if he had, but…. From there it's all business.

It continues to continue, and does not develop.

Fred offers his phone number on Wednesday and Adam takes it, a slip of paper stuffed carelessly in a jeans pocket. Thinking ruefully of his wobbly bank balance, Fred nonetheless suggests Friday for their next meeting and Adam accepts as he would, maybe registering what's being said, maybe already wherever he's headed from here. To buy some pot. Maybe hang out for a while.

When Adam leaves this time Fred opens his door to hear the elevator stop at the ground floor, and then, suddenly anxious, hurries down the five flights of stairs and onto the street. Adam is of course nowhere in sight but Fred heads for the corner where they'd had their first encounter, as though that were Adam's home.

It is still light, another too-warm late July evening, hazy and again uncomfortably humid, shirt-sticking-to-back weather. Fred rushes until he can see Adam's corner and then slows, alert, Adam's familiar figure the only thing he would really see across the street in the milling pre-theater crowd. He doesn't. Stopping in the shadows by the bank on the far side of Eighth as he had so often in the more or less desperate week after the first meeting he waits and mines the constant movement across the way. He registers each possibility quickly and negatively: Not Adam. Not Adam. Not Adam.

But Fred remains. He has just been with Adam, the center of this new edition of his world. He hasn't the slightest intention of picking up anyone else, hasn't got the cash anyway—that's new, he always goes out with enough money just in case, you never can tell when there'll be that irresistible someone. It's a weeknight, not crowded, and there are no new faces that he would pause to consider even if he had the money, or one familiar one he finds intriguing now. But he lingers, standing, walking, looking—looking, even now, he must admit (maybe Adam isn't perfect), for someone new.

He walks the streets he's used to walking, Eighth and Forty-second, the front and side of the Port Authority and the block north. Old hunting grounds. And the old anticipation—anyone might be there this time around, someone ideal—keeps him walking, looking. But if he begins dissatisfied with Adam, uneasy that there is little sex and a lot of money and not much else but small talk, the walk reassures him. As he might have hoped, Adam's memory is quickly burnished to a glow by comparison with anyone he sees on the streets now. The only familiar waiting hustlers are two twentyish ex-con types, slouched together talking and smoking by one of the pillars near the north steps into the Port, posing in the self-conscious manner of men not yet comfortable in a world without walls and hard rules, wary eyes ready to take offense, as they wait to be approached by someone with a more adventurous nature than Fred's.

The two old tricks he sees smile greetings without real expectations—he's turned each of them down repeatedly, requests to be taken home a second time, a couple bucks anyway? Once with each was enough, as once each with hundreds had been enough, hundreds who'd been able (just the one time, briefly) to give him hope of an experience that would relieve him of his desire, lift him for as long as it lasted and a little longer out of that constant state of waiting and wanting—hope he'd drawn from a promising smile, from the depths of dark eyes or the turn of slim hips or the tight muscular swell of a chest. Hope that had been disappointed soon enough. So he walks the streets again after looking for Adam in the only habitat Fred's ever seen him in, although he refuses to think of his own boy as one of these; Adam's young enough his time here can be put down to youth, not corruption. Fred dreads and covets the nasty thrill of seeing him with one of those others, one of those Fred's stood and walked among all these years, who any evening now might buy himself all Adam is willing to sell: The sight, the touch, the tastes and smells Fred would like to have to himself alone. (And there's no question Adam is in this world. He says as much—guilelessly boasting or artfully baiting Fred by noting appointments kept and money made.) Many of them may have already had him—that's how they would think of it, Fred is sure,

I've had that one is what they'd tell their friends pointing Adam out on the sidewalk—had him and enjoyed themselves and filed him away with all the others. They are Fred's competition. Real competition; Fred thinks how many of the others have more money than he, and how can they resist Adam? Walking back up Eighth, looking again at the Adamless groupings of men, young and old, across the way, he stops, moves to the darkness near the buildings as he feels the truth hard like a blow to the stomach. He can't really afford Adam and others can. Any of those others might, any of those simpering old queens or eager predators might have what it takes, the right shade of green to keep Adam happy. And he does not. He is suddenly sad and helpless and takes moments to snap out of it. Maybe (he can tell himself) Adam *likes* him. Likes him and hates all these others. Maybe none of them likes Adam that much, although that would spoil the story of his own triumph and others' envy, one of the many Fred has coasted on these weeks—and anyway Adam's look would always be right. Probably he'll never know; would Adam likely tell him if someone else pursued him as ardently as Fred does? Maybe, to make him jealous, pry more out of him. And then it might be a lie.

Between Wednesday night and Friday afternoon Fred pushes his doubts and disappointment away and lets the stories do their work, convincing himself again that a life with Adam is not only possible but even likely. And he has begun to obsess over something different. Fred's life is largely a day-to-day exercise in masking or resisting or rewriting reality, and one of the results is some distortion of his sense of time. There is no problem with the regular—Monday through Friday nine to five, weekends off—which if anything makes his parallel life easier to live; since he doesn't have to worry about making schedules or even think of odd hours, he has that much more time to be where and what he wants to be: so often in some indefinite but satisfying near future or alternative present. But not thinking beyond the next hour's lunch or the next day's Travel books order leaves him a bit unprepared for the bigger things: Changes of seasons, holidays, his own vacations, tend to sneak up, make the shift from future indefinite to tomorrow without being noticed. (The past, too, the past—his own past seems formless to him, a life lived out of context, his pursuit the only plot and that repeating, without much reference to the rest of the world. Some music, some movies or television shows stick in his mind as belonging to a particular year or presidential administration—and always associated with this or that boy—but even then he has to think hard to remember just when they might have been current, not nostalgia.) Now one of those plans thought of as off in the indefinite future turns out to be imminent: His vacation, and the nonrefundable ticket he already has to visit his mother on what might be (so far from Adam) the dark side of the moon. There are always stories, a story for every occasion, making every unpleasantness livable, leaving every obstacle overcome. It was simple enough when the plot was finding Adam again, making some connection, but now here he is, so far failing to fit any version of himself Fred has created, and just as Fred has begun to think more and more uneasily of Adam's life when they are not together they will be apart for almost a week.

So Fred approaches the Friday meeting with a certain desperation. Surely Adam will show up Friday, then maybe they can meet again Monday, the first day of Fred's vacation; he leaves on Tuesday and he'll be back the following Sunday. So, Monday, and then his plane gets back early Sunday afternoon, if he can impress a meeting that day on Adam—say three o'clock, Fred checks his ticket, he can be home by then—that's the shortest separation he can manage. There is the thought, of course, of a whole day with Adam on Monday when Fred won't be working. But the Adam he's coming to know isn't likely to be interested. What would Fred suggest? A movie? A museum? A walk in the park? A day out shopping might go over well, if they were shopping for clothes for Adam, but that certainly isn't in Fred's budget. Even Fred's well-exercised powers of invention can't conquer the anticipated embarrassment of a day with a bored and resentful Adam, wanting money and to be gone.

By Friday evening Fred has adjusted—he survives, sane, which means he always adjusts—to the inevitable. He's going away and Adam will stay behind, will be living the life Fred knows he lives and seeing the other men Fred knows he sees and Fred will put whatever he can between himself and that truth, will have Adam with him as he usually does now, will be the one Adam wants to be with, the one Adam waits for. Maybe Adam doesn't go with that many others anyway. Maybe he's getting the idea Fred is the one he can rely on. Maybe he's tired of life on the streets and ready to settle down. Fred works through all of these. He will need them. Now that his worries have shifted from how to see Adam again to who else Adam might see he will—he knows he will—seek the reassurance of passing by the streets and corners where Adam has been before, hoping as he hoped Wednesday to register his boy's absence. When home at least he feels some power just from this propinquity: He could rush out any time jealously seizes him to see if Adam's on the streets, doing what Fred wishes he wouldn't. Halfway across the country he'll be helpless even to seek this negative solace. But he will try in his own ways to keep Adam close enough the other possibilities won't matter.

"So. What should I bring you back?"

It is Monday and they are in Fred's apartment. Adam, showered and powdered, is sitting on the bed in his plain black boxers, sniffing each of his very white socks before putting it back on. His mind had drifted off but now it snaps back to what Fred, standing beside him in his striped robe, is saying to him. "You're gonna bring me a present?" Adam's face lights with childlike pleasure, he grins briefly at Fred before returning attention to his socks. "I didn't think about it."

"Leave it to me then," Fred says with a confidence he doesn't quite feel; he has certainly been thinking about it—the gift-giving moment, almost a week away, has been central to his parallel life, future tense, for the past few days—but he hasn't thought of the perfect present. Yet. The presentation moment surrounds the object but leaves it obscured, obscurely perfect, extravagantly appreciated. "Just meet me on Sunday at three and there'll be a nice surprise for you." It's the fourth time he's mentioned an appointment for the following Sunday. Adam had been late Friday, late enough Fred was able to (only joking!) suggest he'd forgotten altogether and just happened to come around. So Fred has turned Adam's forgetfulness into a running joke that Adam now smiles at, maybe politely. A running joke Fred hopes will impress himself and their next date into Adam's mind. He does what he can without becoming a nag.

In spite of Fred's hopes, the heart of their meetings has already hardened into ritual—one he hates to admit must have been formed by the men who, well, came before him: There is the massage. ("Massage my back. Harder. Now my shoulders. My upper arms. Harder. Now my calves. Not like that, push up." Fred bought a little vial of massage oil that he's embarrassed to bring out because he doesn't like the smell and now he just imagines its being right and using it as he kneads Adam's smooth dry skin.) That begins Adam's oblivious concentration on himself. (On his stomach always, bouncing up and down, face buried in a pillow or turned awkwardly to look at the TV, hands by his thighs or under his hips, manipulating himself against the sheets, Fred lying next to him or on his knees beside him, watching, touching the hips, the thighs, the lightly undulating ass, ignored as Adam drives towards his pleasure.) Today the porn movie is on and Adam has the remote, pausing in his movements occasionally to press fast-forward or reverse, looking for whatever he needs as a trigger, his own Adam, before returning to his work. There is only the sensation.

After he finishes, in a quick breathless frenzy, Adam rolls over, slips off the condom, which he drops somewhere, cleans himself quickly with the towel Fred holds out, and then, facing Fred with eyes averted (another clue, but who looks for clues at times like this?), the curve to his mouth slightly amused, he waits.

Fred tells himself that, if Adam is greedy and can barely ever wait to be somewhere else, he is, for many of the moments he lies patiently as Fred fumbles and fantasizes his own way to coming, the soul of sweet boyishness. The nose-wrinkling disdain, the little bit of meanness that brought the nipple pinch, don't reappear, perhaps are pushed aside for the sake of the money—harmony of course is good for business—or maybe Adam's decided—who knows?—that Fred's okay, deserves better.

Adam is always so distinctly clean—freshly washed dick, flaky white trails of strong stick deodorant frosting his armpits; he has sweet, boyish strawberry-gum breath; once his hair has been cut he seems compulsive about it, trying to lay down waves with hair oils and pomades, all slightly fruity and clean-smelling. He has relaxed enough, after the first couple of times, to rest his head on Fred's shoulder. He takes orders well, orders to pose—to roll over, sit, stand, bend over, get on his knees, stick this or that into Fred's face. He has heard them all before, alas, obeys them with humorous resignation. Who can't see the ridiculous in the desires of others? Unless those desires are shared.

But real life never comes near the parallel one. The fact Fred has been aware of from the start—the fact of Adam and other men, that Fred is not the first, the only, the best, with Adam, that this boy is not his, anyone with the cash and the desire can stroke this smooth skin, squeeze these muscles, trace this sparse but growing dusting of hair—has grown like a brushfire in Fred's mind, always nearby, controlled here only to break out somewhere else. Even as they're together Fred finds himself thinking that anyone (with the money) can hover here, knees straddling Adam's legs, hands caressing any, all of him in the name of a good massage. Of course, they can't if he's here with Fred, at these moments he is Fred's, or Fred is his. When Adam's here, Fred thinks, knows, he's not with anyone else. It is a victory somehow, satisfaction that lasts through real time and can be redeemed—it will come again. *If he's with me he's not with any of them.* This becomes, in its obviousness, its undeniable logic, a guiding principle of Fred's life with Adam. The trick is to avoid sentences, thoughts, facts that begin, *if he's not with me....*

So Fred has found himself in phantom competition with those men he knows of but does not know: Adam's other tricks. Some presumably among those he has seen on the streets of Times Square for years and others—the subtle, the sporadic, the casual pursuers of boys, insufficiently obsessed to be conspicuous—he may have seen but never been aware of. In his mind they were always his rivals. They are all his enemies now.

However reluctant he is to leave Adam Fred is excited as always to be going away. Any vacation feels like a life being lived, not pretended, and getting on a plane and flying away is a recurring motif of the alternative existence he spends his days and nights plotting and imagining. He can go for months without moving more than a mile and a half from his apartment, his real world a slice of midtown Manhattan, without feeling trapped or restricted; his mind after all is free to wander. But when the opportunity comes the excitement of shedding his routine and flying away—physically, not just in some flight of fancy—makes him almost giddy. It feels—after months in the self-imposed prison of routine, the same days and hours, streets and buildings, hallways, rooms, doors and windows revisited until each is as familiar as his face in the mirror—it feels like freedom. He has to be in a certain place at an exact time and stand in one line after another and be at the mercy of rules and schedules and still it feels like freedom.

Careful as always he is early, the anticipation part of the pleasure as it wouldn't be if he flew often enough for the crowds and waiting and boredom to be a nuisance instead of a novelty. He allows himself to be herded to his window seat, just behind the left wing, next to a blonde German girl in blue cutoffs who acknowledges him with a smile, stuffs her backpack under the seat in front of her, and almost instantly falls asleep. That's good, of course. He doesn't want to chat. He wants to fly away, and to fly away alone—his way of being alone, Adam hovering in the German girl's center seat. For him Fred would even give up the window.

Denver is hot and dry and—after Manhattan—very clean, except for certain days when the air lays heavily visible, a gray filter over the tall buildings of downtown and the blue-green mountains to the west, some with lopsided shrinking high patches of old snow—up close they would be gray and crusty, like frost in a freezer. The famous new airport—the outside a circus tent made for Ludwig of Bavaria, the inside a frenzied mall—is majestically alone, miles of nothing from the nearest sign of urban life. Fred will pick up his rental car and he will drive through this nothing to the lights and traffic of the sea of suburbs that stretches, flat and dull and seemingly endless, around downtown's tightly packed black and silver towers, money visible, vying with the mountains for attention and for proximity to heaven. He will spend five days shopping and driving and visiting his mother, Adam in tow.

The driving is a pleasure, even more since he does so little of it anymore. He'd lived here once, lived for a time in Los Angeles, both car towns, where freedom was in the ability to get behind the wheel and go, the movement more important than any destination. "Cruisin' and playin' the radio," Chuck Berry had sung to him dozens of times. "No particular place to go." Driving with the radio on—or, now, with the car's tape player stocked with more of what was just right, for him—left the same room for his mind to wander (or soar, he might say). For years driving had been a goal in itself, if the situation was right: If there was plenty of gas and money for more; if he didn't have to be somewhere; if the traffic wasn't slowing him, blocking him, frustrating his attempts to escape; if the music and his mood combined to lift him above the life he wanted to be away from—well, freedom needs a definition, and this was his.

Shopping was trickier. It required money and Fred never in his life had felt he had enough to spend easily, without thought or calculation. Adam had no clue about this: Money was money, you got it and you spent it. Fred had turned the act of shopping for anything much rarer or more expensive than groceries into a little routine of bargain hunting that—necessity instead of virtue made into satisfaction—became its own reward. Shopping was a sport, almost, the cunning pursuit of the best for the least: Trade this feature or that nice touch for dollars off, go however many miles out of your way it takes for the one-day sale or special closeout that makes the trip worth taking. His stereo and VCR, his watch, chairs, towels and coffeemaker, all compromises between amenities and money. The pleasure comes in anticipating possession, in the tiny victories of the good deal; the negative reward is freedom from the guilt of spending too much. But money after all is everywhere, always, being talked about and spent and shown off—not just obviously, in Nikes and cell phones, gold chains and BMWs, but in the air itself, the attitude of, well, why not?—why not go there, eat this, buy that, spend money just because there's something to spend it on, without agonizing or pinching pennies beforehand and wondering even as the money goes if it won't be needed for something else later? Others have money for now and don't seem to worry about later while Fred hasn't enough for now or the future either one. It's not much comfort to imagine those free spenders having regrets someday, maybe.

Even as he pursues each bargain Fred knows this game is not exactly noble. Priding himself as he does on his little coups in a world of people who can't take the time to save so little, he suspects there's something in this, in the shaving off of a few dollars here and loss of a bit of elegance there, that hardens him, shrinks his soul a bit from one that takes sustenance from possessing beauty and quality to one that can't quite afford either one, and settles for something less. So the satisfaction is strained, the victories forced on him by necessity minor, too tainted to bring lasting pleasure. He has stories for this, too, of course. There are stories wherever he needs them.

Fred's time with his mother—the reason for his trip, even if more of his time is spent driving or planning what to buy, for her and this time mostly for Adam—is as always strained, almost formal. There is no one he's spent more time hiding himself from, no one he'd be more unlikely to reveal a bit of his parallel life to. And his day-to-day reality is a bit embarrassing to him, the facts don't make for a chronicle of success he could be proud of sharing, they're of little real interest he's sure to anyone, even his mother, so there you are. Television (there's never anything on worth watching) and the weather (it's too much, too severe, or else there's not enough rain) are topics for discussion when they're together. Family secrets that are not his secrets, the black sheep who is not him, the conditions of aging relatives, his mother's health—safe subjects are few, and rest on the peripheries of their lives, where there's no pain to be awakened.

He would if he could—in yet another version of the second life he does—break down the walls, weave their existence into one life, mother and son together. She is no more capable of this than he is, probably; there are shyness (less than his) and the (he suspects) still-throbbing wound all these years after she discovered a secret (not *the* secret, she thinks he is another gay man, doesn't know the details, knowing it's boys only and not men would cut her like a hatchet). So they both avoid the personal that would bring her pain and him shame; Fred's decades of hiding have seeped into all they say, leaving the truth—*the* truth—with no place to present itself. They bury it together, by mutual consent. He has created for her in his weekly phone calls a modest life—a few friends, a quiet round of movies and plays and dinners—that can be spun in conversation into the truth of him in the city. He does go to dinner and movies and plays but not often. His life in the city all these years has been street corners and boys even when he's at dinners or movies or plays—drugs must be like this, the single-minded lust for one more taste—teasing his mind with what he waits for, what might be waiting for him. Now it's Adam, of course, who keeps him tense with longing.

Still it is a pleasant few days. They go to dinner and for a drive in the mountains, losing themselves as one can in a world different enough from the everyday to become an event, a story, a memory. She has become old and slow and frail, walking with nervous care, gauging every step. She sits in her comfortable chair and dozes off with the television on or a book in her lap. She has a jigsaw puzzle she's worked on for months three-quarters finished on a card table in one corner, and spends a few minutes a day fitting pieces of a large dark building in place. Together they settle, mother and son, into an almost relaxed near-intimacy, rhythmless but calm.

When they are not together Fred drives—not quite alone, of course—and searches for gifts. His mother's are easy, she asks for what she wants—a fan to supplement her noisy air conditioner, a new vacuum cleaner, both giving him an excuse to cruise the suburbs, mall to mall, seeking the best deal. It is Adam on his mind, though, something perfect for Adam. And of course— this being Fred—he keeps Adam nearby, bouncing ideas off him. Again and again an offering is made and as each possible gift leads Adam from anticipation to joy Fred judges how right it all feels, how perfect that potential gift is. Clothes are out. Adam has too many for anything new to be special, and anyway Fred has no sense of his own ability to please Adam's stylish street taste. Fred decides early it will be something electronic and eliminates for reasons of size or cost entire stores except for small displays of practical gadgets. There are Walkmans and portable CD players—he knows these already, but he can't see Adam attached to one out on the street, where he's always ready for conversation. A camera? A pocket tape recorder? These lack that just-right feel, fail to conjure that delighted smile to Adam's face.

By elimination Fred comes to the only—therefore perfect— possibility: A pocket electronic organizer that functions as a calendar and address book, keeps notes and records. It's small enough (a bit larger than a billfold) and cheap enough (the one he chooses has the basics only, but maybe Adam doesn't know that, hasn't even thought of one of these before, Fred has never heard him mention anything like this) to fit Fred's requirements, and, he hopes, has just enough useful, prestigious novelty to be exciting to Adam. The gift moment, the flow from anticipation to pleasure, giving and receiving, comes alive with this in his hand.

But he's barely decided before the qualms begin: This will make Adam's life away from him that much easier. All the names and numbers of his other tricks (his *tricks*, that is, Fred will be something more), appointments and even how much money is involved, information Fred now glimpses scrawled in dull pencil or Flair pen on rolling papers and Burger King napkins, will be indelibly organized for quick access. All that Fred wants to erase from his boy's life will be made more convenient. He buries that thought under repetitions of the gift-giving moment, the anticipation and the reward, himself and Adam celebrating the perfect gift.

By the time he leaves Fred has worked himself up into his usual state of sentimental guilt. His mother is his mother, after all, her love and support have never wavered through all his feckless odd misshapen life, and he has repaid her with distance, with silence on every important point. For her feelings or his pride, something more was needed, and he has never had more. Driving away as she waves from her window he can hear the words he might have said—a parallel life here, too—knowing the moment for saying them will never likely come in the real infrequent face-to-face life the two of them share. When one day it is too late he will have a regret with no hope or comfort.

In his bag is the box for Adam. On his Walkman on the plane he listens to Sinatra, the painful pleasures of songs of lost love and loneliness. "To share a kiss the devil has known," "Tell me why my angel eyes ain't here." There's something adult about this sadness, something, to Fred, inevitable. Pushed into the indefinite future, his mourning for the end of something real and worth keeping lets him anticipate time with Adam and wallow in the end of it all at once. The plane takes him and the perfect gift, his hopes and all he knows in his heart, east, towards home.

II.

PARALLEL LIFE

For a moment on the bus from the airport back to the city the winding congested highway offers a glimpse of the southern half of Manhattan, Twin Towers to Chrysler Building, suspended in a hot-day haze. Fred always smiles at the sight, surprised to be thrilled, in love with the idea of it, of the money and power the skyline represents, in love with the swirling energy, all that humanity jostling and wheedling for space and attention, in love with the things he's supposed to be in love with even if he lives like a mouse at Versailles, in but not of, as near as a sane man could be to a hermit in the midst of that crowded clamor. He's home.

The bus comes out of the Lincoln Tunnel and as always seems to be in some other place, speeding down deserted streets with no sense of the city before climbing a ramp into the bus terminal. Fred takes his heavy bag out the back way, unwilling to risk bumping into any of his old tricks hanging out in front of the Port Authority, having to say where he's been, why the luggage; it's oddly too personal to tell them, a trip to see his mother, a life he would be offended to allow most of them to have connection with, even by a few words of explanation.

His apartment seems like a place abandoned, even after so few days without him. No reason he can put his finger on; a dryness in the air, somehow? Or perhaps he's been away just long enough to make it a bit strange, his view refreshed enough to see it as the cramped shabby place it is. He unpacks quickly, puts away the few things he's brought back, and hides Adam's gift in a drawer within easy reach of the bed. Then he showers and changes and he's ready.

Fred of course is right on time where he and Adam were to meet and Adam of course isn't. Fred waits. And waits. He's lived this moment too often, too clearly over the last week for it to turn up empty like this; he is certainly used to disappointment but there is a heaviness today he doesn't usually feel. It was right, Fred and Adam together; this afternoon, stretching into evening, should have become a memory pastel with mutual pleasure, but here he is, alone. He has hardly been able to think of anything but Adam, of any activity without Adam as part of it, for weeks; his life has been anticipation ever since they'd last parted. So Adam's failure to show up on time today seems particularly unfair; Fred's devotion, he thinks (even as he smiles at his own self-pity), deserves more. Still. It's Adam we're talking about.

Fred rationalizes as he walks and waits, but he's tired enough his stories fail him; the hot streets, the thick odoriferous air, the traffic and noise, the familiar faces and strategies, the street games he has seen so many times—when he should be somewhere else with Adam all these things make him tired. Even his music has no charm, none of that power to smooth reality he relies on. He turns off his Walkman and stands again, this time in daylight, across from the corner he's spent too much time watching lately. Again, though now without much conviction, he adds Adam to the scene. After a while he goes home briefly to check his answering machine for some word, as though his number on that slip of paper, one among dozens, might not have been lost. Then he's out again, it isn't even hope anymore but pure habit. Compulsion. Why change now?

Amazingly, amazingly, two hours late, as even Fred with his inexhaustible excuses has all but given up, ready for food and a nap, there he is, Adam, seeing him first, come swaggering across the street, a you-won't-believe-this grin on his face. Fred melts. He'll believe almost anything.

"Guess where I been." Adam extends his hand for a simple handshake.

Fred shrugs, meeting the smile with his own. "Jail?" Adam confirms it, averting his eyes and giving a little twist of his head, the grin even wider. "No, I was kidding."

Adam nods. "No, really." As they begin to walk off he steers Fred into another little store. "I'm out of cigarettes. Haven't had a smoke all day." Fred obliges, and buys him a Pepsi as well, and they continue down the block before Adam goes on. "I got—me and my friend, we was sellin' just—you know—nickels? Like up in the Bronx, got picked up. My mom had to come get me out." He shakes his head, still grinning, arrest for him too one of the great shared jokes of the streets. "Like, all last night, just got out like two hours ago. Went home, took a shower first."

"So you aren't on probation or anything?" Fred's hinted at this before, not getting much in the way of answers. Now Adam just shakes his head and sips his soda through a straw. "You'll have to go to court though."

"No—way it happened, they only got me on possession, so...." He shrugs this away; possession of marijuana is nothing to him, not much to the law. He turns the full force of his smile on Fred. "You thought I wasn't showin' up, right? Thought I forgot. Stand out here all pissed off."

"You are pretty late."

"Said I'd be here though, right? What's that, better late than never?" He nods, too pleased with himself for Fred to point out the times he hasn't shown up.

Adam's happiness at being out of jail—and having gotten away with something, the charge possession instead of dealing—spills over into his time with Fred. Affectionate is too strong a word but he is less mechanical than before; still thinks first of himself, of course, humping the bed with his usual vigor, but then remembers some of Fred's little preferences, without being asked placing his spent dick on Fred's thigh and curling up enough Fred can kiss his ear and finger his ass at the same time. Small pleasures, significant when they're all that's allowed. When after Fred comes Adam looks him in the eye with another grin Fred feels a difference, feels for the first time he might be in on the joke himself.

Adam bounces off to the shower as soon as they're finished; he's actually forgotten Fred was bringing him something. Fred stands at the bathroom sink and cleans himself with soap and water, eager for the intimacy of a shower with Adam but unwilling to risk asking—stands listening to Adam tunelessly and unintelligibly recite some rap lyric. He's back on the bed in his underwear when Adam reappears, nude but for the yellow towel around his head, looking for a cigarette. "Come here for a minute." Fred opens the drawer and takes out the small box. This still feels right. "Remember I said I'd bring you something?" Adam is all attention now, forgetting the cigarette, removing the towel from his head and wrapping it around his waist as he joins Fred on the bed, not taking his eyes off what's in Fred's hand. "Oh, I forgot. Yeah, matter of fact, you did say that." He takes the box (gold top, black bottom, wrapped in a gold ribbon, not Fred's idea, they'd come that way) undoes the bow with a child's care and concentration, unsure for a moment when it's opened what he has here. He slips it from the taped micro-bubble wrap and turns it in his hands and Fred is happy to see he's impressed even before he knows what it is.

Fred reaches to press the release that opens the top but Adam pulls it away from him as he sees how it's done and opens it himself. "Oh, shit. I seen these. This is like…." He presses the "on" button.

"Little electronic address book. You can keep appointments, notes."

"Yeah, yeah. I seen these." He takes the small instruction booklet, printed in four languages in adjacent columns, glances at it and hands it to Fred. "I *need* this shit," he says with feeling, maybe thinking as Fred did of all those lost slips of paper. He looks Fred in the eye, eight inches away, and makes the moment all it should be. "Thanks, this…. Thanks." His delight is real, unmistakable. "Read how it works."

They spend twenty minutes at it, Adam quickly losing interest in hearing every detail, hurrying Fred through to the points that interest him, setting the clock and date functions and making entries in the address book—Fred's the very first, for doing the right thing. (Adam's mother and sister are next, but for now no names dragged out of the pockets of Adam's jeans.) Adam's presence, the few inches that separate them on the bed for these moments, the boy's almost hairless forearm brushing Fred's as they lean together over the device that has brought them this close, is the reward Fred had planned on.

There is space for password-protected secret information and Adam seizes eagerly on this. "What password should I use?" he asks, as for the moment they are that close, sharing secrets.

Fred knows better, but he hopes his honesty will show Adam he's worthy to be trusted with any secrets. "You should decide that for yourself," he says, a bit moved by his own sacrifice of the moment's intimacy. "We might not always be on good enough terms you'd want me to know."

Adam accepts this without a word, concentrates on the tiny lighted screen above the rows of keys and quickly enters something Fred cannot see. "What are you going to keep in the password part?" Fred asks.

"If I tell you it won't be a secret," Adam answers. The moment is just about over.

One of the recurring elements of Fred's parallel life with Adam is the moment when Fred's routine is interrupted by Adam himself, in person, on the phone, Adam dropping in as part of the everyday. On Wednesday, as he rinses the supper dishes the phone rings and the possibility of Adam—never far away, of course—slips through his mind, but even then he doesn't quite recognize Adam's voice, which sounds harsher on the phone.

"Yeah, Fred, wha's up? It's Adam." He adds a little giggle after his name as though it's too obvious to need mentioning. There are street sounds, cars and voices, behind him.

"What's up?" Fred, scintillating as always. "Everything okay?"

"Yeah, yeah, just chillin'. It's mad hot out here though."

"Where are you?"

"Right over here. Forty-third."

"Oh. Well, you want to come over?"

"Sure. Okay." There is a pause. "I need cigarettes." Nothing's free.

"I'll meet you downstairs, go get some."

And so it begins. It may be that Fred is only three, four blocks from where Adam hangs out, and if they've established anything it's that Fred can be relied on for the small things, for cigarettes and soda, and it's too easy, too convenient for Adam not to call when he's around and needs something.

Fred is wearing a robe over his underwear so he has to dress again, put wallet, keys and change in his pockets, get his shoes on, make sure his hair is combed. Still—no surprise—when he comes out of the elevator there is no Adam waiting on the other side of the big picture window facing the street, no Adam in sight when he steps outside and looks down the block. The pleasure, the anticipation he'd felt at the moment—another step closer to Adam, an unscheduled visit that could lead to others, to a habit of Adam at Fred's—dissipates in irritation as he stands and waits in the early evening humid heat for Adam to show up. In his own sweet time.

It's five minutes before he picks out the familiar walk heading his way, recognizable among dozens of the wrong sex or size or energy. All Fred's clouds lift as the figure moves closer, quick and confident and coming to him. Adam looks even slimmer than usual in a skin-tight ribbed tank top and baggy Guess jeans above another new-looking pair of white Nikes. "You bought my cigarettes?" he asks as soon as he's close enough to be heard, a grin of welcome enough to keep that from sounding rude.

Fred shakes his head. "What took you so long? I rushed to get down here…. Come on."

Adam ignores this and starts ahead of Fred across the street, to the little store around the corner. "I'm thirsty, too. Been out a hour. No, two. More."

"Doing what?" Fred thinks he knows the answer but at least Adam seems to have made no money or he could buy his own cigarettes.

"Just hangin' out. Chillin', you know."

They buy Newports, Pepsi, potato chips. Fred promises him a sandwich when they get upstairs and winds up carrying the small paper bag out and back to his place as Adam fiddles with the cigarette pack and lights one.

Across the street Adam slows, lifts his arms across his forehead and sniffs himself, wrinkling his nose. "I stink," he exclaims with feeling. Fred is thrilled. Too-clean Adam smells like a boy for now. He wants that, Fred does, to smell Adam sharp from the excitement of the streets, even (it briefly is in Fred's mind) against his will: "Nah, nah, chill. Let me at least shower first." No, no shower, just you.

But once they're in the apartment the hope of this, of spontaneity, of pleasure outside the formula they've established, disappears; Fred won't even ask, certain both that Adam would refuse (the nose wrinkling again, the words "I stink" that thrill Fred to think of again, embarrassment and fastidiousness) and that the request would lower Fred in his eyes—the word "nasty" Adam's used before would taint the request and adhere to Fred. No. He will sniff around for evidence of Adam, whole and human, but won't ask for this, not now (they will be close enough someday that….); for the sake of his position in Adam's eyes he won't ask now.

Fred offers to make a sandwich while Adam's in the shower. Processed turkey and cheese, not the Swiss he himself prefers but as Adam insists, "Yellow cheese, you know, like Cheez Whiz."

"I have Gouda, I don't have any American cheese. Or Cheez Whiz," Fred says.

"Wha's Gouda?" Adams sniffs the chunk Fred holds out to him. "Yeah, that's okay." Then with a twist of a grin he adds, "American cheese, that's what I want. I'm an American." He looks to make sure Fred has gotten the joke—he has, filed it as proof of Adam's precocious wit and charm—then heads off to the shower.

Fred doesn't know what to expect next, what Adam has come for. Was he bored out there, wanting a break before returning to work the streets? Did he just want to relax, take a shower, watch some TV and talk with someone he knows by now to be sympathetic? Or is it money he came for, as it's always been before? That would be fine with Fred, excited by the thought of natural Adam even as he washes that wild street odor off himself a room away; the thought of it is enough for Fred. He brings pillows out and throws them on the futon but doesn't put down the sheet—that would be a mistake if Adam were to see it and decide Fred's interested in him for only the one thing.

Adam's secrets weigh always on Fred's mind: Where he's come from and where he'll go next, who he sees and how he is with them, what he wants and worries over when he's alone, most himself. Is he complex, created of contradictions that will coalesce into something solid as he becomes a man? Or is he, as he sometimes seems, like a shark, moving forward every moment, money not food the goal of each exertion? It is little things Fred looks for and hoards as he spots them, jokes about cheese, revulsion at his own body odor. There will be others. If he isn't quick or clever enough to follow Adam into the world that swallows him when they separate, Fred can do a little snooping here and now—the bathroom door's mostly shut, Adam's toneless singing rises above the splashing water—Fred checks the jeans left folded on the chair. The organizer is heavy in one pocket, already with a half-inch scrape on the top. And with it, in spite of it, a couple of phone numbers written in heavy black pen on a lined sheet torn from a small notepad—men's names maybe waiting to be entered on the little keyboard. Fred rejects the urge to throw them away, Adam probably is used enough to losing things he would think they'd been dropped somewhere, if he ever thought of them again at all. And who knows, they might be friends, nothing to do with that world Fred found him in. Could be.

The other pockets are unrewarding—a single key on a knotted cord, several wadded dollar bills and thirty cents in change, a plastic bronze-tinted token from Show World, the largest of the porn-and-sex shops on Eighth, a stick of Wrigley's spearmint gum folded almost in half. He's excited to find a wallet—plastic Velcroed shut—but inside are only the stub for a bus ticket to Philadelphia, dated a month before, and a Medicaid card in a woman's name—Adam's mother? Sister? Or did he steal it? Find it? Who knows?

Fred is shaking his head over this clueless haul when Adam calls from the bathroom, shouting over the noise of the shower. He quickly puts the wallet back, refolds the jeans onto the chair, and takes a few quick steps to stand outside the half-open bathroom door. "I didn't hear you?"

There is a metallic scrape as Adam pulls the shower curtain open a few inches to stick his head out, hair dripping, skin gleaming wet. "I said heat it up, okay? The sandwich. I like it hot." He pulls his head back in without closing the curtain again and Fred goes to put the sandwich into the oven. Some like it hot he thinks—food, sex, weather; he could work that up into a little joke for Adam but it's already too late, too much thought over, and if Adam never heard of the movie the effort would be wasted to start with. Again he comes near embarrassment and pulls back just in time.

The water is turned off with a squeak and the curtain pulled wide and Fred turns to see again the thrilling sight of Adam, casually nude—could it be he really doesn't care about being observed, watched, by men he knows want him? The long legs and torso, the dick jerking back and forth under its dark triangle as he vigorously dries his hair, the ass—when he turns and puts first one foot, then the other, onto the side of the tub to dry his feet—muscles visible, the cleft just discernible, dark, moist, clean, a finger could probe it and come away smelling of soap and boy. Fred smiles at his own porno fantasy and turns, reluctantly, before he's noticed watching, to take the sandwich out of the oven.

Adam sits at the table, towel around his waist, legs entwined with the chair's, bare feet toe down on the floor, and eats the sandwich in large bites. He'd asked for Pepsi first, then decided orange juice is better for him. Fred sits, he hopes casually, on the bed, propped up by the pillows, and divides his attention between Adam, on his right, and an old episode of *Cheers* on the TV on his left, until Adam's boredom becomes obvious. Fred likes *Cheers* and had hoped Adam did, too, but after a few moments tosses him the remote. "Look for something you like. I don't care about this."

Adam is used to remote controls and barely pauses at each station before going on to the next, an instant long enough for judging. When he lingers for a few seconds at a Chinese language public access program Fred barely has time to make his little joke—"That's the one we want"—before he's off, not responding, control in one hand, sandwich in the other, his expression a mixture of blankness and concentration, even satisfaction from the very act of pushing the keys.

"How long were you out there today?" Fred asks, making conversation, certain Adam's forgotten he already said.

Adam shrugs, not taking his eyes from the screen. "A hour? I don't know. Couple hours." He stops at MTV, jiggly videos, and sets the remote on the table, stuffing the last of his sandwich into his mouth and settling back in his chair. Taking a long gulp of orange juice he makes satisfied sighing noises, patting his stomach. "That's better." He looks at Fred and smiles. "All I had today was cereal, Fruit Loops, and we ran out of milk."

"Dry Fruit Loops?"

"Yeah, that sounds bad, right? Plus I had a slice when I came out, is all." He smiles at Fred again and finishes the juice.

"I wanted to make some, you know, some money, but there's nothing out there. Too early. Plus, middle of the week." He shrugs slightly at the well-known qualities of the middle of the week and looks frankly at Fred, having made himself perfectly clear. "So. Wha's up?"

So. It's the money after all. The shower and the food, but mostly the money. Maybe the company too, but Fred is always reluctant to accept what he most wants to believe. He shrugs and replies, "What's up"—an answer as clear as Adam's request—adding, "How much you need?" Since this is not one of the scheduled meetings he hopes for a bit of a reduction, a version of that quantity discount he's never gotten around to mentioning.

And Adam after a moment's hesitation says, "Thirty-five?" What Fred would consider extravagant for anyone else is, to Adam, a bargain. But asked, a question, perhaps negotiable.

So Fred a bit reluctantly expresses his desire to get some control over his own money; between cash and the things Adam has begun to expect he feels it flowing away, like water from a faucet stuck on full. "How about thirty?" he asks, but Adam is ready, his questioning tone was only a second's weakness; before he finishes the prelude to his argument ("Nah, nah, come on, I got to....") Fred relents, embarrassed, to seem small about a few dollars. "Okay, okay. Thirty-five's fine. It's just, you know, what I've got has to last to payday." The step, the step to saying no, being firm with Adam, is one he can't take, he tells himself the time still isn't right, they're on good terms but not that good, Adam still doesn't trust him enough to have a serious talk about the way things have to be because Fred can't afford them any other way. Adam has called him out of the blue this time, if he can't count on him how likely is that to happen again? So this time, this time. Then maybe later....

And so on to the usual, sweat and quick, familiar moments, Adam in spite of the heat fresh from the shower. When they're through he takes another, splashing in and out quickly. Then, with the towel around his waist he takes the organizer Fred gave him and sits at Fred's phone to make some calls. Fred is ten feet away and the television is on but he hears enough. Men's names—Hector, Lou—a bit of confusion about who Adam is ("Light-skinned black, remember? You took me in the Korean store for cigarettes?") and pleas of poverty ("I'm fucked up tonight. Seriously"). Fred listens and understands and feels what is important is not to seem to care.

And how much does Fred care? Not as much as he tells himself he should, if this is the grand passion he likes to think himself capable of. There had been those long evenings waiting for Adam, standing and walking and watching for the familiar figure who in his second life was never far away, but even when they'd ended in failure Fred had been able to go home and sleep. None of the bereft stomach-turning emptiness of lovers in songs and books. Never once did he wake in the middle of the night unable to calm his misery; he could turn over and close his eyes and drift off every time. Never has he stopped in the middle of work, caught unawares by some image of Adam, overtaken, as by a seizure, by a certainty of loss he could barely push far enough away to continue what he was doing. That would have been something.

But then why should reality wreck his routine? The intense life with Adam was from the start the life in Fred's mind, Adam's physical absence only a drawback—but then one might say his presence, refusing to play out Fred's scripts, is a drawback, too. The real object of his passion from the start has been that Adam he keeps with him at all times, smooth and agreeable, giving a smiling, Fred-friendly face to the greedy, hurried, demanding reality. How could he miss the physical Adam—the one who rarely showed up on time, if at all, who went out looking for money from men—when he had the Adam he wanted (giving enough, not asking too much, always sorry for his previous excesses) at his elbow, his command, every moment? The possibilities that second Adam presented spilled over to burnish the image of the real boy, who had, after all, provided raw materials for him. Not all the raw materials; the outline of the two of them together, of their parallel life, is the one Fred has carried with him down the years, shaped, sometimes on the basis of pure wish and speculation, to fit how many other boys? Dozens, certainly. Hundreds? And now the space Fred had prepared for *a* boy is filled to overflowing with *this* boy: Adam's face and body, his voice and manner, his curly hair and dark skin and long legs and slender smooth arms, the determined walk, the long fingers fussing at his hair, his tricks of speech (the hard syllables, street slang like "mad" for any extremes—"mad busy," "mad pretty"—"no doubt"; "dog" as a verb; "word to mother" the standard oath; "for real"). He's filled that space too well, was the first in years to make it his. Fred won't give him up easily. His parallel life was made for an Adam.

Now that Fred has (by his standards) an actual relationship to live in he of course doesn't know how to go about it except the way he always has: He visualizes each encounter, every conversation, in advance only to find reality has little resemblance to what he has prepared for, so easily slipping away from him; relives meetings even as they go on, and after, softening the hard unwelcome edges while beginning to experience, as hope and another chance, the next. Adam, he may someday realize, is always Adam, perhaps predictable to anyone who sees him as a type: Street kid, school dropout, smokes dope, sells drugs and his body, hangs out with older kids, loves money and clothes and late hours. He is not so predictable to Fred, who insists on an Adam who fits the story he has carried with him all these years, an Adam who cares—or will care—for him more than for the life out there, who can be counted on to say and do the right thing—not always, but often enough, often enough. Too often already Adam doesn't. For these occasions there's next time.

"I'll be around Friday," are Adam's last words to Fred on Wednesday night, with the implication that they'll get together then. Fred takes it that way, the two of them are settling into something regular and understood, although the understanding is still all his; so far Adam seems to understand that he will show up when he wants to and take away more than Fred wants him to have. The time has come, Fred thinks, for a talk, settling things. Making clear the time they'll spend together and the money that will be exchanged. Fred of course had done this already, but only with himself, with that Adam he keeps handy at all times.

At work Fred has quit dropping hints and settled into what must look from the outside like himself as he's always been. He can still bring Adam in, in his mind only, for a guest appearance or two every day, shown off, mysterious and tantalizing, something for gossip to hang from, but there are no more hints, no teasing references. Fred's initial giddiness has run up against the real Adam and the fact that parallel lives never meet; his secret is a secret again.

Frank and Greg, the only two at work who might ask, or even realize there's something to ask about, don't. Frank—expecting perhaps his own discretion in not inquiring about others will save him the embarrassment of being asked about his own problems with money and a sickly mother and juggled girlfriends—smiles at Fred occasionally as though they share something they had not shared before, but does not ask questions; Fred appreciates both the smiles and the silence. Greg, probably relieved Fred hasn't repeated his almost-confidence, never goes near the personal, keeping every exchange bland and businesslike, professionally cool.

Fred's working mask is, he thinks, back in place, though with no real idea what others say or think of him he can't be sure how effectively he keeps his secrets. He looks in, not out, to find an image of himself.

Friday evening begins (in Fred's version, before the fact) with Adam's call coming at just the right time—after Fred's shower and nap—when both of them are hungry enough to want to eat out (somewhere cheap, Adam doesn't seem to have expensive taste in food at least)—who knows?—maybe even going to a movie, Adam might stay the night; waking

116

up next to him is a constant in Fred's second life. Even in the shower he has the phone handy, ring turned up, so he won't miss the call he has already taken in his mind a dozen times. But it doesn't come when he's ready and he isn't prepared for this wait—what has he learned from his years of small disappointments? Not to plan for the worst. Adam didn't mention a time, Fred is trapped here with no backup plan to amuse himself. After a while his hunger is stronger than his desire to live out his fantasy but he can't go out for something for fear of missing the call—even a slice of pizza, how long does it take the phone to ring and not be answered?—and there's nothing much in the house to eat; he hadn't planned for this, counting on the parallel life to be reality this time, hope overcoming all that experience. He fixes himself a peanut butter and jelly sandwich and waits some more, suddenly a prisoner, a prisoner of the telephone, Adam might be three blocks away or in the Bronx, might have lost the number or decided there's just as much money, more, to be made without calling anyway, but Fred doesn't dare budge for fear of missing him, as though the thread that binds them is so slender it may snap at this, at one missed phone call, and never be connected again. This night's waiting is doubly annoying since Fred can't find firm higher ground, can't claim Adam had given him a time or even his definite word, just that phrase, "I'll be around Friday," not a promise, maybe no more than thinking out loud, saying what Fred wanted to hear. Once again Fred took what was—or wasn't—there and built himself a story that turned out to have no life outside his mind.

On other nights he's been able to claim the small comforts of the streets, to move back and forth, watch lives pass by, add the vicarious richness of that world to whatever stories were passing through his mind, he's had the freedom to walk off his nerves and recently the hope each time he approached Adam's corner of perhaps seeing him there this time. Now he has four walls, nothing much on TV, boring food, a phone that won't ring, just will not ring.

All the usual stories—other, better versions of the evening, tales of Adam's perfectly good reasons for not being there—seem sour; Fred has let his guard down, he was just so sure this night would work. He doesn't give up until nearly eleven, hot and desperate for some stimulation beyond the apartment and reruns of television shows he hadn't cared about the first time. He picks up his Walkman and, listening from outside his door even as he locks it for the ringing phone that would bring him relief, bring him rushing in to forgive all at the sound of Adam's voice, goes out for the first time this Friday night to walk the streets.

He almost expects to see Adam, he always almost expects him on that corner, perched on the hydrant, but he is nowhere to be seen. Tonight Fred does not hang back on the quiet side of Eighth Avenue but walks through the alert, shifting crowd; he sees a few he knows among the many he's seen before, but no one bothers him, no one makes the sort of eye contact that requires him to stop and talk, stop and say no, stop and fob off importunate requests with a couple dollars and a lie. He passes not quite invisibly down the streets he's spent so much of his life on, hunting and hoping, among the kind of people he has most planned to be among, although there is not a soul he sees here tonight he wants to be with or talk to. This whole world of men and boys, men and other men, has been edited and enhanced in his mind so the reality can't satisfy him. Certainly not tonight, when he's waiting—how can it be? Again?—for Adam.

Through the headphones Fred listens to Neil Young's thin harsh voice, maybe made for disappointment, and is able to smile at the mirror he finds—"Helpless, helpless, helpless, helpless." "I keep searchin' for a heart of gold."

He walks around for forty-five minutes, an hour, with no Adam, no Jeff to ask about Adam, before going home, seeing as he walks the blinking message light, hearing Adam's recorded voice—there will be something on his answering machine. Of course he is not surprised to be disappointed by the indifferent red zero. No calls.

He could go out again, but he's tired. He sits on the edge of the futon and flips uninterested through all the cable channels and then sits and stares at whatever was on first, not even quite sure what it is. There is tomorrow. He could go out, do something during the day and be back by evening to wait again for Adam's call. It will come, there's money to be made so it will come. The way it might be is there but Fred's too tired to take any comfort dwelling on it, the possibility of pleasure sometime in the future. He brings out his sheets and pillows, makes the bed and turns off the TV, closing his eyes on Adam, again, Adam where he isn't.

Sounds, real sounds, intruding into a deep sleep, always seem to be just what they are. A ringing phone is a ringing phone and Fred is sure who is on the other end of this line even as he fumbles to answer before the machine picks up. Out of the corner of his eye he sees the clock on the night table: 3:35. Better late than never.

"Hello?"

"Yeah, Fred. Wha's up? It's me, Adam." Again the little giggle at the mention of the obvious, his own name.

"Yeah, yeah. What happened?"

"What? Oh, nothin'." As if answering an accusation. "We just chillin' is all. Listen—"

"Oh.'Cause you said—"

"Some shit came up. Listen. We're out here on Forty-third, we wondered could we come over for the night."

We? "Night's almost over. Who's we?"

"My man Michael is all. Just, you know, hang out till morning."

Fred thinks as quickly as he can half-awake but there's no chance he'll say no. Is it a good sign Adam feels he can bring a friend over, or is it taking advantage? He wants Adam to himself but he's always curious; all those years on the prowl makes any opportunity to meet a new boy seem too good to pass up. "Where are you? Forty-third?"

"We'll be, like, two minutes, okay?"

"I'll come down."

"Yo, Fred, Fred. You could buy some Newports?"

Fred is in front of his building, pants pulled over his pajamas, twenty dollar bill in one hand, keys in the other, five minutes before two figures appear from the Eighth Avenue end of the block, making their unhurried way to where he stands. Maybe it's just because it's the two of them unaware of having an audience their movements are almost the opposite of the streety space-filling exaggeration Fred sees so much of; they lean towards each other, close as much smaller boys on a playground, almost bouncing off each other, puppy-like, finally spotting Fred and approaching with more of a swagger, Adam grinning, Michael smiling with the confidence of one who knows a secret: Adam has told him about Fred. As they shake hands Fred makes the sort of instant judgment he's made thousands of times over the years, yes or no, safe or dangerous, likely or not: Yes, safe, and of course likely, since he's with Adam. Michael is dark—darker than Adam—but his olive complexion and fine features are Hispanic instead of black. He is Adam's age, round face with a small mouth of the sort that forms an easy pout, short straight hair, probably slim build hidden under the usual baggy jeans and a light blue football jersey worn loose outside the pants. Adam has on knee length cutoffs, a plain white T-shirt and his own pair of white Nikes, maybe not new but very clean.

"Late as always," Fred says to Adam, trying make their meetings sound more regular than they've been, anxious to impress even this stranger with how close they are, on teasing terms, and maybe to put himself between them a bit, instead of being the one outside.

Adam ignores him. "You got anything to eat? We're starvin'."

"Just something for sandwiches."

Adam and Michael look at each other. "I want cereal," Adam announces.

"Yeah, yeah," Michael agrees. "Cocoa Puffs." They both grin as though Cocoa Puffs are a shared joke.

Fred doesn't ask to be let in on it. "Let's go to Smiler's." The overpriced convenience store is the only one open nearby and Fred walks between the two boys, half a step back. "You just got down here? This late?"

"We was hangin' out at my house. Just, you know." Adam makes a smoking motion, exaggerates holding a breath and exhales ecstatically. Both boys grin.

"You come around here much?" Fred asks Michael.

"Just lately is all. We come down together." Another not so welcome glimpse into Adam without Fred; he brings his friends down for three-ways—probably very profitably. Tonight's Fred's turn. "Mostly we just hang out." Michael has a soft thick accent, part Spanish, part the hard black sound he's picked up on the street.

"Nothing going on out here this late, is there?"

Adam might say he came down specifically to see Fred, might say it just to score points, but, "Weekends there's sometimes people be out mad late, but not tonight," is his answer. Followed by the more unwelcome, "I made some of my best money late like this." Fred is careful not to show how bothered he is by another boast about Adam's moneymaking skills. But for the moment he realizes he isn't so bothered: For the moment Adam is with him.

It isn't hard to spend Fred's twenty dollars, plus the four singles Adam has wadded in his jeans pocket. Cigarettes, Cocoa Puffs, whole milk because Fred only has low fat at home ("I hate the taste of that shit. I want real milk."). Chip-a-Roos, American cheese in case Adam does want a sandwich, rolling papers, two packs of gum—it adds up fast, although the bag Adam holds under his arm as he lights a Newport going out of the store doesn't look like much.

This near dawn on a weekend the city is barely moving, only half a dozen vehicles per change of light on Ninth Avenue, mostly early delivery trucks and an even higher than usual percentage of taxis. There are a few late drinkers and partyers, some members of the non-suit-wearing classes going to or from work, the earliest dog walkers. Those who are truly of the streets—the shuffling homeless, the bluntly criminal, the mumbling, wild-eyed, tic-y weird, all present by day of course but half-hidden in crowds, easy to slide over—have no camouflage at this hour. An ancient man in a tattered gray sport coat, too-large black slacks held with a twine belt, sleeps in a recessed doorway, his bare feet—swollen and cracked, veins so visible his skin seems almost reptilian—splayed on the sidewalk. A middle-aged black woman Fred once mistook for a prostitute sits on a discarded couch on his block, rocking back and forth mumbling, he knows by now, about the angels who keep her down.

"You was sleepin'?" Adam thinks to ask as they enter the building. Fred puts a finger to his lips, worried how voices carry in the predawn quiet, and doesn't answer until they're in the elevator.

"I stay up late weekends but not this late."

"You didn't go looking for someone else when I didn't show up?" This with a sidelong grin that Michael picks up.

Fred looks Adam in the eye and shrugs, unsmiling. "No one interesting around." Adam's grin wavers, perhaps he's trying to decide if Fred is seriously able to pass him off for some casual trick, or if Fred is teasing his confidence. This could be a mistake of course, Adam might be trying Fred out, as Fred has been Adam, and he might have expected some proof of Fred's devotion. Nah. Suddenly Adam turns to Michael and raps out two rhythmic lines that Fred barely catches a word of, from some song he doesn't know, changing the subject as effectively as possible, from Fred to the two of them.

Upstairs Adam takes charge, emptying the bag and (trying to show Michael how at home he is here) on his second guess finding the spoons and two large plastic bowls to pour the cereal into. Fred stands in the doorway to the main room feeling unnecessary and rather pleased at this, Adam acting like he belongs.

Adam's question in the elevator is all Fred needed to be sure—not that he had doubts—that what these boys expect here is what he himself expects. Sex and money (definitely money, but then definitely sex, too, so how can Fred complain?) is the plan. All Fred has to do is wait for Adam to take the lead; he'll suggest

122

Fred put on his dirty movie, or he'll switch to the all night adult channel. One way or another Adam will bring the subject up, that's the etiquette here. Of course it could be expensive but for the moment Fred is free to wonder what's underneath those loose-fitting clothes of Michael's, what the three of them will be together. The presence of someone new and attractive, the certain anticipation of pleasure to come, add up to a perfect moment in sex. Before the disappointments set in.

Fred picks up the remote control and turns on the television, turning it down because of the hour and leaving it on something he recognizes, one of Clint Eastwood's Italian Westerns, he isn't sure which one, he's never seen any of them all the way through, but they should have the right amount of blood for his guests. And he knows some things about Eastwood and these movies, mildly interesting stories that might mildly impress.

But Adam, coming in and establishing himself on the bed, quickly pulling off his shoes and dropping them on the floor, propping a pillow up behind him, barely glances at what's on before picking up the remote and beginning to troll for something else. He pauses at MTV to eat a couple of spoonfuls of cereal and then goes on. Michael is at the table, cereal box and milk carton at his elbow, and Fred, with so few choices, joins Adam on the bed, using a second pillow to support his back. They go through cartoons, reruns of seventies sitcoms and *Dukes of Hazzard*, movies featuring mindless violence or mindless jokes, programs in Spanish, Japanese, Indian, and what seems to be one Chinese dialect with subtitles in another. There are lots of ads, some masquerading as real programs— ads for skin cream, kitchen utensils, song collections, psychic readings, peace of mind and for getting rich from selling real estate, presumably to people who don't watch the same late-night programming.

Fred's mind is not on the television. He feels Adam next to him, their legs touching. And there's Michael. Michael's no Adam but Fred would have noticed him, at least, would have circled him with interest if they'd been on the same stretch of Eighth Avenue some evening. He is young enough, for one thing, Adam's age, and if he doesn't have a look Fred would linger over if they were passing on a stairway or sidewalk he is available and therefore—Fred is conditioned this way—attractive.

Adam winds up with a *Lethal Weapon*——not nearly as interesting as Eastwood in Italy but with much more inventive sorts of violence—and, having decided, proceeds to ignore it. Through a mouthful of cereal he asks Fred, "You know what food stamps are, right?"

"Sure. They've been around for years." He is instantly suspicious.

"You never used them?"

"I always, you know, worked. I had enough money I never needed to."

"Yeah, but you could, right? I mean nobody'd say anything."

"Well, I mean, I'm not going to, I don't have any reason to. Why—"

"'Cause I got a bunch we wanna sell," Michael blurts out, half standing to dig several coupons out of his front pocket. "Like, for half what they're worth." Then, showing some natural salesmanship, he adds, "Less."

"Come on." Fred turns to Adam. "Do I seem like a stolen food stamp kind of guy to you?"

Adam has a mouth full of Cocoa Puffs and almost spits them out laughing. "No. No, you don't, matter of fact." He wipes milky crumbs from his chin.

"Well?"

"We just thought, you know. Money for us, save you some." Adam shrugs and Michael stuffs the stamps back into his pocket. They both return to their cereal.

Maybe this was the reason for their visit, maybe Fred's blown it already, but no, they both seem barely disappointed by this refusal, making small talk while they finish their cereal. Fred stirs himself; hating to leave Adam's side but hating even more to leave a mess he takes the bowls into the kitchen to rinse, puts the milk in the refrigerator. He hears some movement in the next room and when he comes back he's a little put out to find Michael has moved from the chair to the bed but then Adam says, "Come on, there's room for all of us," moving as far as he can to his side of the futon and giving Michael a little shove towards the other. "You can get right between us."

The boys are pleased, expectant, as Fred climbs over Michael to settle snugly between them on the narrow bed. They know and so does he. He has been here before, on other nights, in other beds or this one, with other boys, singly or in pairs, everything understood. He doesn't kid himself, it isn't him the boys want, it's sex for its own sake, money, both, and he is the one they'll use, the one they'll let themselves be used by. If they were alone, jerking off, or in a circle jerk with others their age, it would be part of growing up, a boy thing, expected. His presence doesn't change that. They lack whatever brake it is— shyness or modesty or revulsion or fear—that for others forms a barrier, keeping this from being a standard relationship of boys to interested men.

Fred has never—as he knows others do—provided drugs or alcohol to speed things up. Adam and Michael have done that themselves, smoking a joint or two before they ever got here, although it probably doesn't make any difference. They're fifteen. Everything is ready. And when after a moment Adam again picks up the remote and says, "Which one's the porn channel?" Fred doesn't hesitate to answer.

The boys are used to this; they pretty much ignore Fred, each goes his own way, unselfconsciously delighted, as the boys in Fred's experience tend to be, in the pleasures they can take from their own bodies. They use the video for inspiration, talk and laugh and brag about their sexual adventures—with girls only, nothing about what they do (except make money) with men ever comes up—and finish quickly. Then they are dutiful about arranging themselves for Fred, but he can't concentrate, he's distracted by their giggly chitchat and has to shush them— jovially, he hopes—then close his eyes and wish Michael away before he can come.

It is exciting and disappointing; once his curiosity is satisfied—Michael is what he would expect, slim, solid, butt a little big, dick small—Fred wants him to go away so he can have Adam to himself. But they're in for the night, Fred dozes off as they watch TV, the boys eventually falling asleep themselves. When Fred wakes up Michael is at an angle between himself and Adam on the far edge of the futon. Fred's wanted to wake up with Adam of course, but now he's just out of reach, just beyond where he can be studied and sniffed at, some sleeping secrets sought out. Fred props himself up and looks at his boy, curled on his side, his light blue boxers tugged down to reveal one pale hip, present but unreachable.

Fred is used to living alone, or at most with one boy, shadow of reality, cut to his specifications. It doesn't seem to occur to Adam or Michael that spending time here might not be something permanent, they settle in quickly the next two days; Michael had seemed a bit tentative when they'd arrived, asking permission at first even to use the bathroom, but now he like Adam acts right at home. They are together in a way that seals Fred off from them, boys and all that street stuff together. Fred and Adam certainly have nothing comparable—Fred wants it of course, for himself and Adam; that sure sense of being part of a pair the world cannot penetrate or separate is what he's wanted since that first Sunday approach to the new boy resting on the fire hydrant, dark glasses and cigarette and cap and attitude all impeccable. He's seen it day in and day out, lived himself and Adam together in a way that isolated them from anyone else, Adam's friends or anyone. But what he wants to have with Adam is a version of what Adam really has with Michael and surely they'd see rejection of Michael as a slap at both of them. Fred feels trapped again.

Michael is fine, breezy and agreeable, but he's not Adam and his presence becomes annoying even though he himself is inoffensive; Fred can't possibly indulge his parallel life with this third person in the way, a distraction, it's like trying to sing with someone else's voice in his ear—Adam's song is discordant enough as it is. And Fred can never let annoyance pass unnoticed and he won't take Michael's unwelcome presence out on Adam. He knows himself, and hates it, he's seen this in others and despises it, the impulses and the cowardice and the very look, but it will be him: Thin-lipped, curt to the point of rudeness, he will find fault at every opportunity in an attempt to make Michael seem impossible. His barely concealed anger will take a while to be noticed since Adam and Michael will be in that world of theirs, and then there will be confused sidelong glances and growing uneasiness and finally some sort of resolution; one of them—probably Adam, it would be his place to ask—will try to find out what's wrong. There are other ways of course, ways Fred thinks of as normal, as everyone else's methods of dealing with unwelcome guests; he could lightly and humorously make it clear he'd rather not have them both around, he might say, "Look, this apartment's just too small for three, I'm the quiet type, you two together are just too much for me." No harm, no hurt feelings. But he can't bring himself to this, he almost believes what he wants to believe, that he can isolate Michael from Adam and bring Adam to himself, make them a pair. So thin-lipped and curt he is, part of him knowing he looks just that way, angry and short-tempered, part of him thinking he can put Michael in the wrong. He goes on.

Michael cooperates, sort of, through klutziness, spilling Pepsi on the kitchen floor, dropping a cigarette that burns two tiny holes in a sheet on the bed. By Sunday afternoon they have gone out and come back several times, Adam and Michael, returning with cash and the story of how they made it selling fake cocaine to kids from New Jersey, a story of stealing sunglasses from a Korean store, Michael distracting the shopkeeper as Adam slipped the glasses into his pocket, but not fast enough, both of them having to run—laughing all the way, no police in sight to worry about—to escape the sharp-eyed shouting old man. They take turns trying to imitate his accent cursing at them.

Michael goes into the shower and Adam sits next to Fred and says, "He thinks you don't like him, right?" Guaranteed to make Fred feel guilty, defensive.

"I guess I'm just too used to living alone. You're fine, of course, you know how much I like you, but the two of you—"

"No, that's cool, that's cool. You should have said."

"I felt bad. I didn't want to—"

"No, no. That's cool. We'll go and I'll be back late, you know, if that's okay."

So it's done without Fred having to say a word to Michael about it, just as well. There are awkward moments, Michael out of the shower, Adam whispering to him in the bathroom, television and weather small talk as Michael dresses, quick good-byes. Fred does feel bad, once it's over and they're gone. Michael had been fine—he'd even suggested (before Adam and Fred's talk) that the three of them go to a movie that night— it was just wrong for Fred, having him there. Michael would have been one of those he brought home only once, the spark wasn't there, and the truth is—always was—that Fred has no real interest in any boy who can't keep the spark alive.

And Adam in fact does return that night, Sunday, late, around the time Fred usually goes to bed. He has gotten enough money from some unspecified somewhere to buy fried chicken from a Chinese restaurant and he attacks it eagerly—dried out stringy leg and thigh with greasy French fries—turning down Fred's offer of a plate in favor of tearing the paper bag open, squeezing in three plastic packets of ketchup, and plucking out shreds of meat and limp red-smeared fries. It turns out he can't stay; he's meeting Michael, who's with a trick, and barely keeps Fred past his bedtime.

The phone rings the next morning, just as Fred is getting out of the shower; he leaves wet footprints on the floor, drying his hair as he pads over to answer it before the machine picks up. Adam, sounding a bit bleary, high on pot or just sleepy, loudly tries to make himself heard over the morning traffic: He's still out, he's broke, he's tired. "I could stay at your house

128

while you're at work? I'll probably sleep all day, when you get home we can eat, maybe do something, you know, if you want." Do something. Adam's own euphemism.

It is a moment Fred has longed for and dreaded; he's thrilled but knows this dream come true doesn't feel like his dream. He has to add that seamless connection he has assumed in every moment of his real life in order to mask his doubts, his awareness of the risks. Has Adam in their real time together ever failed to ask for more, too much—more money, more sneakers and clothes and attention, Fred waiting on him like a servant or a mother? Does Fred even trust him? He wants to trust more than he trusts, of course, wants to believe more than he believes. He feels the risk, he has risked before and lost. So he hesitates but not for long; this is yes or no to Adam, not to a single favor. "Where are you? I have to leave soon," is his reply. As good as yes.

The next two weeks are tantalizing, like a sketch of what Fred has imagined, Adam close but not completely there, calling at all hours, showing up unannounced, wanting a shower, a few dollars, a slice of pizza, but not quite willing to hang around, except to sleep, when Fred's at work. Fred feels like a man with a dance partner who won't learn the steps. Fred knows the steps, hears the music, Adam's part and his own. If only Adam would be willing to learn his rhythm at least.

The first and last time they eat out together is this Wednesday, at a cheap Chinese restaurant behind the Port Authority—half a dozen tables, chairs with orange plastic seats, mirrors on both sides to make the cramped dining space look larger. The young woman behind the counter that separates the customers from the cooks seems unusually unsure of her English, or maybe it's the argument she's having with a scruffy black man dissatisfied with the amount of hot sauce she's poured on his fried chicken. "That's why I don't be giving them a hard time, they make a mistake," Adam says, his look lingering on her as he and Fred sit down after giving their order and a thin Chinese man in a stained white apron takes over the argument from the stricken-looking girl. "It's too easy to hurt their feelings."

Fred seizes on this, proof of Adam's kind nature, and files it away, should anyone come along he can share it with. A moment later as Adam starts on his two thick pancakes of egg foo yong and Fred his chicken and broccoli Fred realizes they are being watched by a man his own age, dark and heavy, thinning black hair slicked back, a canned ice tea in his pudgy fist and a smirk on his face, sitting alone at the next table. Adam sees him, too, his reflection on the mirrored wall, and becomes silent, self-conscious, eating fast. After gulping down half his food, washed down with Pepsi, Adam says, "Let's get the rest of this wrapped up. Let's go." Fred doesn't argue, hearing the urgency in his voice, but takes what's left to the counter to be put in a styrofoam box and a plastic bag. Outside Adam takes his own leftovers and walks back a bit to the knot of homeless men and one sleeping woman waiting for the nightly visit of a food truck sent by a Harlem church. He says a few words and one of the men takes the food. "I hate to waste it, all these hungry people," he says as he rejoins Fred back at the light. Another memory to cherish.

Halfway down the next block Fred gives up hoping Adam will volunteer information and asks, "Who was that guy looking at you back there?" He assumes the worst, a trick, one of Adam's too many.

"He's always tryin' to talk to me. He lives over in, like New Jersey, wants me to go out there." He shakes his head. "That's like, too far. I don't want to get stuck out there, fuckin' New Jersey." Not the perfect answer, but still, someone who wants Adam but can't have him—even if only for logistical reasons— fits right in Fred's second life.

So for a time Fred's routine before and after work is hostage to Adam's whims: The pre-work phone call isn't repeated that week so every day Fred's home as early as possible, waiting for the phone to ring; if it doesn't he goes out once, twice, three times, even late, looking for Adam still but now with some confidence: There is a connection, he's a regular, relied on— isn't he?—more than any of Adam's others. He can believe that.

Even if Adam is around they don't make much contact—a nod, maybe a word or two, even Fred can't pretend to fit into Adam's life on the street; Fred just can't afford him every time he's out and if Adam's looking for a trick talking to Fred will only keep other men away. Still. For Fred being this close is something. The stories continue to flow.

Friday night Fred has plans—take Adam to eat then back home for the usual. But Adam is nowhere to be seen from early—Fred passes by on his way home from work—to as late as eleven. Fred isn't worried, of course, not even concerned; the night is pleasant, cooler than others recently, and not spending money on Adam means he has money to spend, not that he would on anyone else, but the possibility brings memories of successful nights, Fred on a weekend with cash and the possibility of a new boy.

He goes out a little after midnight for one last pass down the usual blocks, past familiar faces and new ones that barely register. For the first time it is Adam who makes the approach, he sees Fred and comes up, hand out, smiling, even though this is his own block, so to speak; he is by himself on Eighth, in the middle of the block north of Forty-second, and they walk back to the Deuce like old friends. Two of the men lingering near the corner eye Adam appraisingly but he looks away and shakes his head. "All these homos out here want me," he says softly to Fred in a tone of slight disgust. Fred is thrilled by this, of course, a confidence that separates him from "all these homos out here."

Adam is hungry and they start off in search of a deli open this late. "I was in New Jersey with another guy and these two girls," he says. "I fell asleep in the hotel room and they left me." So he doesn't object to New Jersey on principle.

"I hope you had some money."

"Nah, nah, I was stranded out there. I had to, you know, hitchhike, then I got this bus driver let me slide. Like, you know, 'Yo, B, I'm fucked up out here.' He's like, 'Okay, okay.' Black dude."

"How'd you wind up in New Jersey?"

"It was—they wanted to go there. It was the girls' car, so…. But I was mad anyway. There was one of them was real pretty, she was the one I wanted to be fucking with, but she wound up on the bed with my other friend so I had to fuck with the other one."

"Then you fell asleep."

"I didn't eat since this morning, either. I'm hungry like a motherfucker." He grins with justified confidence.

The narrow deli a block from Fred's apartment is always open. Adam orders ham and American cheese on a roll and watches to see they give him enough of both. He starts eating as soon as they're outside, giving Fred his soda to hold while he takes a big bite from the sandwich. But instead of going towards Fred's building Adam starts back the way he came. "I'm gonna, you know, hang out for a while."

"I thought—"

"Maybe I'll come over later. I only just woke up, I wanna, you know." He takes another big bite, pushes the rest of the sandwich back in the bag, and retrieves his soda. "Thanks for the sandwich. I was hungry like a motherfucker."

The next call doesn't come until Monday morning, while Fred is again getting ready for work, but that's all right. Fred read a lot into being separated from "all these homos," and Adam's comings and goings the previous week seem to have settled into a comfortable irregularity; Fred's been able to think all weekend of an Adam just close enough, a phone call, a block or two away, but not for the moment making demands or costing any money. When he does call early Monday Adam's decided on something, and then this is how it is for another couple of weeks: He spends his nights on the streets, Eighth Avenue, the Port Authority, somewhere, he moves around—as on those nights before they'd met when Fred would glimpse him and then he'd be gone—and doesn't give Fred the details. "Just chillin'," he'll say when asked. "Hangin' out." Early in the morning, after Fred's awake but before he leaves for work the phone rings. "I'm comin' over, okay?" It's okay. A few times he borrows the boom box Fred keeps in the bathroom and takes

132

it out overnight; those mornings the first sign of his approach is the bass of the radio, thumping down the block before Fred can recognize Adam, shedding a friend or two as he comes near. Radio or no he keeps Fred waiting as he saunters down the block, cheerful and vague about his night, always claiming to be broke, sometimes needing cigarettes, cereal, a single cheap cigar he'll hollow out to hold the nickel bag of pot he's brought back. Not without misgivings Fred leaves him in his apartment for the day. In the evenings Adam is asleep, torso bare, blue or white or patterned boxers, tangled sheet he's kicked off in his dreams. Fred, home from work, usually has time to read the paper, pick up the pants, socks, shirt Adam's dropped wherever he took them off, maybe push his sleeping boy enough to one side he can take a nap himself before Adam wakes up, logy and crabby, stumbling wordless into the bathroom to piss, farting a few times, hawking loudly into the toilet, needing a cigarette, a shower, something to eat.

Fred feels what he wants is close, very close.

Their evenings together are short, with never a doubt of Adam's going out. He claims appointments, makes phone calls to numbers stored in the little organizer Fred gave him (never referring to where it came from, there should be a bit of a bond between them in the fact it was Fred's gift, but Adam seems to take it for granted, as he does everything he receives from Fred, and Fred can't very well bring it up, how often can he ask, "So do you use that thing I got you?"). He never tells Fred much more than he's meeting someone, maybe Michael, maybe a trick, Fred gets only the briefest idea and knows prying won't be welcome. It may be that the streets intoxicate Adam with the excitement of possibility the way they did Fred for so long—for Adam it's the glamour of it, of danger, sex, money, of thieves and whores, drug dealers and addicts, seeing himself, his own minor scams and hustles, fitting right in that dark swaggering corrupt world.

There are a few moments of what Fred is able to think of as tenderness; they have their price, but then they would. He and Adam have already eaten these nights, Chinese takeout or

133

leftovers or sandwiches, and Adam has taken his shower, but instead of beginning to examine his clothes to see what's clean and compatible he sits or lies on the open futon, damp towel around his waist, chatting aimlessly. After a moment he'll roll onto his stomach and say (sticking with a line that works) "You could give me a massage?" He has a little smile, the satisfaction of a success he can assume in advance, as Fred strips down to his underwear (no reason to pretend) and begins. It isn't Fred's only disappointment that these few times are so little different from his first with Adam, so little different, he's sure, from anyone else's. (Adam once, not bragging, very matter-of-fact, put the number of men he's been with at sixty.) He is disappointed by the certainty that Adam will expect cash or yet another new something; Fred gives him ten dollars or so every day ("I don't like you going out without some cash in your jeans," he's said, somehow liking the sound of it, the implication) and feeds him and keeps him in cigarettes, but that seems not to count, the calculations start at zero when it comes to what Adam can do for Fred.

But once they're finished there is time—not much, but enough to convince Fred it means something, that he and Adam are becoming more than the sum of these few quick sexual encounters and what he can afford to give—time to talk (briefly, Adam soon becomes antsy for the streets), time for what Fred can call tenderness. Maybe this is one thing Adam doesn't share with all those others; this talk of living with his grandmother, and later in a group home, of childish successes of looks and charm and intelligence, of almost being caught by the police joyriding in a stolen car with a friend, of robbing a drug dealer's house a year or so earlier. All these stories seem—if not meant only for Fred—meant for someone Adam at least feels comfortable with.

Beyond that Fred takes what he can get. He tends to hover, to watch Adam eating, he knows he shouldn't, he knows better, but the way the small main room's arranged Adam at the table eating can be kept in sight only when Fred is standing, and that generally means he's in the doorway from the kitchen, behind his eating boy. Adam doesn't seem to mind. They find movies, sports they can both watch. Adam's sport is basketball, he can recite—Fred assumes accurately—achievements of players from years when he might have been thought too young to notice and can pass easy judgment on any name he hears, interrupting an off-season basketball review to give a commentary on almost everyone who comes on-screen. "He's steppin' up in the league" is the phrase he repeats enough for Fred to remember.

One night they're watching preseason football highlights on TV; football is Fred's sport, his only one, he's seen enough to pretend he knows a lot about it and in fact he knows a fair amount. Adam has a football story. "I scored a touchdown once for my school team." He puts a half-chewed chicken wing in his mouth and skins off the remaining meat, dropping the stripped bone on his plate and wiping his fingers and mouth with a ketchup-reddened paper napkin. "I was, like, eight." He turns and favors Fred with a little smile as Fred tries to picture eight-year-old Adam, with his gap-toothed smile and absolute confidence. "I was the running back? I took the ball, like, the ten yard line." He puts his hands, balled into fists, in front of his chest, elbows out, and begins to move his head and shoulders back and forth, dinner table running. "I started one way, got away from the first couple guys, then like this, then boom!" He mimes the easy run down the field, the last few yards with his arms raised for a touchdown. He looks at Fred and grins again. "I could have been, you know, good, I'd stayed in school." He shrugs and picks up a couple of ketchup-drenched french fries.

Fred is charmed and touched; the shift of emotional weight he longs for and sometimes feels, from the passionate to the fatherly, wells up, but he is accustomed to keeping his emotions to himself and aware showing them is dangerous with someone as knowing and grasping as Adam. He puts a hand on his boy's shoulder and squeezes instead. "You could have been a lot of things. Maybe it's not too late." The feeling lingers.

"I could still get back in school next month," Adam says through french fries. Could be, Fred thinks; then, you're having too much fun.

One day they're walking back from the Chinese place on the next block, Fred as he would be carrying the bags, thin white plastic holding brown paper holding Adam's favorite, moo goo gai pan with lots of extra packets of duck sauce. ("They don't give you at least five of 'em you shouldn't go back.") Suddenly Adam, bouncing along with his usual confidence, slows to a stop, surprised, even uneasy, and walks over to the curb, looking across the street at one of the crowd hurrying in the other direction. Fred moves next to him. "That's my father," Adam says, almost to himself. Not proud or excited. Surprised.

"Which one?" It's rush hour, there are dozens of people in the direction Adam's looking.

"Over there." He nods his cap at anybody and everybody. "With the hat on."

Fred looks. He sees hats, tries to find one on the man he thinks of when he thinks of Adam's father—Adam's father is his black family, his mother is white—but no one stands out. Adam doesn't talk much about him—he was a pimp, has been in prison, is a man who likes drugs. "Well, go talk to him," Fred says. "I'll wait here."

Adam hesitates, eyes on the figure he still sees across the way, receding into the distance. He licks his lips and for the first time in these weeks Fred's known him seems uncertain, he is a boy always but now is so young Fred is startled by his confusion. Adam turns away, shaking his head. "He might be on his way somewhere."

"You can't just say hello to him? He's your father." Adam is embarrassed, something else in him new to Fred. He shakes his head. "I'll go, like the first of the month. He gets his SSI and gives me a few dollars. You know." He mumbles the last of this and pauses, licking his lips again, anxious. Is this a defense of his father? "Come on. I'm hungry."

The night before he's supposed to appear in court on the drug charges that made him late the Sunday Fred returned from his mother's, Adam is anxiously trying to plan his day in court.

"I should wear a suit and tie, right? You think the judge'd be impressed, see me there all dressed up? Know I really take this shit serious." *Se*rious.

"Don't get too fancy, he might wonder where you got the money."

A small smile, his eyes waver, uncertain if Fred is joking. "Nah, nah. Just. You know, light colored suit, nice tie."

"You'd need someone to tie it for you," says Fred, thinking of course of himself.

"I can tie a tie." The smile turns to a familiar grin. "I learned it in church, I lived with my grandma." The word "church" is struck hard, he knows how improbable this is. "I remember, too. I can tie one good." Fred's fatherly side swells again at the thought of Adam—how old? eight? nine?—in some black church youth group giggling with the other boys as he learns the twists and loops of tying a tie.

One afternoon Fred returns home around five as usual, to find Adam still asleep, as usual, sheets tangled around his slender legs, boxers twisted but not enough to reveal anything, the smell of farts and old cigarette smoke lingering stale in the thinly air-conditioned room. He puts down his bag and stares for a moment; all the affection he's stored for this boy becomes so much easier to feel, to believe, when Adam's asleep than when he's awake, scheming and demanding. We're innocent when we dream.

Fred is startled from these thoughts by the phone. This is the hour for credit card and long distance offers but this woman's voice is wary, even annoyed. "Somebody beeped me from there?" she asks flatly.

Fred looks at the sleeping Adam. "Um, let me check. What's your name?"

"Myra."

Fred puts his hand over the receiver and sits on the bed, putting his free hand on Adam's shoulder and shaking him hard enough to wake most people. "Adam. Adam. Wake up. You've got a phone call."

Adam shakes him off and tries to turn onto his side but when Fred holds him still he wakes up enough to protest. "Chill, chill."

"Phone call," Fred says again. "Did you beep someone?" This gets Adam's attention, he opens his eyes and lifts himself halfway on one elbow.

"Who is it?"

"Someone named Myra. You beeped her?"

Adam looks confused and uncertain as he has so few times before. "That's my mother," he says, sounding almost frightened.

"Well, did you beep her? Here." He tries to hand off the receiver, but Adam pushes it away.

"Hang up." His voice is a whisper, urgent.

"Adam, it's your mother," Fred whispers back. "I'll go in the bathroom, I won't listen."

"Hang up." He rolls over onto his side for real now, his back to Fred and the phone, and Fred stands reluctant.

"Nobody who's here now," he says, too polite to hang up without a word. Myra isn't and the click is loud in his ear. When he turns back Adam seems already to be sleeping again. He's embarrassed to be found here, Fred thinks, in the company of someone like me. That's a side of Adam never glimpsed in any of the stories Fred's spun for himself. Present but never accounted for.

An hour later, barely awake, Adam stumbles into the bathroom, eyes half open, hawking phlegm and spitting in the toilet as he starts to take a piss, and looks to where Fred is sorting clothes from the hamper. "Not my jeans, okay?" he says thickly.

Fred lifts a stiff dark denim leg and sniffs it: Vinegar and smoke. "These are filthy."

Adam shakes himself and hitches one leg up slightly to slip his dick back into his boxers. "I mean dry cleaned. So they won't fade and shit."

"So I should start going to the dry cleaners every week, too?"

Fred intends this to be peevishly humorous; of course he likes any connection with Adam that sounds regular and domestic, but Adam's in a sleepy child's touchy mood. "So, don't. I—or my mother'll do it. I can take 'em myself. Shit." Like Fred's too lazy or too cheap to do it, doesn't care enough for him, that old familiar blackmail.

"Oh, I'm kidding, for Christ's sake. I don't mind." Another defensive recovery from a failed joke, Fred trying to avoid conflict. "You want dry cleaning, you get dry cleaning." He tosses the jeans and another tangled pair from the heap of clothes into a separate pile: Dry cleaning. He tries again, in a tangential direction. "Extra duck sauce with your Chinese food, double stuffed Oreos on hand, dry cleaning. Admit it, when it comes to all these little things you like, I'm your man." He hopes this will work as another little joke, not the plea it sounds to his own ears. But Adam seems not to hear. He snorts something back from his nasal passages, clears his throat again, deeper, and spits again before flushing the toilet, then shuffles back towards the bed, scratching his head with one hand, his butt under the boxers with the other, saying no more.

"I'm your man," Fred says again, under his breath, shaking his head in that chagrin that seems especially acute because it's known only to oneself, the near-humiliation of the close call—the misbegotten joke almost told, the nasty gibe thankfully unheard. Adam didn't seem to register his words at all. Fred is not yet quite so abject, maybe, as to be begging for Adam's affections with reminders of duck sauce and laundry.

Perfection is for dreams, waking or sleeping dreams, and most of the time Adam is hard, wide-awake reality. He is petulant and demanding, greedy and fickle, and Fred knows, picking out nuggets of charm and vulnerability, that their shine is partially from the contrast to most of Adam's life. Very quickly the bloom fades; as the days pass Fred's little jokes bring fewer smiles and more irritated twists of the mouth, his attempts to please even less gratitude than before. Maybe, Fred thinks, it's Michael's influence, maybe that was a mistake; if Fred had been able to keep his annoyance to himself Michael could have stayed around, even become his ally. Well, maybe. It's too late now. Briefly, briefly, he can see the two of them together slowing Adam's plunge through the night, his endless thirst for excitement. But Michael will not be back, even if he were there's no reason to think he loves the night any less than Adam, there's no satisfaction in thinking of him. Maybe he whispers in Adam's ear, "How come you hang around that faggot Fred all the time?", drops hints to make Adam embarrassed to be so often in Fred's company, playing on his pride, his independence, his boy's need to be just another boy. The point is there to be made, Michael has reason to make it.

Fred has parts of Adam's past now, that grandmother, the foster home, the father he won't walk up to, but Adam lives in the now and referring back to them, inserting himself somehow as a meaningful link of Adam's story, won't work: Adam doesn't, wouldn't, see him that way.

The man who brought him here has more claim on Adam's memory. Fred has his story too, and can't use it for himself. Adam was riding into midtown on the train one Sunday afternoon seven, eight months before, nothing much in mind, when he caught sight of a single pinky fingernail, grown an inch long and painted with gold polish. He knew what that meant; telling Fred the story he demonstrates, smiling, holding his own trimmed and clean nail up to his nose and sniffing loudly. Adam was seduced just like that, although he made the approach, fascinated; the exotic, tinted with gold and a promise of excitement, was it all took. Within days he was living with this man—named Blue, for some reason Fred never asks—in an apartment over the hustler bar Blue managed. So at fourteen Adam was living above a gay bar behind the bus terminal with a man who referred to him as his husband. Not a resume Fred can easily fit onto the boy in his parallel life. But Adam tells it with regret—"Fuckin' Blue. I'd still be in school I hadn't met him"— and left Blue after a few months for (surprise) the promise of more money on the streets.

What Fred is able to tell himself now is that Adam went through this, through Blue and the bar and the streets that came after—three or four months of hanging out around Times Square before Fred met him, using at least as much as being used, another relentless street shark—without ever letting the life he led touch anything inside him. He is there, pure somehow still, for Fred, for someone, his heart waiting to be opened, all he has done disturbing only the surface of his life while he has remained whole underneath, a boy waiting to be discovered.

Fred's neighbor down the hall is a chubby effeminate Hispanic man with hennaed hair and a yappy poodle. The thought of his seeing Fred with Adam is somewhere on Fred's list of minor potential thrills, his sure envy the sort of boost Fred craves: See what I've got you can't have. The time comes one evening as Fred and Adam are leaving together, Adam to his streets, Fred to buy groceries. Fred, hearing the door down the way slam and the click and jingle of the dog's claws and collar in the hallway, tenses in pleasant anxious anticipation, hoping Adam finishes patting his hair into place and admiring himself in the mirror before the chance is gone. Fortunately the elevator is on the main floor so they are on their way out before it's climbed to the top.

It starts out as good as if it hadn't been planned: Fred and Adam step out the door, Adam says he needs cigarettes and Fred answers, "The apartment always smells like smoke anymore." Enough information for anyone, and Fred is gratified to see the appraising glance directed at Adam before the elevator arrives and the man—he and Fred have never more than nodded, no names, not even small talk—picks up the dog and opens the door. They ride down in silence until Adam reaches out to scratch the dog around its ears and says, "Poodle, right? I like dogs." He's rewarded with a little smile and somehow the balance has shifted. Is Adam flirting here, by smiling back? Is the eye contact long enough to be *meaningful*? Fred's satisfaction, his tiny victory, is suddenly empty, even threatened. But what can he do or say? Adam would pretend only innocence here, whatever is in his mind. What's that, be careful what you wish for?

And what is on Adam's mind? For all the intimate knowledge he likes to think he has, what Fred has really become expert on is the little tricks Adam uses to get what he wants. None of them is subtle, just difficult to argue with; he's manipulated his way through life so far and is very good at it: Maybe he does have a party to go to, no clean white sneakers to wear, a present to buy, a debt to pay or else. Whatever the claim it will either cost Fred—gullible Fred, credulous Fred—money, or (less often) give Adam an excuse to go somewhere else, or (more often) both. For Fred there is no lasting pleasure possible; he cannot for long forget the lies, the too much money being asked for and spent, that it could as easily be another man in his place and maybe will be soon.

The next weekend, the third after Michael, is as close real life comes to the one Fred lives out in his mind. Weekends he feels more able to cope with Adam, there is none of the worry of what might happen while he's at work, no need to be in bed early or up early the next day. They might go out together, although Adam has shown no interest in even going to a movie with Fred and now refuses to eat with him anywhere but in the apartment—permanent reaction, Fred guesses, to the staring fat man in the Chinese restaurant. But at least they're in together, Adam back at the usual time near dawn on Saturday and Fred, happy not to have to rush or worry, able to go back to sleep beside him.

Fred wakes up mid-morning and, with Adam asleep within sight, has a few hours of peace. He eats and reads, cleans the bathroom and watches television, careful to keep quiet although he knows by now Adam will sleep through almost anything. He might get dressed but he has hopes that when Adam wakes up they will, as Adam says, "Do something." They don't seem to do much, only one bit of intimacy in this week of Adam's constant coming and going and Fred's spending and giving.

When Adam does wake up Fred is propped up beside him on the bed having tuned in the end of *Woodstock* on one of the cable stations. Fred's mind is wandering as usual; he's trying to remember just where he was and what he was doing while so many his age were making this history in the mud. The specifics are lost, he knows he was thinking about sex, looking for it, then even more than now turning the slightest possibility into stories he could almost believe.

"What's that?" Adam's question, thick through sleep-clogged sinuses, is the first sign Fred's had he's awake.

"Woodstock. You hear of it?"

"Nope." Pause. He scratches his head. "Maybe, somewhere." He jumps out of bed and walks quickly to the bathroom. Hawking and spitting punctuate a long piss, followed by the rushing of the water from the sink and the toilet and the thump of his hurrying back to the bed. He fluffs his pillow with one fist, wraps himself in the top sheet, and feels around on the table next to the bed for his cigarettes and lighter, pulling the ashtray near.

Fred doesn't look at him, he keeps his eyes on the screen, but all his consciousness is anxiously directed to the boy behind him on the bed: What does he think of what we're watching? What am I going to say about it? This is typical of Fred; in his second life scenes like this are a daily occurrence, himself in a position to teach Adam some of the things he knows about. In reality he has no clue how to make this grainy footage of a muddy mob, this music so far from anything Adam listens to, interesting. So he is aware of Adam next to him, watching, judging, and tenses for a reaction, sure it will be negative, searching for something that will impress. When after only a moment Jimi Hendrix comes on, it seems like salvation. Fred settles back and glances at Adam, smoking, scratching one foot with the other under the sheet, unimpressed.

"Jimi Hendrix? You heard of him?" Adam shrugs, still sleepy, so Fred has to go on. He is unfortunately shaky on facts, chronology, all but the basic outline. He was busy when all this was happening, busy his whole life with things important only to himself. What boy, boys, was he obsessing about in August '69? Twenty-five years ago. Had he perhaps been in another bedroom with another bored boy, even then enough younger than himself to make the difference important? Their music at least would have matched, then the music of the young was his,

143

but even then knowing about it was an affectation, there was only the one thing he really cared about.

"He was one of the heroes back then. Sang, played guitar. Look at him. Ignored the whole race thing and just made his own music. He died young. Drugs."

"Was he rich?" Leave it to Adam to know what counts.

"I don't know. I suppose. There was always money for the stars."

"If he was rich how come his fingernails are dirty?"

Fred had registered the orange headband and white suit and guitar and is too surprised by the question to do anything but try to discern the state of Hendrix's fingernails in the grainy details on the small screen. They *are* dirty, as a matter of fact, long, with smudges visible near the quick. He's lost Adam, any chance of his being the boy he should have been; if all he sees of Woodstock are money and poor hygiene there's no hope Fred can impress him with the little he knows about the sixties, the world he himself passed through, after all, with blinkers on. And somehow, taking this little defeat in conversation, Fred has lost the chance he and Adam might as he'd hoped "do something" today. Adam doesn't bring it up, and Fred can't establish the mood, even for himself, with this tiny, unexpected failure on his mind.

The weekend almost ends right there. Adam is hungry, he wants to watch something else, and after Fred's warmed up Chinese food for him he decides he needs to go home to see his mother. He missed that court date and wants to see if there's a warrant out for him. He wants home for a day or two, Fred supposes. Even for Adam there can be too much of life on the streets.

Before he's finished eating Adam has made his plans and—as always with him—the decision requires instant action, as though his intentions won't survive any delay. He takes a steamy shower, sticking his head out from behind the curtain a couple of times to call for Fred to find him clean socks and underwear and to iron the shirt he plans to wear. Once out, towel around his waist, cigarette in hand, he fusses with his clothes: Does the touch of yellow on his shirt match the yellow of the swoosh on his Nikes and the canary details on his new L.A. Lakers cap (chosen just because that color matched that shirt, but now he isn't positive)? Again as always when ready to go he's in too much of a hurry to slow down; he bounces from one end of the small apartment to the other, Fred leaning out of his way.

Then, dressed (the yellows matching perfectly to Fred's eye), and with the few things he wants to take along to his mother's in a plastic Duane Reade bag, Adam pauses, hesitates, not looking Fred in the eye, in a way Fred knows and has come to dread. "Yo, Fred, I'm fucked up," he finally says, looking now at Fred with an almost embarrassed smile comprised of the knowledge that he's had plenty of money and wasted it, that he's asked Fred for too much too often, and of course of the steel certainty that Fred will give more now. "You could give me money today, when I come back, like Sunday, we'll do something, we'll be even."

"How can you go out every night to make money and never even have train fare by the time you get in?" A right answer, not refusal, not a lecture, not angry—exasperation, an almost humorous bit of headscratching.

Adam's smile becomes a grin. He shakes his head. "There's always something. Like this cap, or, I see what I like, I buy it."

Fred, now feeling slightly foolish at still being in his pajamas in spite of having been awake for hours—made foolish by his vain hopes, the failure of the little story that had brightened his morning—walks to the dresser where he has his wallet. He knows just what it contains, what bills in what denominations. Adam moves close, craning his neck slightly to see for himself, and Fred turns his back ostentatiously to hide it.

Adam makes a little disbelieving sound with his tongue, his look changing from eager greed to mischievous smile. "Like I'm gonna rob you or something," he says, and goes to the hall mirror to check his look once more. Fred follows behind him, holding out three tens—too much, more he knows than he can actually afford, but maybe enough to secure Adam's promise, Adam, whose usual response to whatever amount Fred thinks is adequate is injured indignation: "But, but, but," followed by his current list of expenses.

This time he takes the money, wordlessly shoving it into his jeans pocket with barely a break in his study of the mirror. Fred knows why, what's different this time. It is the first significant exchange of money for, well, nothing—the first time Fred's handed over this much without Adam doing his part, perfunctory and hurried as it is, for Fred. He hesitates. (Isn't Adam more to him than sex for money? Shouldn't he let this stand as proof of what else there is between them? Or does even thinking that just make him more of a sucker?) "So, Sunday you'll make this up, right?" he asks, with no idea if that's the right thing to say.

Adam looks at him, expressionless. "Yeah. We'll do something, then, free."

Well, prepaid. Fred feels vaguely apologetic and apologizes vaguely. "Just—you know, the money's always so important to you, we should keep it—"

"Nah, nah, that's cool."

"Just keep the accounts straight, if I have to pay you every time, I mean." Hint, hint.

"That's cool, I said. You got to look out for yourself sometime, right?" The smile seems real, the money's in his pocket.

Fred should be able to feel the freedom of an afternoon off from Adam, but nothing is quite right, all the little things nagging at him turn every possible story sour. The connection with Adam, the one he'd thought would only start as sex for money but then grow, has seemed to shrink instead since that afternoon—a golden time it seems now—when Fred came back from vacation with his little gift. There has been no change that has felt like an advance. Well, one, maybe. Could it be, he thinks again, Michael was the possibility he'd missed, the link that would have made the difference? If he'd made friends with Michael, just not been so selfish, then the three of them might have become a unit. The thought dwindles in futile improbability. He knows more likely it would have been two against one, more hectic, certainly even more expensive. And anyway it's too late now.

Adam of course may simply be on to Fred, whose usual ways of relating to boys have never worked for long. And Fred is old enough—though barely—to be Adam's grandfather. Not a thought he'll dwell on, one he's rarely approached before, but true. So what does he have for Adam? If he can't manage the actual conversation he conducts so effortlessly in his second life, if Adam has no interest in his advice or his experience, what's left? Money. For sex. Or for the promise of sex.

This failure to connect on the level Fred has seen as natural, even certain, has left him with the best part of a stranger in his home. Every day the dangerous possibilities of leaving Adam alone in his apartment are present as Fred leaves and stays with him through the day. What will he find when he comes home? The first real clue comes when he puts the key in the top lock, the one that can only be locked from inside or with a key Adam doesn't have. So far the lock has been secure every evening, and each time the relief is palpable, a shedding of real worry. The other, less likely possibility—Adam and friends will be there to rob him of cash and credit cards—never feels as real as coming home to a looted and deserted apartment.

But what can he do? Adam still seems like all the raw materials for the boy Fred wants him to be, he won't risk losing that; as long as something better is possible he can't bring himself to put an end to his own stories.

Fred's tense Saturday night and Sunday are filled with serious stories, he and Adam sitting down to settle the truth between them for good. They go gratifyingly Fred's way. Adam, it seems, has his own doubts, has never had anyone he could count on to keep promises. People leave him, they let him down, and now that he's found Fred he just can't trust his luck. The hesitations and evasions are reluctance to believe he's found someone genuine at last. Well. Fred smiles at himself as he spins this line, knowing how much he wants to believe, knowing the conversation (some of the words, phrases he's heard from Adam turn up, make him sound like himself) will never be heard anywhere but in is own mind. Knowing the only comfort he can come up with is too good to be true.

By the middle of Sunday afternoon Fred is expecting Adam. That is all he's doing, essentially, as he reads the Sunday *Times* magazine and checks the TV schedule in hopes there's something to take his mind off the wait, and what might happen after. *Woodstock* again. Exhibition football. Movies he'd never watch if there were any choice. He settles down with the remote in his hand, his mind of course elsewhere.

Sunday, Adam has said, not morning or evening, just Sunday. And even that might not be true, Adam is in no way reliable about time, but Fred would like some idea. He has no options, he will wait until Adam shows up and either redeems his promise or sits down for that talk Fred's been rehearsing. Fred waits through football (another mock opportunity to show off what he knows), a true crime reconstruction (his stories of crimes grisly enough to impress), and mindless automatic scrolling of channels, each glimpsed long enough to be rejected.

Finally, when he's given up hope anything could drive Adam from his mind, he comes across a rerun of a black-and-white TV series he remembers from his youth. He recognizes it instantly, thirty-some years on, the concerned, handsome face of the man with the rifle as familiar as if he'd seen it yesterday. He might not have remembered so well if the man hadn't had a son. The boy was slender, serious as his TV father, sweet smooth face, slim long-limbed body; Fred then, near the beginning of desire, had imagined under the plaid shirt and Western jeans the most attractive of the chests and backs and legs and butts he'd seen in after-gym showers, and had used this boy—or what he created from a few weekly glimpses of him in the cramped square of a small black-and-white TV—had made him a friend, and more, one of the first to exist oblivious out there in the world at the same time he was being remade as something of Fred's own. Now Fred finds himself waiting for the boy's appearance, through the usual Western TV show tough talk, dust and horses. And then there he is, standing in the doorway, smiling shyly, his soft voice with that crinkle Fred remembers, his big dark eyes and open expression heartbreaking. But this isn't what it should be; as Fred stares at the screen the years do not melt away, he sees himself as he was all those decades ago, watching what could be this very bit of film, weaving a fantasy not unlike those he's caught in now, and his thought is not, how far I've come, but, how little I've changed, still making a life from the spaces between what might be—just, barely, at the farthest limits of the possible—and what is. Instead of being nostalgic, though—and he might be, the boy is everything he remembered, like any beautiful thing a pleasure to contemplate—he is embarrassed, for himself then and for himself now, always inflating the most unlikely desires until they float before his eyes, float like the truth.

Adam shows up around eight, slightly high and in a hurry. Someone's waiting downstairs, he can't stay, they've got a chance to make some money right now but he needs, well, not too much, "A little twenty dollars," and when he comes back he and Fred will do something. Word to his mother. Fred even now doesn't say no; why risk the money he's already given Adam by refusing this bit more, he's guaranteed nothing if he says no but a yes gives him Adam's word. He fishes the "little twenty dollars" from his thin wallet and with—as he knows and cannot help—thin-lipped poor grace hands it over. It is Sunday evening but Adam promises to be back soon.

He returns in fact about three in the morning, earlier than usual but late for Fred on a workday. And the first words out of his mouth are, "I'm fuckin' exhausted," an answer and a defense against the request Fred hasn't yet made.

Fred is tired himself—groggy, awakened from his sleep—but not too tired to be angry. "You did make me a promise," he says. Aware he's never badgered Adam into anything and isn't likely to now, it's to salvage a bit of his own dignity he even tries.

Adam of course is indignant. "I'm fuckin'.... Damn, you can't wait till I get some sleep? Let me.... When you get up for work, wake me up then, we'll, you know. I ain't doin' nothin' now. Shit." He stomps off to the bathroom and Fred lies back down, frustrated but now excited by his expectations, by his shot of anger. Adam returns and silently strips to his shorts, flopping on the other side of the bed and seemingly to fall asleep almost immediately. Fred is awake now, replaying their last few encounters as they were and as they should have been, aware above all of Adam's presence—warm, sleeping, smooth skin, firm flesh. Then Adam moves slightly, onto his back, throwing the arm nearer Fred over his head, and Fred has one of those spells when all else—regrets, doubts, sense—disappears into desire. In his life he has given in to more than his share of these moments of promising lustful curiosity, although he has tried to respect Adam the few nights and late afternoons they've been side by side together, not really invading his sleeping boy's intimate space no matter how much he's wanted more than the morsels Adam has sold him. The most he's allowed himself has been to gently work the sheet Adam usually keeps himself wrapped in loose enough that they're both together under it, leaving his body and Adam's separated by only the bits of cloth they wear. It's best when Adam's back is to him, his legs pulled up; inches away Fred can mimic his position, feel his heat, imagine the contact, touch his knee to the back of Adam's leg in a way that might be accidental, one casual hand on his boyish hip, although even this is too much, at least the shadow of violation, but it gives such breathless exhilaration, this almost-touching, this near union.

Now it's something else, a possibility that sends a wave of desire through Fred: Adam, always so clean, deodorized and powdered, has been out since early evening, wearing himself out pursuing the dangerous thrills of city streets on hot August nights. How has it left him, another night of the Deuce? Fred waits, tense, listening and looking for any sign Adam might not be fully asleep, but he's stolid, slack, oblivious. Fred leans closer, careful, careful, until he's two inches away, cheek by bicep, nose in armpit, and inhales. The acrid damp sharpness of sweat almost makes him gasp. It's just what he wanted, Adam as he is without the soap and cologne and the latest clothes and sneakers. Underneath he is this, a boy, smelling of energy and life—of sex, to Fred, in a way somehow more pure and authentic now; unwashed, unconscious, natural, he's more the real thing than he's been before.

Maybe sensing Fred near, Adam moves suddenly, the arm pulling back, his head lifting from the pillow. Fred falls back quickly, looking at Adam, who briefly, briefly, on one elbow, opens his eyes (Fred's sure seeing nothing), rubs his nose and coughs before settling back down to sleep. Fred joins him, soon enough, the excitement calming into a plan to wake Adam early enough to collect on his promise.

Fred is disappointed but not surprised of course when the real morning is so different from his hopes. He wakes early, remembering the other times when the still soundly sleeping Adam simply refused to be awakened, and knows that's the most likely story this morning, futile attempts to wake an Adam who will not stir. Fred considers just letting him be— leave things where they are, don't risk antagonizing him more, come back and start over in the evening. Maybe, he thinks to himself with a smile at his own helplessness, he could bring a little present to smooth things over. That decides him, he becomes almost angry at the thought Adam might require, after all Fred's spent on him and done for him, another gift to bring him around. And there is the deeply thrilling possibility of burying himself, briefly, in the rich human odors of Adam as he is; maybe Adam would allow him something for just that reason, maybe it would never occur to him presenting himself unwashed, rank, could be anything but an insult. The joke for once would be on Adam.

Oddly enough Adam comes around immediately, surfacing from his deep sleep as though to something urgent. He looks at Fred, then at the clock on the night table, and fumbles briefly for a cigarette before thinking better of it. "Damn, it's like…. When I went to sleep?"

"I don't know. Like, three hours ago. I just woke up, getting ready for work."

"So? Wha's up?" Adam slurs the question, his soft voice sleepy, clogged.

"You promised me something this morning?" Fred hopes making it seem a question will soften the intrusiveness of waking Adam for sex. Even though it was Adam's idea.

But Adam returns to his earlier indignation. "You.... Damn! Like you can't wait, or—"

"I already waited. You're the one who suggested this morning. You got in you said—"

"You're just scared I'm gonna cheat you, your fuckin' money, right? Like I—"

"You're the one who said this morning. Remember?"

"I don't feel like it now though." Then with the sly shadow of a smile he adds, "It's my birthday, too. You should be buying me sneakers and shit."

"Your.... It isn't your birthday." Fred's sure Adam's birthday is in May, but now that he thinks about it he isn't so sure. Maybe it didn't really come up, maybe Adam had been lying to seem older.

But his tone is unrelenting. "Sure it is. You think I'm lyin' about that too. Shit."

"All right, all right. Hey, forget it. We'll talk about it some other time. Tonight." And with that Fred stalks off to the bathroom.

His thought, as he turns on the shower, is that Adam might join him. The door could open, Adam come in, strip off his shorts and stick his head around the far end of the shower curtain, reaching out one hand to feel the water temperature, complaining the water's too hot or too cold before climbing in. Fred can hear the metallic slide of the curtain rings, feel Adam's nude shoulder nudge him aside as he reaches to adjust the water. But there is no door opening, no change in the air or the closed bathroom noises. Fred will finish his few minutes in the shower still alone.

Or. When Fred comes out of the bathroom Adam might be waiting on the open futon, mind changed, ready with a few conciliatory words to keep his promise. But in the small main room there is silence, the smell of fresh cigarette smoke,

Adam awake but not even turning to look at Fred, who's finding excuses, as he stands wrapped in his towel, to delay dressing. Adam could still change his mind. Hope. Hope.

It is Fred of course who can't take the hostile silence. He sits on the bed, leaning on one elbow next to where Adam presents his indifferent back, hoping his presence so near will provoke a response. It doesn't. "You know I don't want to make you do anything you don't want to," he finally says, admitting defeat. "But you did make me a promise."

There is more silence before Adam responds. "I promise tonight. I'm tired, I…. Shit."

Well you are awake right now, Fred thinks, saying, "All right, you're tired. We can talk about it tonight."

"You act like you own me and shit." Adam, sounding dangerously aggrieved, rolls onto his back inches from Fred.

Fred isn't going to have this discussion, it's too far from anything either of them should be saying. "Oh, Adam. Come on," he says unthinkingly, "Don't you know how much I like you?" Like. He won't use the other word, how could he? "And I guess we can get something for your birthday, too." Then he leans forward—it's only inches—and puts his face against Adam's stomach, cool and hard under the sheet, puts one arm around his waist and gives him a hug. Looking up at Adam's face, at surprise turning to distaste, he sees what a mistake this is, one of those he may never quite forget or recall calmly. It is something from his second life, where tenderness is expected and affection returned, where misunderstandings are untied like the simplest knots. Adam of course is elsewhere.

Fred sits up and reaches for his clothes, covering his embarrassment with a flurry of movement and talk; maybe he'll look as though nothing has happened. "Well. We can talk tonight. Anything special you want for dinner? I can stop on the way back. I got your dry cleaning back yesterday, it's in the first closet there. I should be home the usual time." He is aware of Adam not looking his way, not responding, of a coolness he hasn't felt before, not a passing mood but a harder, growing thing, a spike of frost in Adam chilling all he sees of Fred. Or maybe he's wrong. He doesn't think so. Before he leaves he makes one last try. Offers one last bribe against disaster. "If it's your birthday maybe we can do something. Go out, buy you some new sneakers." Too late, he thinks, no matter what it is it's too late.

It barely occurs to Fred he might not go to work today. Hope and helplessness, habit and a stubborn refusal to give in to his fears send him out as usual. And what would he say to Adam? Even more than usual it's habit that keeps him functioning at work. His mind races in a tight tiny circle, barely deep enough to be controlled, to be kept from spinning into words actually spoken rather than forced over and over through his mind. Habit and pride—he is very proud never to be out sick, never to miss work; under all the life of hunting the streets there are parts of him that he wants others to see, he wants to see, as defining his *real* self: Responsible, reliable, solid, consistent. He works every day, even today, his mind careening. He allows himself no excuses.

But inside there is the circle, thin first then thick then thin again: The thin, the unconvincing, is the little hope there is a connection, he and Adam, something that will keep the boy with him—surely it was there once, maybe, briefly, once— and if not there is at least the promise of more, Adam will have sneakers, clothes and money, and where else can he find such a convenient place to stay? The thick, though, the thick harsh likely part of the circle his mind travels all morning is the dread he's built from the look in Adam's eyes, the tone of his voice; all Fred has done is so obviously not enough, Fred himself is not enough, it's all gone wrong, something will happen and it will happen today. Fred relives that thrill hours before Adam fell asleep, of leaning forward, fearful of being sensed so near and inhaling for the first time the odor of the Adam always kept from him, that dank sharp underarm smell of all his energy, all his tough secret night living, unwashed and unhidden. Somehow after that nothing between them could be quite right.

Fred can barely keep himself from making excuses and rushing home, at least calling in hope the familiar sleepy voice will answer, confused and barely coherent, wanting only to return to sleep until Fred comes to feed him as usual, keep his promises. Or if the thin hope is misplaced calling to have the phone ring unheard in an empty apartment, stripped of whatever's worth having. At least he would know.

He makes it somehow until eleven-thirty, over three hours of something that feels and tastes like fear, before he slips into the empty downstairs office and makes the call. The circle spins as, breath short, mouth dry, he dials the number. If there's an answer—there could be an answer, this panic could be him not Adam—he'll say he's coming home for lunch and would Adam like Chinese food; he'll be giddy with relief to be able to say it. One ring, two, three (maybe Adam's asleep, it wouldn't be the first time he's slept through a ringing phone), four, and then it comes, the fifth ring, and it's barely an instant, another ring, before Fred's moment of brutal certainty: The answering machine picks up after four rings. If there were still an answering machine it would have.

The shock is so complete, the knowledge so clear there is not even the space Fred always has for a cushion of daydreamy possibility to form, that space he makes or finds in every fear or threat or pain: Maybe it's only, it might be, what could have happened is…. After these weeks when the second Fred and the second Adam have been available every waking moment, ready to be fit into any reality, there is no buffer to dull the dread, this is too close, too hard, knife to bone. Fred has left himself nothing else.

So he makes an excuse, he needs to run home for lunch and to let the building super into his apartment, that sounds plausible, he hopes is said like truth, not like the hasty panicky lie it is, and he hurries out to the subway, too anxious to waste the extra five minutes walking home.

Already on the train he sees how he might begin to come back. His look reflected in the window opposite is to him stricken and sad; it is an image he might use, might even strive for, at other times, times when he felt further from being stricken and sad than he does now and could revel—from a distance—in the stories he could weave around his own (pretend or at least not deep) pain. Even now he's peripherally aware of others who might notice his look and think he's a man with a secret sorrow; that would be respectable, he could live with their respect for his loss, respect from the jean-jacketed Puerto Rican girl in wild corkscrew curls and clunky jewelry, the stiff black matron in the nurse's aid uniform squeezing lotion from a tube onto the back of her hand. Both glance at him and away, uninterested.

Fred looks closer, though, as the train shrieks and bounces the minute's ride from east to west, at his face reflected dimly in the tunnel-darkened window. He does not look at himself in mirrors, he looks at the hair comb or the trim of the beard or the neatness of the clothes, but never at himself full in the face, looking back. Now he does. Now he does. It seems a sketch of himself, pale and insubstantial, a washed-out film run over the rush of blacknesses beyond the window. It looks like he feels, all his stories still for once, almost still, pushing their way back from habit but not taking over the way they will when he is emptied of real pain, emptied of anything to block his ability to sustain mild pleasure with harmless fantasy. (Usually harmless—isn't it?—he would be better off this minute if he'd kept the truth always in mind, but that trade-off, truth for pleasure, or more often simply for comfort, has always been dangerous.)

He isn't empty now, that part of him he's accustomed to filling with whatever feels good, the part where others live their lives, is so crowded with pain and disappointment even his few halfhearted visions of revenge or recovery lie limp, uninflatable for now. He's used to spending all his passion on what might be. Now what inescapably *is*—Adam's lies and treachery, his own foolishness and refusal to defend himself—defeat him altogether, leave him without the will or resources to comfort himself with anything. He feels insubstantial as the face he sees staring back from the window opposite.

As he approaches home another thought strikes him. Maybe someone's still there, maybe Adam's with his friends, waiting for him, to take his cash, credit cards, whatever. Fred slips his wallet into the mailbox before going up, a precaution. He gets off a floor early and creeps up the stairs to silence, approaching his door trembling, listening for the slightest creak or whisper, barely able to fit the key into the lock, not even trying the top lock he is certain will be open. He turns the key as carefully as he can, still listening, still to nothing, and pushes the door open. After a moment he sticks his head in, looks around and, suddenly seized with another wave of panic, the thought someone might be behind him instead, on the stairs leading up to the roof, he hadn't looked there, where Adam or a friend could be waiting to jump him, he slams the door, the fears that seconds before were inside now shut out in the hallway.

It's just what he expected, disaster, holes in the cabinet where the VCR and receiver and tape player had been, all the papers from his desk strewn around the room, a towel, Adam's, the yellow towel he's thought of as Adam's, in a wet heap on the floor, both closet doors open with clothes spilled out, phone jack hanging empty. The first sight is confirmation of all he'd thought since the phone went unanswered, but it's a fresh shock all the same, he stands in the middle of the room not knowing where to look first. He thinks of things now, his most expensive possessions, what's most precious to him, though he doesn't often consider values that can't be counted in money. He doesn't think of Adam as the great loss, tries not to think directly of Adam just now; it is pure humiliation, last night's promise, this morning's hug.

And it all has to wait. He's made an excuse for a brief absence from work, and after a miserable look around to estimate the damage he hangs the wet towel up in the bathroom to dry—noticing the little boom box he'd kept there is gone, too, another small loss (usable, saleable), another small blow—then stands for a full minute at the door, listening for some sign of danger outside, before carefully opening it and hurrying out and down the empty stairs to retrieve his wallet and return to work.

157

Fred spends this afternoon even farther removed from what he's actually doing than usual—lost for once in a reality, the intensity of pain, loss, embarrassment far more insistent than any well-rehearsed daydreams. It isn't exactly Adam he feels the loss of, he's spent weeks trying to erase the simple fact Adam of course was never his to lose. The loss is in the humiliating way he's been reminded of this, that he's a dreamer whose dreams are lies, that he's a fool: His losses are pride and money, not Adam. He can't even quite work up the righteous outrage of the victim: He knew the risks, he saw the warning signs, he couldn't say something like this hadn't happened before. There isn't much comfort anywhere; facing reality when reality is what you've been trying to avoid gives cold comfort, if any.

Adam has changed his mind, he immediately regrets what's he's done and is waiting for Fred with all he'd taken when Fred comes home in the evening. Fred tries that out briefly, can't make it work as more than a joke, a joke on himself, and on the way home stops at an electronics store, he'll start by replacing the phone and the VCR, that's what he can carry back on the first trip, the phone at least will be there so if anyone calls who isn't Adam he'll be able to answer as though nothing's happened, he won't have to explain. If Adam calls—Adam will call, curious or gloating, both, he will call sooner or later—well, he'll see what happens then. Entering his building Fred again is seized with fear, he spends a moment looking up the open stairwell for faces, movements, then, again, with a churning stomach, gets off a floor below his own, seeing, sensing, nothing amiss before quickly going up and in.

He hooks up the phone and begins to clean up, that's the next thing, putting his home back in order he will feel some control of his life returning. At first things get worse as he begins to count up what's missing: A checkbook, he'll have to go to the bank and put a hold on a dozen check numbers; a favorite sweater; not just the VCR but the cable box and remote. There will be phone calls tomorrow about that, expensive lies and explanations. No one to blame but himself.

Weeks from now, months, Fred will be looking for that missing sweater, maybe, or a shirt or pair of gloves he won't even realize are missing until they are not there, and he will find some small possession assumed as part of his life is gone and all this will hit him again, not as hard, each realization a softer but distinct blow, a new insult on top of the others. The violation, the pain of the loss, will be fresh every time.

That very night the new phone rings and Fred, certain who it is, answers, all but in a panic at the thought of Adam's voice—what? Threatening? Ridiculing? There is silence on the open line. Fred is almost pleased, absurdly, to think of Adam on the other end, puzzled, surprised, wondering how this quick recovery is possible. As though this were an achievement.

By the end of the week the things of Fred's life are again where they belong, the new among the old. New receiver, tape player, phone, VCR. Everything thrown around back in place. There is a feeling of accomplishment in this, odd and secret, putting things in place is satisfying in itself, and Fred, as always priding himself on getting good value, balancing the features he needs against cost, is convinced what he has now is just a bit better than what he had. Plus—and here is the story, there is always a story—Adam, had he stayed, had things continued as they were, would have cost so much more than this, that's the thing; the way Fred was spending he would have claimed this much, these hundreds of dollars, in no time. So looking at what happened Fred can tell himself he's better off, saving money in the long run, while Adam's worse off, losing out on all he would have wound up talking Fred into.

It's thin and unconvincing, this logic in the service of pride, calculating a new winner and a new loser, but there it is, all Fred can manage, and he trots it out once he returns to himself; the loss, the embarrassment, the anger are too much without stories to soothe them: Stories of revenge (his own), regret (Adam's), how things might have been different and might be bent back into shape in the future (Adam, sick or injured or arrested, could come to need and appreciate Fred). Fred's hurt and anger push these thoughts aside, but they linger in that wishful part of his mind where all those rosy stories originate. And he remembers Adam, Adam: There's that crooked tooth and the beautiful long legs, and the grandmother and the touchdown run, there's all that useless boyish beauty.

For the first few days the fear stays with him, impossible to talk away. Once the idea someone might be waiting to jump him—around the hall corner, up those stairs, even on the fire escape—has taken root in his mind, he worries shadows and sounds everywhere. Leaving in the morning and returning home at night he creeps like a criminal, a guilty man about to be caught, studying shadows and holding his breath as he turns corners. Home is a fortress in enemy territory.

His soundtrack, the music Fred carries on his hip and in his mind, is inadequate for this, music can keep him where he wants to be but can't take him there, can intensify, prolong whatever pleasurable state he's in, but can't create one where none exists. Resilient as he is it's difficult for Fred to create anything satisfying for the first few days. For all his experience at enhancing reality, replacing it with something more comfortable, livable, this has left him flat, even when he can think of something else the nagging disquiet is constant. Music for a time is without charm, without power, he cannot catch the spirit of the songs, ride it like a wind that carries him higher.

Friday night Fred goes out a couple of times, halfheartedly looking for someone, telling himself it's time to get back in the game, put Adam behind him and start the search, the wait, once more. But even if he were to see someone worth the money and effort (and he doesn't), it isn't time yet. Adam is with him as much as ever, as heavy on Fred's mind now as any time since they'd met. His need to drive out the pain makes these stories, revenge and regret, more urgent than those that just please his vanity, but still they add up to the two of them, bound together now in bitterness and anger rather than affection. Fred, being Fred, slides back from the hurt condemnation of the first hours, days, after the robbery. Maybe, he thinks, I shouldn't have said this, done that, let him see me so plain. He remembers his little gibes, teasing Adam about his demands, why hadn't he been a man about it, said what was bothering him, even said no once or twice, Adam might have respected that. What could have happened instead was....

The call comes Friday, very late, late enough it can only be Adam. Fred is shocked by the ring into a panic he knows is ridiculous, his heart begins to pound and his breathing becomes tight and hard. He simply can't handle the pressure of human opposition, the defenses he marshals so effectively in his mind disappear, he's reduced to stammering uncertainty when he faces a real person's real reactions, especially angry ones.

He takes a few deep breaths and answers the phone, expecting traffic noises, hearing instead an almost-familiar rap beat loud in a nearby room. "Hello." He has to force the word up, rasping through his too-heavy breathing.

There is a pause before Adam speaks, very softly. "Wha's up?" To Fred this sounds mean-spirited, triumphant, spoken through a smirk.

"I guess I should ask you that." Another pause, breathing over the distant music. "I don't think I deserved what happened, after all I did for you." He's disappointed to sound a little whiny, delivering this between more deep breaths.

"You got new stuff already?"

"Pretty much."

Another pause. "How come you're not mad?"

"Mad? Of course I'm mad. You think just because I'm not yelling and calling you names I'm not mad? That's not my style, is all." And Fred briefly sees himself as *having* a style, cool and controlled.

"Nah, it's just.... You sound like you're all nervous and shit."

Or not cool. "I've got a cold. But of course I'm mad. You had no right to do that. I always treated you with respect, you should have respected me." Fred has calculated this; "respect" is street currency, treasured, and he hopes the word, the concept, will resonate with Adam. But all it brings is another pause. What else can he say here, since yelling isn't his style? "How many people did you have helping you?"

"A couple of my friends was there is all." Adam sounds annoyed to be asked, as though it's none of Fred's business.

"Then what, you just sold my stuff?"

Adam doesn't bother to answer this at all, maybe there was only one point to the call and he gets to it. "I wanted to ask, I mean. You called the police?" *Po*lice. Once Fred would have been charmed by this.

"The police? No."

"Why not?"

Why not? What was he going to say, the fifteen-year-old boy I was having sex with stole my stereo? "That's not my style, either," he says.

Another pause. The conversations Fred had rehearsed for this moment hadn't included the purely informational. And none of this is an ending, not a proper one, he needs some final word that will have meaning for both of them. "Respect" came close, but nothing had really worked when this conversation was going through his mind and nothing occurs to him now, nothing that resonates even to himself. "You still hang around down here?" he asks. It is not an idle question—this is Fred, this is Adam—but neither is it a prelude to a meeting. Information.

"Yeah, you know, just now and then, now." Then, maddeningly, "I gotta go, okay? I'll call like, next week."

It's Fred who hangs up now, not saying or waiting for good-bye, something he will remember and doubt Adam even noticed.

III.

THE CONVERSATION

Is that the last of Adam? Not in Fred's mind, where the two of them had come together with such intensity that the time since they met—weeks only, not even two months—seemed like a life. Thinking about Adam has become a habit powerful enough Fred can't pull away. He's so used to finding something like satisfaction in the thought of Adam's being near he gravitates back to it in spite of the mess reality turned into. Billie Holiday sings "Ain't Nobody's Business If I Do" in his ear one morning as he walks to work, and he tries that out, holding on to Adam in spite of all that's happened, all sense, all the odds against any good outcome. "If I should take a notion to jump into the ocean…." Could Billie Holiday spell masochism?

What Fred saw reflected in that subway window was not quite the man in his parallel life, not the one next to Adam in all the stories. Fred knows him though, this is the cross he has to bear, himself as he is, not young enough, charming enough, witty enough, having nothing (except money, and not nearly enough of that) to offer the Adams of the world. He might have strained to see a romantic, even tragic, face looking back, but he knows all he saw was himself. It's an odd kind of realism that pulls him back to Adam, to the empty, false, finally humiliating fantasies Adam inspired, but maybe the tiny thread of possibility they hung from is the best Fred can hope for this late in life. What more, what better can he expect from the streets than those few moments with Adam when he felt near to breaking through that membrane between his two lives, joining the real and the ideal? When Adam talked about his grandmother, his accomplishments, hadn't Fred been his confidant instead of one of "These homos out here?" Wasn't that something? Maybe with another chance Fred could … well, something might be different.

So their conversation continues, Adam's impossible presence conjured up in stiff chance meetings in which he pays the price for what's happened. It's important first of all he know what he's lost, he's lost Fred—where will he find anyone who'll care for him that much, do as much for him; why, they might still have been together in a year, two, three, and how much more than what little he carried out of the apartment would Adam have been given by then? Fred's new mantra.

Once Adam has learned his lesson the breach can be healed, once he realizes how wrong he's been he can begin to atone. All Fred's initial anger and hurt are eased by being woven into typically improbable but soothing tales of Adam, chastened and contrite, becoming the suitor, wanting his second chance. These begin as background, blotting out the pain, or perhaps poured over it, smoothing its sharp edges, but soon enough of course— they're so much more comfortable than hate and bitterness— they come to him first, the comfort of healing displacing the pain it was created to heal. Doing just what it was meant to.

But Adam will not leave him, cannot be pushed altogether out of his mind or reduced to being just another memory. For Fred a return to the streets as he'd prowled them before means the chance—thrilling and frightening, a danger and an opportunity, feared as much as looked forward to—of running into Adam. But not going out, not trying to resume his life, means never moving past Adam at all. Is there a third possibility? Could Fred at this point change his life, inspired by this disaster to pull away from the streets he's made his home all these years, away from his fixation with what boys might be there, might be available, might at long last be what he's been waiting for? The thought crosses his mind, it's a big city, a big world, Fred could spend his time on so much else. He tries out other lives, running them through his head with himself in place; he might—what?—volunteer? He finds himself answering phones at a crisis center, stuffing envelopes for some politician, the cheerful energetic cog, always helpful, agreeably efficient. Well. Maybe if he were the one who solved the crises, directed the campaign. The stories don't work when he's a cog.

Other thoughts—practical thoughts—of what he might do with his time and his energy drift by and keep on drifting; he still reads, can't get much interested in television, has tried movies and plays, which are too expensive, and friendships, which don't take, don't work, he has none of the hooks that attach one person to others. By now his parallel life has had its hold long enough no new reality can compete, can offer the pleasures of Fred's stories. The work, the planning and effort and discipline of becoming a new person are like mountains he'd have to climb. Should he change his life? Must he change his life? If so the change would not be from the streets to some shabby salutary office, some minor good works. Real change for Fred would be transition from his own world into everyone else's, and by now he wouldn't know how to begin. And why bother when he has no incentive, no certainty the life he would come to live would be happier, more satisfying than his is now? Maybe he should get a cat.

So the streets win again, not that there was much doubt; he will do what he's done before, retrace too-familiar routes down too-familiar streets, looking again for what he so recently thought he'd found at last. Time and again he will approach certain blocks and corners with rising hopes, will circle and hover, rehearsing words he's rehearsed before, worn out in fact, without ever quite mastering them, convincing himself he can succeed with whatever attractive available stranger he finds. Once again he will work at detecting boyish qualities in some new young man, may be lucky enough to be surprised someday to find someone who's nearly the boy he wants, more surprised than he ever is to be disappointed.

Summer by now is almost over, Fred's hot Adam summer; the unpleasant edge of heat and humidity is gone, and with it that feeling of never being quite dry, that faint pervasive city scent of rotting fruit. The streets can be walked in comfort again, better weather meaning one less distraction from the life in Fred's mind. The first few nights he's out the hope/fear of seeing, approaching, being approached by Adam is never more than seconds away; memories of Adam, tortured hopes for Adam, fear of Adam's potential for scorn or gloating elbow aside any other stories Fred might develop. With time he knows Adam himself will move aside, move from the front of his mind to the background, become past tense, part of the flow of his life, a memory among memories, barely distinguishable from so many others. Right now awareness of that is just a device, like thoughts of a vacation in the just-foreseeable future. It hasn't the power of pain or danger, doesn't soothe like the new Adam stories, but it has its uses.

When there's no sign of Adam the first few nights Fred's back out it's easy enough to let fears and expectations recede, conversations that had been tense one-sided rehearsals for their next meeting become stories among all the others. Fred sets out every night to find someone new, that's what he tells himself, that's why he comes out, why he's spent these years seeking eye contact on crowded sidewalks, standing uncertainly in shadows near someone who might respond to an offer, purposefully stalking lone youths first seen in the right place, with the right look of calculating uncertainty, to make them possible. But at first there seems only the one real possibility. Adam. Adam. Adam. (Of course Fred doesn't see anyone more than just passable these nights, no one to set his heart beating faster, bring out all his hunting instincts, send him into his hovering, scheming dance of attendance. There are no potential Adams, that makes a difference.)

So he is still out late Sunday afternoon, at a point familiar from all these years of frustration: He should go home, it's time to eat, he's got things he'd planned to do this weekend, he's tired. But. It's such a nice day, the streets are crowded, somewhere here, among all these young men who are not right there just might be one who is; how can he leave that chance for the sake of a hot meal and a few household chores? Maybe, just maybe … well, it's his story, same plot, familiar characters, the usual words and setting. And when this young man wonders why Fred refuses to let him get closer it will be time for the story of how recently Fred's heart had been broken. Yes.

So Fred is thinking of one more pass down his usual streets, by now more for the echoes of past hopes, of expectations from years before than any real hope for today. And there he is, Adam, in that playground on Forty-third Fred passes occasionally as a diversion from his regular route, he and Michael the two youngest of a half dozen playing a strenuous game of basketball. Adam is clearly having fun as he bends from the waist guarding a heavyset Hispanic of thirty or so, sweat dripping from his slicked-down black hair and Fu Manchu moustache.

Fred hurries past unnoticed, this image—Adam, grinning, loose-limbed, bouncing on the balls of his feet, blue overalls over yellow T-shirt, blue cap for once front to back for the game, Fred miles from his mind—another one that will stick. Fred's relieved not to be seen even as he spins the inevitable stories of how that might have gone, Adam seeing him, stopping perhaps in mid-dribble, thrown off his game by surprise, embarrassment, leaving the game to trot down the street and catch up to Fred all … well, all *something*. That lost instant loops through Fred's mind, cut off before Adam reaches him and the story turns into all those other stories; by the time Fred gets to Ninth Avenue Adam's moment of recognition and surprise, noticed by all around him, his decision he must talk to Fred, his flustered flight from the game and down the street, have already played out half a dozen times. That dries up quickly, and Fred tries to examine his feelings past the initial adrenaline rush. He knows what his emotions should be, and the hurt and anger that have been clouding every moment since he'd rushed home in a panic the Monday before can't be ignored, but beyond that he can't sort out what's real from his tangle of stories and hopes and daydreams. He tries to find something as he moves down the block, but what comes to mind is secondhand, scraps of other people's words for situations that are only vaguely the same; yet again he's stuck with lyrics for feelings. "I know I should hate you the whole night through, instead of having sweet dreams about you." "I don't have happiness and I guess I never will ever again." Songwriters know how to make the sadness of failed romance sweet, and it's easier to fit into the moods they've described than to dig deeper into his own pain, or past it, to find shapes that are his own.

The actual music in his ears is something else, he turns it off as he reaches the corner. Some other time he could appreciate the dirty innuendo of the Rolling Stones' "Stray Cat Blues," the sleazy decadence of "Dead Flowers," but today that's all wrong, the wrong tape to indulge his angry sense of loss. He goes to Forty-second and begins to walk east. Through the block-wide parking lot opposite the post office he can see the basketball court, Adam with the ball now, recognizable from this distance by the clothes at least, although Fred would like to think he'd know this boy anywhere by now. He stops and watches. Adam dribbles and feints, passes to Michael but it's slapped away and the sweating fat man takes it for an easy layup. Fred smiles; his Adam was better than that, a schoolyard Jordan, not just another kid who liked to play. Fred enhanced them both for the lives he saw them living.

The game is over and there's a flurry of handclasps and backslapping hugs, towels and cigarettes brought out, the fat man takes a quick look around then seems to light up a joint.

Fred can almost hear Adam demanding his turn and after a couple of quick tokes the man passes it and bends to retie his shoes as Adam takes his own drags, slower and deeper, before handing it to Michael. The man stands and the three talk, giving still-jealous Fred a sudden conviction this overweight guy with the silly moustache is one of Adam's tricks. But no, probably not anyway, they don't seem to be paying that sort of attention to each other, the man's is not the attention of real interest, and Fred tells himself that of course it's not his problem or his business anymore, if it ever was.

It's late enough the shadows are lengthening into darkness as the players make their way out of the small park, splitting up as they reach the street. Fred is tired and hungry and tries to find some version of an encounter that will feel real and right. He runs through them all, from telling Adam off in an angry confrontation to listening to apologies and, maybe, forgiving. He knows any of them would end in fact with Adam asking for a few dollars. Could he start saying no now? Probably not. Even now. He'd still wrestle with any likely excuse, thinking of fairness, benefit of the doubt, not hurting anyone's feelings— even Adam's. Even now. Suddenly the chance they might see him, Adam and Michael might come his way, becomes a threat. They wouldn't avoid him—he didn't call the police after all, didn't yell on the phone—they'd see him and the thrill of trying for one more score would be too much to resist. They've started back towards Eighth, oblivious of him, and after a moment of pure curiosity—where were they headed, what would they do not knowing he was there, watching?—he decides the risk is too much. He turns back towards Ninth and home.

He manages to stay in for a while, eating, ironing the clothes he'll wear to work tomorrow, but in his mind he's followed them, walked, still walks, behind Adam and Michael, approaching them or being seen and approached, running through every scene of the past week, from the angriest to the most bittersweet, still rooted in his small rooms because the reality of this meeting could only turn out wrong. They would be without remorse or respect—he's heard them after getting away with something, winners without pity. They would be wolves, cunning and merciless. Still. Won't he see one, both of them, face-to-face, sooner or later? What will happen then?

Isn't something possible with Adam? Isn't it, even now?

By seven-thirty it's begun to rain, as the Weather Channel had promised, and Fred, as he knew he would (the question was how long before he gave in) puts on his light jacket and breaks out a cap and umbrella (maybe he can hide even if seen) and heads for familiar blocks. The rain isn't heavy, there's no wind, quite a few people are still out, clustered under overhanging signs and in recessed doorways instead of spread out along the sidewalks. Fred walks past their original corner, his and Adam's, deserted now, and from there moves up and down the rain-shined streets, deliberate among those hurrying or huddling, looking for Adam, expecting him at each corner just as he was a couple of hours before, overalls and yellow shirt, baseball cap for once on backwards.

The stories remain the same, the plot doesn't thicken or thin out, it is what it is, what he needs it to be over and over again, different locations and onlookers for their conversation the only adjustment.

This time Adam is at Forty-second and Eighth, a thin yellow nylon jacket added to the outfit, the cap turned back the way God intended. Michael is nowhere in sight. Adam is where the sidewalk meets the street, foot traffic hurrying by swerves to avoid him as he stands in deep conversation with a young man Fred has seen here before who seems to be selling drugs, not himself. After a few seconds the two move back to the shadows near the fried chicken place and a quick exchange is made, Adam buying a small bag, probably pot, before a brusque handshake-and-backslap good-bye. Then, before Fred, on the far side of Eighth, can even think to follow, Adam ducks down the stairs to the subway and is gone. He got some money from somewhere is Fred's first, jealous, thought; he reminds himself he has to dismiss this from his mind. Then the question is if

Adam's actually catching a train or just finding a quiet place to smoke a joint in the dry recesses of the subway. It is fifteen minutes before Fred's convinced Adam is indeed gone for the night.

The rain has stopped now, even this part of this city can smell fresh after a summer rain, it's almost enough Fred can feel a possibility of change for himself. But he walks the familiar blocks one more time, checking the small groups on all the usual corners, backs retreating down side streets, likely smokers alone in the shadows. Maybe there'll be someone new, a new beginning to put him in a proper frame of mind to face the week. Or maybe Adam has slipped out some other subway exit, is lurking out here somewhere looking for a quick score, not at all particular who he goes with to get it. "You new out here?" Fred would ask. "What's up?" And Adam would smile, nerveless, in on the joke. "Just chillin'. You know. Lookin' to hang out."

But then ... nothing. Fred's life resumes the form it had before Adam—the wait, the hunt, hope and frustration—except, at first, Adam is the real object of the search, his presence anticipated at each approach to certain corners as his voice is every time the phone rings, Fred filling in all that would come after as always, in an endless loop of possible conversations, all of course the same conversation, a whole life that might be, right there next to the one that is. But days turn into a week, two weeks, without Adam standing on any of those corners or making a single call. For a while the time he's been gone makes his appearance on any given night seem more likely: He's due, he's bound to be back any night now, on the corner where they first met, on the basketball court, glimpsed walking on this side street, eating chicken wings in that restaurant, somewhere. Then, as enough time goes by that Fred can't quite count the days since that last sighting, his conviction that Adam's return is imminent fades. Michael's gone, too. They must have been locked up, something's forcing them to stay away. Adam's movement to the background, to past tense, continues, slowly, but he is still nearer than any of those actually around, still the one who captures Fred's attention, the one no one else has stepped up to replace. Fred's pain is reduced to a memory of pain, the anger to a buzz, Adam to the pleasure he might have been—was, occasionally, briefly.

Fred's first glimpse of light, of possibilities after Adam, comes two weekends after the basketball game, on a Saturday night that feels enough like autumn that he's out in a sweater, one extra layer against the overcast, not-quite-raw evening. He walks the old streets in the old way, living his life of habit made into satisfaction by what might be, and when he sees someone excitingly familiar, a young man watching the crowd passing on Eighth Avenue from one of the side streets, he's ready. Fred has to reach for a name, it's been years, literally, but this one kid he remembers, a face retrieved from the multitudes that have passed through his daydreams and his bed, that's a good sign even if what he recognizes is a grown-up version of someone who was only almost right even years before.

Fred has walked a quarter block past the corner before he decides he'll take no risk by being cool, strolling around the block and coming back so if seen he won't appear too anxious; he might return to an empty street and no sign anywhere this wasn't the wrong person altogether, even simply his imagination. He stops and turns and walks slowly around the corner, trying to fill the memory out with a name. Angel? Maybe. Angel. He tries it with the face as he remembers it but it's been too long, the feeling it's wrong is just as strong as the feeling it's right. He'll fake it, not for the first time.

It's the same person, the right one, he's sure of that as soon as he sees him again, leaning on one of the red lamps by the subway entrance watching two crackheads next to the pay phones across the street arguing over the custody of a pipe, hurling the usual epithets—"asshole," "motherfucker"—in the strangely enervated tones of crack smokers deep enough in a binge even anger can't pull their minds away from the high. Fred coasts to a stop, waiting to be noticed, and is rewarded with a double take and immediate smile of recognition. "Yo, yo, yo. Wha's up?" They shake hands. "You remember me, right? Angel?"

"Of course. Saw you from the corner. I wasn't sure you'd remember *me*. Fred, right?" Nobody remembers names out here. Although it turns out he had remembered this one, at least.

"Fred. Right. I couldn't think. Fred. Wha's up, Fred? It's been a long time."

"I've been around."

"Yeah, well...." Angel smiles a familiarly embarrassed smile and admits, "I been upstate, a two-year bid, like. Thirty months. Been out awhile, but stayin' home, right? Lookin' for work and shit." Fred calculates it must have been more like six years ago they'd met, Angel must have been seventeen, eighteen then, but up close he seems impressively youthful, his face still smooth although the boyish softness has settled onto the cheekbones as it always will with time.

"That's a long time," Fred answers sagely.

"Well, you know." He changes the subject quickly. "So what's up? What you been doing?"

Fred shakes his head and tells the truth. "Not much. Working, hanging out. Not much at all."

"Shit. I had an excuse. You got no excuse."

Fred shakes his head, no doubt looking a bit embarrassed himself. He could, almost does, offer Adam as an excuse, extending what was into an actual life he might have been living: "There was this kid named Adam. That just ended recently." He rejects this, not that he won't ever use its hint of romantically dark disappointment, but it's too soon, too genuinely painful to present quite yet as something it isn't. "I never did live a very exciting life," he says instead.

Angel smiles, looking him in the eye in an open, even affectionate way that's startling out here, where the calculating gaze is standard. Fred is actually made uncomfortable by this sign of an authenticity he can't quite understand; are Angel's memories of their few times together that different from his own, are they of some connection Fred never felt or doesn't remember? All those others who've come in between—small attachments, modest affections, business transactions that didn't even pretend to be anything else—could have added up to enough to obscure something real that far in the past. Not an Adam, but maybe what was worth remembering in an Angel.

Fred smiles back, feeling his own look softened by Angel's, and does remember an odd fact or two: Angel was the one who'd mentioned reading *Down These Mean Streets* and *Soul on Ice;* that alone, that he could name two books he'd read, would have made him memorable out here. And there is the name, the name. Looking in Angel's eyes Fred recalls a moment of intimacy half-remembered across the years, Angel confiding that his real name was—well, not Angel, though Fred doesn't remember what it was right now. Street names are usual, for Angel to confide the one his mother gave him was not. Maybe there was a connection there, Fred and Angel.

But this is now. Adam is gone and Angel seems perfect for this moment: Fred doesn't have to deal with all that awkward first meeting stuff. There's none of that little doubt and worry of being with someone brand-new; no stranger ever feels completely safe. And if Angel's not young, by Fred's standards, he's young enough, looks even younger, and, in a way, can be made younger in Fred's mind. That's one of the virtues of living in one's own world as much as Fred does: He can move yesterday's reality to today, can remember that Angel was much younger when they first met, was, perhaps, new to all this, maybe brand-new the first time they met, so why not go back to then, all the years fading away. "How do you do?" Fred can be asking this fresh face. "What's a nice boy like you…?" They talk for a moment and walk away, the three of them this time, Fred and Angel, and that boy Angel was, younger, young enough not to be concerned with what Fred's been doing with himself all this time.

But the past is past. If there was some real affinity between Fred and Angel it's been lost, though Fred knows if Angel had meant much to him he would remember, however many years he had to look back. Still, he's able, as they meet, chat, walk the couple of blocks to his apartment, to create what it might have been—something not so easily forgotten—and what it might be again. It's the usual story, now with Angel in the place Adam has occupied for the past few months, but it doesn't last, by the time they reach Fred's building it's falling apart, reality intruding too rudely to allow Fred the space to create this parallel world from what he doesn't know and what can't be disproved. Angel is married now, mid-twenties and married, settled and clear-eyed about the boy he was. "These guys want you to be their son or something, like you're gonna be friends for life, but that shit don't last, they're always lookin', always out there lookin'. Even if they meant it at first, just any little thing, some new boy, they move on. Talk about friendship, want to help you out, this and that, you always know that other shoe's gonna drop." Nothing personal, he wouldn't be saying this if he were talking about Fred, but he isn't because whatever was between them wasn't what Fred would have wanted, or remembered—it was mostly this kind of talk, probably—and Fred wouldn't have cared enough to try to embellish it with promises. Angel is what he is, and honest about it, but nothing he gives will open a world Fred can move into, live in, like the world he had with Adam. And when the moment comes Angel's too thin, too much hair, not sensual or needy enough to indulge Fred any more than some new kid who has no clue how to tease the imagination instead of only the dick. As they talk afterwards, Angel blunt and anxious about money and women problems and his kid's school, Fred can see they may have had a connection after all, but it was this one, a simple human bond, sharing problems and confidences. Something like friendship. The sex was separate, ordinary. No wonder he hadn't remembered more than the face and the name.

He takes Angel's number, maybe he won't lose it right away, he likes Angel, thinks he might call him some especially empty, hungry night when the pleasure of the talk might outweigh the bad sex. Might. Won't. For someone who thinks and plans and imagines how good it can be, bad sex is too depressing, downright unfair. Fred won't settle for it willingly no matter how much charm and sweet nature goes with it.

So. Angel. Not nearly good enough, but also not so bad—others have been, Fred shudders to remember—as to drive him back to the streets immediately to find someone else whose company might obliterate the experience, a cold drink to wash away a foul taste. Fred stays in for the rest of the evening, and the next day he's calm enough to keep the possibilities at bay: Some perfect boy could be out there right now, just for a few minutes, just a quick walk and he could make sure. That old siren song. He stays home instead, goes to the store, reads, cleans house. Angel is not much in his mind. Adam is not quite flushed away, he keeps approaching, he's seen at a distance, quietly returning, as to home.

Work is what it was before. All the color and enthusiasm that the possibility of Adam had added to Fred's days have faded, leaving, when he reflects on it, a bitter embarrassed residue. Those things he thought he might say and do to startle/impress/titillate his co-workers have to be pushed away, excesses that make him grateful once again he does most of his living in his mind. Usually he's regarded from a distance and can think of himself as too mysterious to decipher, but even he is sensitive enough to tell when this isn't true; the first week or so his pain must have showed. Frank is willing to be sympathetic but as always doesn't push. "Rough week?" he asks the Thursday after the robbery. "Oh, yeah," is Fred's answer, backed by a sense of how stunned Frank and everyone here would be by the magnitude of his loss; he has an impressive secret, never mind what the impression would be. Fred can just about manage to see himself in the eyes of others—after all, they don't know the truth—as romantically disappointed, not quite bitter, even admirable, bearing up without complaint the way he is. He keeps that in mind for the sympathy, refuses to see the other reactions that would accompany the truth. It's a story that takes a while to feel plausible even to himself, and in the meantime he detects a certain watchful recognition—these are the only people who see him every day, his mask is not inscrutable—that something has happened, although Frank is the only one who mentions it. Greg may have some idea, but never betrays a hint of concern; Fred is surprised by the realization that this careful ignoring of his possible problems may mean that Greg doesn't like him. He is briefly hurt by this, but then the real opinions of real people never affect him that much, unless he wants them for sex, and he makes a point of forgetting it; those confidences Fred had imagined directing at Greg are the most firmly suppressed of the things he might have said.

Time passes, and does its work. By the week after Fred's encounter with Angel he tells himself he's back to the life he'd lived for years. It's all almost familiar, but there is a difference; Fred can't quite return to what he was before Adam because he can't quite recall what he was then. Adam was such a presence in his stories that without him, or some replacement with his power, they feel empty, too weak to give even that illusion of satisfaction that kept Fred going through all those months, years, when there was no possibility in his life rich enough to make the reality seem as dry and flat as it is now. This is why Adam can't be sent away altogether, why those chance meetings, Adam's remorse, Fred's forgiveness, reconciliation, become a standard thread of the story. Adam might show at work needing Fred, ready to apologize. So many things might happen.

But of course they don't. Fred returns to the search, that wait for perfection, or a street substitute he can fool himself with. He has hopes but won't be surprised when there's no one else out there even as close as Angel to what he's looking for. He already knows the most attractive of the old regulars and his reasons for not being interested in them again, or at all, and for now everyone new falls short somehow—too old, too homely, too grungy, too aggressive. Wrong. Maybe he's more critical—who can improve on his persistent memories of Adam?—but more likely he's letting the objections he's always had, the understanding of how little he was settling for, make the decisions that have in the past been overcome by accumulated lust, by loneliness, by his ability to convince himself some particular kid might be better than he seemed.

The Saturday after Angel Fred goes out late in the afternoon, not the right time, he can't remember picking up anyone interesting at this hour, but his old sense of the endlessness of possibility makes it worth a try. He passes the usual blocks and corners, nothing to make him pause but one more old trick whose name he can't remember hitting him up for a couple dollars, making the walk so far a total loss in cash and irritation. He goes through the bus terminal, his eye caught by someone else he'd been with once, someone experienced enough to deliver wet kisses and blow jobs like a machine set too fast; fortunately he's occupied in what looks like business and Fred hurries by without being accosted.

He's planning to go home, come back in an hour, two, when there's been some turnover and an evening crew will be here, but then he passes a young man by himself near the north steps to the terminal. No luggage, one thing to look for, so he's not just off a bus waiting for his ride. Waiting for something, though, he has the air, so familiar out here, of waiting to be approached.

Fred passes him, walks up the short flight of steps to the terminal entrance, turns and looks back. A little too old, early twenties, but fine otherwise—black, very dark, short, hair cut close to the skull, with a build that can only be guessed at—very slender, probably—under the loose black Yankees jersey and the Levis bunched around the scuffed high-top white Nikes. The face—Fred glimpsed it in passing, now sees it from his vantage point at the top of the stairs in one-quarter profile—is smoothly eager, ready to smile. He's looking around, jumpy, impatient, a good sign, Fred thinks; this won't be complicated, not a chore with the sort of extended small talk he's no good at, this is someone who seems as anxious to get on with it as Fred is himself.

Of course there are preliminary worries. Fred checks to see who else might be interested in this kid. One or two of the other regulars are near the stairway but don't seem to be paying attention to Fred's quarry. The fact that they are present slows him a bit; he's unwilling to risk their seeing him rejected, if it comes to that, a matter of pride, part of staying separate from all those others. But this young man has stimulated the hunting instincts Fred hasn't used these last couple of months: His stomach tingles pleasantly, he feels a testosterone/adrenaline rush, he can already see and smell the body under the shapeless clothes, can feel the smooth chocolate skin, the firm thighs and stomach, the pressure of hands and mouth and whatever else might bring him pleasure, as he imagines predatory animals anticipate the taste of flesh even as they stalk their prey. It seems a long time since he's had this particular thrill.

But the meeting itself is too easy, hardly a conquest, the beginning of disappointment; the jumpiness Fred noticed was from impatience, not the nerves of a novice. As Fred takes a few steps towards him the young man, perhaps alert for any movement in his direction, turns and, seeing Fred looking his way, releases the smile he was waiting to use and moves to meet him halfway. The smile is very nice, white teeth sparkling against the dark skin, but not for a stranger, unless it's a stranger you have very little time to sell to.

"What's up?" There is no original conversation out here.

Fred shakes his head, wondering if second thoughts should be in order; he's unnerved by a direct approach with none of the usual dance of positions staked out, looks exchanged. "Walking around. Just on my way home. You?"

A shrug and a glance, aware of bleak possibilities, at the uncrowded sidewalk around them. "I gotta get back home, too. I live, like, Long Island City. I need, you know, some cash. Thought I might see somebody I know...." He looks Fred in the eye, sure they understand each other. This flat-out approach, the experience it shows, drains any possibility of romance that might be left in their meeting—Fred feels the loss of a richer life being led from here—but it also puts him on solid ground. There's none of the need to be tentative, hint around, worry about misunderstandings. The relationship has been defined for him, money for—well, out here? two strangers? it's obvious what for. And he is much more relieved than disappointed that this is starting out just as it will end up, no mystery but also no pressure, no illusions, no tiny hint he might have found another Adam to tiptoe around and obsess over.

"How much you looking to make?" Fred asks.

His name is James, not Jim or Jimmy, James, and he's not even quite as young as he'd seemed, in his mid-twenties, Fred calculates, as James rattles on about himself, trying very hard to seem young and innocent, serious and stable—he lives with his mother who doesn't like him in the city or late getting home, he's going to junior college and works part time—while making his city life all too clear: "I usually hang out in the World Trade Center, the bathrooms there, but the cops been around too much. I don't like the Port, the cops know me here, but it's too early for bars." And so on. The few asides about school and his mother's strictness seem like hollow tries for respect, but then who knows what incompatible lives, each with its own authenticity, can be lived side by side? Fred's not the one to say.

All the experience implied by James's monologue is belied by his actual performance; he is, after all, just a kid picking up cash the quickest way he can, and like so many others feels little need to work for it. He undresses nervously, apologizing for his torn undershirt and the noticeable odor of his feet and underarms ("I walked all the way up from the World Trade, I couldn't even borrow a token.") And then he lies still, quickly refusing Fred's simple requests ("I don't do that"), all his energy directed to trying to maintain an erection he flops helpfully against Fred's leg, small assistance to Fred's imagination, but soon enough the fact of someone else, attractive, naked, penis rubbing Fred's skin is enough.

So. James, working his way through college. He gives Fred his number and the best hours to call, oblivious to the lack of interest that must be clear in the way he's hurried through washing up and sped on his way. Surely he must wonder, if he gives out his number to all these men, why he still has to stand

180

in men's rooms, on street corners, waiting to catch someone's eye. He hopes for the best. But then, so does Fred.

On his way home from work one afternoon the following week, planning a quick pass by his usual hunting grounds, Fred sees, walking half a block ahead, a familiar look and walk, the back of a head he's sure he knows. He moves quickly to catch up, so sure it's Adam he forgets he'd made the mistake once of thinking someone else was this boy he wanted to see. He skips across the street at the light, hurries past touristy congregations on the sidewalk, steps into the gutter to make up ground, all the while keeping his eye on the head, in a brown cap today, a maroon football jersey with a name and number Fred can't make out as he dodges and weaves his way down the rush hour street, keeping his steady, oblivious goal in sight, like a sailor following a star, like himself. He pulls close finally, breathing hard. And with no idea what he'll do next. All the reality he's tried not to think about since Adam became an abstraction comes back to him: The last time they were together Adam lied and manipulated him while Fred made desperate promises, useless against the inevitable. Adam's call, for information only, to find out if the police were after him, colder perhaps than no contact at all, was the last time they'd talked. The things Fred knows for sure about meeting Adam again now are that there will be no apology he can believe and that Adam will ask him for money. He cannot feel safe.

The head he's following has stopped at the light at Eighth, too much traffic to cross against, Fred's chance. He slows instead, the heavy breathing as much from sudden uncertain emotion as from exertion. There is anger still, fear of losing what little there is left of wounded pride—could there even be threats here, some public embarrassment Adam might decide he deserves? But then there's the boy he's spun all these weeks, and the reality that inspired him, and of course Fred's endless lust, memories of the long legs and smooth skin and all that comes with them. He halts now three feet behind a slender boyish figure, short curly dark hair, long neck, long wedge of a back. It isn't Adam.

And Fred is relieved, almost giddy, there's barely a trace of disappointment at finding the subject (even now) of most of his stories is still lost to him, has disappeared, perhaps as irretrievably as the past itself. He knows why he'd want it otherwise. He knows what part of his mind longs for Adam so much it's created him here out of this near thing, out of desire and resemblance and the possibility of living out one of the too-many stories, sliding directly from fantasy into fact. He knows there is still nothing else, here or in sight, to fit into that space Adam had filled.

Fred can still see the humor in himself, smile at each breathless pursuit of a wrong thing, wonder (with hindsight) how he ever expects anything but disappointment. His small gaffes, his quickly pumped hopes, as quickly deflated, his grand dreams dependent sometimes on a single glance that doesn't come, or that has no meaning when it does, all can seem funny if he stops to think about them. Until the embarrassment sets in.

His encounter with the almost-Adam has put the real one back in the center of his mind. He goes out early Friday evening but can't find the appeal of his usual routine, the same streets and corners walked in about the same order as he trolls for someone new. He's impatient with the usual. After a pass or two without spotting a single interesting face he begins to walk south. It's cool but not cold, the slightest breeze, the kind of night when most of the world has better things to do than ignore the odds and continue in some half-hearted search for a trick. He heads for the downtown streets he's sought out before.

Once again he knows what he will find there, part of the pleasure is that there will be no surprises, although now as before he's come to look, not to participate. He's not one of these people, though they represent a world he might still be part of; a few adjustments in himself, his decisions, his preferences, the way he spends his nights, and these streets might become his natural destination, the place he belongs. He considers this almost every time he comes down to the Village, the Lower

East Side, the parts of town that seem to fit the person he knows himself to be at heart—the heart under the heart that lusts and obsesses, sends him on wild-goose chases and midnight sorties seeking some new boy. If the heart that lives down here, a heart that has no say it seems in how he lives his life elsewhere, could only free itself, why, who knows what he might become?

He walks east, past crowds with places to go, past clubs and theaters and restaurants and bars, famous destinations, he might stand and watch comings and goings that will be written up and talked about tomorrow, he might linger and watch. He doesn't.

There are little knots of people outside one of the exclusive velvet-rope clubs he passes; for a few days they'll say they saw so-and-so there, a distinction, never mind they couldn't get in themselves. But Fred moves quickly by. He goes into a bookstore, a video store, but barely pauses to look around. Here again the movement is as important as what he's moving through and every interruption is an irritant, disrupting the flow of his mind, which is as always speeding through a parallel world all its own. The soundtrack here is from the same pool that accompanies all his life: Tonight he's heard "Body and Soul," "Something to Remember You By," "Where or When" from one tape, "Have You Seen Her," "Nothing Compares 2 U," "You've Got a Friend" from another, each song for as long as it lasts, maybe seconds longer, like a tributary adding to the flow of a river, a spice bringing out the flavors of a stew, powering and enriching the stories that roll on in his head.

He circles through the busiest streets, the ones he knows will be full, taking pleasure as he has before in something he is not quite part of; knowing this world is here, his if he's ever ready, is enough.

He's beginning to feel tired as he turns west, towards the Hudson. If he were to feel at home anywhere this should be the place, Christopher and streets leading off it, between Seventh Avenue and the river. But he's here alone, by choice, and does not even imagine joining any of the groups clustered on corners near the PATH train entrance, outside the dim jeans-and-leather bars. It's all too gay, for one thing; that difference he's always felt is difference from this, too, gay men and boys of no interest, he's always looked for the space he can fit into next to straight boys, and any of those out here are too much for him: too experienced, too knowing, probably too expensive. He can't help picking out certain faces and attitudes as he passes, it's what he does; inevitably he slows long enough to see if a glance will be returned; this blond kid, maybe twenty, here after sunset in a leather vest and dark glasses, has that waiting look, but then he's ambushed from behind by a black queen his own age and they go off giggling, appearance belying reality.

The pier off Christopher is crowded at this hour, but not busy. The pace is slow, the life calmer than the downtown world just a block or two east. Here the gentle slapping of waves on the pilings and the sun fading in the sky over New Jersey overwhelm city voices and lights just far enough away to be ignored by anyone looking in the right direction. Fred walks to the end of the pier, stepping over barriers only because others have, and finds a spot for himself, looking down at the few lights dappling the wide black river. He hears conversations around him only as a murmur of voices that could be gay or straight, friends or lovers; everyone seems peaceful out here. He looks at the river and imagines another life, another self to live it, but only shadows come to him, nothing even as steady as the lights bobbing on the ripply water, nothing near the satisfying life he brought up time and again with Adam for inspiration.

Still, he tries. He would live near here, with a view of the river. He would have an apartment others would envy filled with things others would like to have. There would be a boy. He would have the time and money for the world's routine pleasures—theater, travel, leisurely suppers out. The soundtrack to this life would be, well, "I Love the Night Life," maybe. "Sweet Dreams Are Made of This." The occasional "Walk on the Wild Side." And when the time came to say good-bye he would be strong enough for "By the Time I Get to Phoenix," "How Insensitive." He smiles at the thought—being missed, being regretted, another second life. The person he might have been, might be, might still become. Or not.

It's near closing time for the pier, the same gentle pace that brought the crowd taking it away. A big retriever chasing a Frisbee cuts in front of Fred as he strolls back towards the street and when Fred catches his eye begins to bring the yellow disk to him before being whistled back to his owner. Fred would have a dog, too, living down here. Maybe two. Maybe a cat as well, all the reliable company he would need for these nights when he didn't know what to do with himself.

It seems unnatural how completely Adam has disappeared from Fred's world. After those weeks that seem in Fred's mind to have stretched into something much longer of Adam being no more than a day or so away, likely to call or show up at any moment, there's no trace, no sign, no word, no more mistaken sightings, no mysterious phone calls that might be him, playing, teasing. More weeks pass without him and still every time Fred's phone rings there's that twinge of expectation, Adam jumps into his mind, and every time he returns to the streets that thrill of possibility returns—with time slighter, briefer, but never completely absent: Tonight Adam might be around again. Nothing. Fred sees Jeff once, not looking his best, shaggy, a bit strung out, with that bleary too-many-sleepless-nights look of a fecklessly adrift drug user. He hints that Fred should take him home but there's no chance of that. It's a couple dollars for information, only Jeff doesn't have any; he hasn't seen Adam since that day he introduced him to Fred, he says. Maybe, maybe not, maybe he doesn't remember, maybe he's been asked not to say. Fred tells him he needs to go home, get himself together. "Oh, *yeah*, yeah." Jeff sounds like there's no chance he won't, right away, like it's Fred's mistake to imply there's any problem. Well. What can Fred do? There are too many Jeffs out here for him to get involved.

Time, Fred tells himself, that's what it takes. Time heals all wounds, makes all losses bearable, makes the most futile set of habits feel like nature's plan. Life before Adam, as long as Fred didn't think about it too much was—not comfortable, certainly—it had come to seem inevitable, he'd lived it too long for anything else to be as right as nights of cruising the streets and days of living the life he didn't find there. Adam has blown all that up somehow, and now he's gone, and the old way— built-in disappointments and all—no longer seem inevitable, or even possible, in quite the same way. But time will pass, is passing, and Adam will fade, is fading, the old life will again become life. That's the way time works.

It's a Monday morning, six o'clock, Fred, awakened by the radio alarm, is drowsily listening to the news headlines and trying to remember the weather forecast he just heard when the phone rings, startling and awful as a gunshot. It can only be one person. Fred's instant reaction is senseless panic, as if the ringing were an intruder's voice shouting in his ear. Nothing is right, how could it be, he's been robbed and apparently forgotten and now, as Adam's being transformed in his mind into something safe and distant, available for long casual chats, there's this ringing telephone, like a dawn assault. Still, he answers it, breathing deep, hoping not to embarrass himself by sounding as shaken as he feels. "Hello." Out in one quick breath, no chance for wavering.

"Yeah, Fred, wha's up? You know who this is, right?" No little giggle this time.

"Adam." A deep breath. "Didn't think I'd ever hear from you again."

"Yeah, I got locked up right after—you know." As though it were the time that had come between them, instead of what that "you know" represented. "Only just got out."

"I didn't mean because of how long it's been."

"Oh, yeah, well, you know."

"That's all you got to say? 'Well, you know.'"

"Things happen, I don't know. It was this one kid's idea."

Fred almost hangs up here. This one kid's idea? But this is Adam. "Come on, nothing could have happened if you didn't say yes, right?"

"Okay, I'm sorry." There it is, the inflection of a child forced to apologize, followed by a brief pause Fred refuses to fill and then, "Listen, you could come down a minute? We could talk?"

He could have said no, anyone else would have—no one could blame him for saying no to Adam now, not even Adam, maybe. But instead it's, "I'll be down in a few minutes," and underneath the fear, the recognition of all that might go wrong, Fred's convinced himself that even now there might be hope of something for the two of them, even as he wonders if he isn't making a mistake he tells himself he couldn't have said no. He has to see Adam again, if only, he thinks, to try for a last word that ends their conversation, a last word that settles something, but he knows the dreams he once had are not dead, he feels them rising yet again, against all experience, those stories of the best that might yet be. And he truly believes he has to give Adam a chance—not to explain, come out with a real apology (as if)—but a chance to do what his macho fifteen-year-old pride might allow, maybe no more than make a sideways gesture of regret, let Fred know he realizes his mistake, but without any hint of the abject that might make it harder for him to stand up in his own eyes. That, and Fred can actually believe Adam would gain some sort of higher ground, even allow himself to feel wronged by being denied this meeting, refusing to see him somehow proof of Fred's meanness, unfairness, cowardice. Adam could think that way, Fred would be uneasy in his own mind knowing that he might.

Of course all that's in addition. Nothing matters except that Fred wants to see him.

Still, he pauses before opening his door, listening for that creaking floorboard, some whispered hint there's someone out there, waiting to grab him, push him back in, add some new humiliation to the list. He's sure Adam was calling from the street, though, and with trembling fingers snaps the locks and goes quickly out into the empty hallway.

Adam's in front of the building when Fred gets off the elevator, only the second time he's been there first. Is this a good sign, his forfeiting that little extra show of his power? Maybe he's changed. He's framed in the big front window, back to the building, wearing a black leather jacket, bigger than it needs be, a tan watch cap pulled low over his head. Fred hesitates, thinks of drugs, of weapons and robbery and danger. He takes a nervous reassuring breath—they will be on the street, people on their way to work or school pass even as he worries about the possibilities, and he doesn't have to ask Adam to come up, doesn't have to allow him any of his former privileges.

Adam turns at the sound of the door. Fred steps outside, letting it close behind him, and climbs the two steps to the sidewalk. Under Adam's coat a very clean striped button shirt is loose over baggy new Levis. The high-top white Nikes look new. The watch cap is pulled so low over his forehead only a smooth oval of face shows—from eyebrows to the top of the shirt that cuts off any glimpse of his neck; even his ears are covered, only his eyes, nose and mouth are left visible, and to Fred this face he's known so well, now shorn of context, is suddenly a mystery: Only the barest humanity shows, darkness and youth, the essential Adam hidden from him more than ever.

Expressionless, not quite looking him in the eye, Adam takes Fred's offered hand, a simple handshake, discouragingly limp. He waits for Fred to begin.

"So, you been in jail." Fred hopes he doesn't sound as though he cares.

"Yup. Locked up." The D and the P's struck with familiar force, the lips almost curling into a smile, eyes averted, at this most common of street jokes, funny as always just because it's so expected. Fred doesn't laugh and Adam is uncertain enough to explain without being asked. "Me and Michael was selling drugs up in the Bronx. They checked up and we both has these little warrants."

"And now you're back."

Two Hispanic men with heavy canvas tool bags pass; Adam waits until they're out of earshot before answering. "Not—it won't be like before, I'm gonna be on probation and shit, I can't be hanging out all night, living wherever." Fred can remember when this would have been the perfect answer, even his version, in one of those stories that turned the real Adam into his own by providing something to force him to be good—to be Fred's, Fred's alone. Now it might even be Adam's attempt to let him know he's changed, imply things will be different. But now it's too late, Fred thinks, isn't it? Could he ever forget enough of what's happened for Adam to return to his life as a real possibility? And of course it's six in the morning so presumably the end of Adam's night. Like before.

"When did you get out?"

"Friday. This is my first time back here." He looks down the street towards Eighth, towards Times Square, as if towards home.

There is a pause. Fred could fill it with, "Well, you want to come up for a few minutes?", as he once would have as automatically as he'd agreed to this meeting. "You back in school?" he asks instead, to fill the gap.

"I'm supposed to start next week." Supposed to. In other words, no.

They stand a few feet apart, Fred studying Adam as carefully as Adam avoids looking him in the eye. They might be strangers, enemies. Fred wants what he's wanted from the first glimpse of Adam on that fire hydrant on the corner two blocks from where they stand now. For all he remembers of his life he has had one basic story—himself and a boy together, somehow enduring. Details (even the identity of the boy has been a detail) have shifted over the years, with fashions in clothes and hair and music, from home to home, coast to coast as he has moved from there to here, restless partially because the story as it fitted into each place got old, needed new surroundings to make it fresh again, to make it seem possible. A few similar weeks strewn about Fred's memory had been as close to the story come true as those first weeks with Adam; none had been closer. Even after the robbery it had straggled along, the story with a life of its own, the connection kept alive by Fred's desperate need to believe in it, this near-last chance, and now that it seemed the story with Adam was nearly dead at last, here he was again, smooth tan cap pulled low, as if to make himself new, perhaps possible again.

"So you're back living with your mother?" As always small talk defeats Fred; no one could believe his interest from the questions he thinks to ask.

"My sister's house, just, you know, for now."

The conversation stumbles on, two strangers, anyone who heard them would assume, being polite. All the questions but one are Fred's; Adam asks only if Fred has found the beeper Adam had been sure he'd left there once. That last day? Fred hasn't seen it. Is this all this is about?

After moments of this, desultory, hopeless, Adam says what Fred has known from the first sound of his voice on the phone that morning he would: "I just need enough for carfare." Asking perhaps only enough to prove something, to gauge Fred's anger or forgiveness or guilt or gullibility.

"I only have a few dollars on me." Fred had been sure enough he'd be asked to bring money along, nervous enough about Adam's intentions not to bring much. He reaches in his pocket and pulls out a five and a couple of singles. "What, seven dollars is all."

There isn't even a flicker in the blankness under the cap. "Thanks." Adam takes the bills without looking and shoves them into a pocket of his jeans, then looks around as if for an excuse to leave. He sees one, a police car stopped at the light waiting to turn the corner in their direction, and seems slightly unnerved by the sight. "So, um, I guess I'll see you around, okay?" He shakes Fred's hand quickly and with another look at the police car, now driving slowly down the block, turns towards Times Square and hurries off, quick, confident, eyes straight ahead.

The police pass by without a glance. Fred stands shivering slightly and watches Adam recede. He would have followed once, of course, caught up with a smile and an offer of a little money in exchange for a little more time. That occurs to him now, he sees it happening, himself even quicker than the boy on his way back to familiar dirty intoxicating streets, Adam turning at the approach of hurrying feet and knowing he's won another chance. Fred sees them together, himself leaning back against the railing of the subway entrance at Eighth, nodding as Adam explains: He'd given people Fred's number and somebody'd called that morning, wanted to come over, only he brought friends, two, three others, once they were inside things just happened, he would have stopped them if he could. And now he wanted to get away from all this, off the streets, back in school, find another way to spend his time, other places not so dangerous, temptations with surer rewards. He's changed. Fred sees those eyes now, not evasive, looking into his from under the tight-fitting cloth cap barely darker than Adam's skin, brown eyes for once honest, seeking, not sharp and grasping. Changed.

It isn't much more than a minute before Adam has disappeared, crossing the street and rounding the corner at the end of the block. Fred watches as long as there is something to see, echoes and visions of himself and Adam fading as the morning chill becomes too much to ignore, a reality that drives him back inside to get ready for another day.

ALSO FROM SALTIMBANQUE BOOKS:

THE SWITCH, by J. Boyett

Beth used to be a powerful witch, till a meth addiction burned her powers away. Her daughter Farrah thinks she's nothing but a loser. But Beth thinks maybe Farrah would change her mind if she had to spend a few days in her mom's shoes—and when she gets her hands on a new source of magic, she decides to make that happen....

THE UNKILLABLES, by J. Boyett

Gash-Eye already thought life was hard, as the Neanderthal slave to a band of Cro-Magnons. Then zombies attacked, wiping out nearly everyone she knows and separating her from the Jaw, her half-breed son. Now she fights to keep the last remnants of her former captors alive. Meanwhile, the Jaw and his father try to survive as they maneuver the zombie-infested landscape alongside time-travelers from thirty thousand years in the future.... Destined to become a classic in the literature of Zombies vs. Cavemen.

COLD PLATE SPECIAL, by Rob Widdicombe

Jarvis Henders has finally hit the beige bottom of his beige life, his law-school dreams in shambles, and every bar singing to him to end his latest streak of sobriety. Instead of falling back off the wagon, he decides to go take his life back from the child molester who stole it. But his journey through the looking glass turns into an adventure where he's too busy trying to guess what will come at him next, to dwell on the ghosts of his past.

STEWART AND JEAN, by J. Boyett

A blind date between Stewart and Jean explodes into a confrontation from the past when Jean realizes that theirs is not a random meeting at all, but that Stewart is the brother of the man who once tried to rape her.

THE LITTLE MERMAID: A HORROR STORY, by J. Boyett

Brenna has an idyllic life with her heroic, dashing, lifeguard boyfriend Mark. She knows it's only natural that other girls should have crushes on the guy. But there's something different about the young girl he's rescued, who seemed to appear in the sea out of nowhere—a young girl with strange powers, and who will stop at nothing to have Mark for herself.

BENJAMIN GOLDEN DEVILHORNS, by Doug Shields

A collection of stories set in a bizarre, almost believable universe: the lord of cockroaches breathes the same air as a genius teenage girl with a thing for criminals, a ruthless meat tycoon who hasn't figured out that secret gay affairs are best conducted out of town, and a telepathic bowling ball. Yes, the bowling ball breathes.

RICKY, by J. Boyett

Ricky's hoping to begin a new life upon his release from prison; but on his second day out, someone murders his sister. Determined to find her killer, but with no idea how to go about it, Ricky follows a dangerous path, led by clues that may only be in his mind.

BROTHEL, by J. Boyett

What to do for kicks if you live in a sleepy college town, and all you need to pass your courses is basic literacy? Well, you could keep up with all the popular TV shows. Or see how much alcohol you can drink without dying. Or spice things up with the occasional hump behind the bushes. And if that's not enough you could start a business....

THE VICTIM (AND OTHER SHORT PLAYS), by J. Boyett

In The Victim, April wants Grace to help her prosecute the guys who raped them years before. The only problem is, Grace doesn't remember things that way....Also included: A young man picks up a strange woman in a bar, only to realize she's no stranger after all;
An uptight socialite learns some outrageous truths about her family;
A sister stumbles upon her brother's bizarre sexual rite;
A first date ends in grotesque revelations;
A love potion proves all too effective;
A lesbian wedding is complicated when it turns out one bride's brother used to date the other bride.